"*Separate Fountains* is similar to another young adult classic, Harper Lee's *To Kill a Mockingbird*. Both books explore racism in a small southern town. Both have a young girl as the main character who witnesses a morally strong father take a stand against hatred."

BETSY SPEARING
Media Specialist, Leon County Public Library, Tallahassee

"*Separate Fountains* is a very well written book. The characterization is exceptional; it reminds me of Jem and Scout in *To Kill a Mockingbird* by Harper Lee."

CATHY HENDLEY
Media Specialist, Bloomingdale High School, Tampa

"By turns moving and amusing, *Separate Fountains* tells the story of a sensitive girl's growing up in Jonesboro, Georgia, in the aftermath of World War II and the prelude to the Civil Rights Movement. The story of Katie Jane's education in class and racial bigotry is history written from the heart."

JANET G. BURROWAY
Professor of English and Creative Writing, Florida State University

"*Separate Fountains* is a realistic presentation of race relations between blacks and whites in the South in the 1940s and 1950s. I highly recommend the reading of *Separate Fountains* by all Americans to bring about an understanding of what life was like in the South prior to the Civil Rights Movement."

DR. JAMES N. EATON SR.
Professor of History, Founder and Director of the Black Archives Museum
Florida A & M University

"Patti Wilson Byars's *Separate Fountains* is in many ways a gift to society—a gift of knowledge and insight into a slice of America's history. Based on her experiences of growing up in the deep South of the 1940s and 50s, Byars opens the window to her family's values—opposing the Ku Klux Klan when it was unpopular to do so and treating African-Americans with respect and dignity when it was dangerous to do so."

DIANA BOGAN
Reporter/Book Reviewer, Sarasota's Weekly Planet

Teachers: For a free Guided Reading Plan for *Separate Fountains*,
please e-mail your request to Byarspatti@aol.com

Separate Fountains

Patti Wilson Byars

HILLSBORO PRESS
Franklin, Tennessee

Copyright 1999 by Patti Wilson Byars

All rights reserved. Written permission must be secured from the publisher to use or reproduce any part of this book, except for brief quotations in critical reviews or articles.

Printed in the United States of America

07   06   05   5   6   7

Library of Congress Catalog Card Number: 99-71546

ISBN: 1-57736-132-6

Cover art and illustrations by Barbara A. Psimas

Cover design by Gary Bozeman

Separate Fountains is a historical fiction novel, with its roots in stories told by the author's parents and other relatives. Names, characters, places, and incidents are either the product of the author's imagination or are used fictitiously. Any resemblance to actual events or locales or persons, living or dead, is entirely coincidental.

Published by
HILLSBORO PRESS
An imprint of
PROVIDENCE HOUSE PUBLISHERS
238 Seaboard Lane • Franklin, Tennessee 37067
800-321-5692
www.providencehouse.com

To Mama and
Daddy

and

To the good and decent people of Jonesboro who were part of
my family's life and part of this story.

Contents

Preface and Acknowledgments ... ix
Prologue—Images from the Past ... xi
Part One ... 1
   1. Home ... 3
   2. Jonesboro ... 12
   3. Taking Ardella Home to Colored Town ... 24
   4. God Works in Mysterious Ways ... 29
   5. Down the Red Dirt Road ... 38
   6. Walking to Jonesboro ... 50
   7. Cletus Jones's Drugstore ... 69
   8. Sometimes Secrets Have to Wait ... 83
   9. The Klan ... 91
  10. Hot Water ... 115
  11. The Peach Packing Plant ... 128
  12. Trouble ... 136

Part Two ... 145
  13. A Different Kind of Trouble ... 147
  14. New Routines ... 165
  15. Helping Ardella ... 179
  16. A Miracle at the Gypsy Camp ... 195
Epilogue ... 204

Preface and Acknowledgments

Separate Fountains started as a memoir of short stories I wrote when Mama lived with me the last few years of her life. She was always retelling our favorite family stories, and I decided I should write them down for memory's sake. One story led to another one—and thus, *Separate Fountains* developed.

I have many people to thank for the development of this book: my Aunt Dorothy for our long-distance telephone conversations and her constant encouragement that I could write a book; my friends, Mary Ann Twyford, Drollene Brown, Toni Duchi, and Noreen Wald, for their helpful critiques and suggestions; and my editors, Deborah Sims and Mary Bray Wheeler, for believing in me and the story I wanted to tell.

Last but not least I want to thank Barbara Psimas, an art student at Tallahassee Community College, for bringing my manuscript alive with her artistic talent.

Prologue

Images from the Past

The lovely black woman on the television held my full attention. She mesmerized me, but I wasn't sure why. Charlayne Hunter-Gault turned her head toward Jim Lehrer, and suddenly I remembered—I saw her as she had been in 1961, on the University of Georgia campus, as the first black female to enter the college. I shuddered as I recalled the dramatic scene we had shared as students.

January 5, 1961. The campus was quiet.
January 6, 1961. The campus was in chaos.
Federal Judge William A. Bootle ordered the University of Georgia to admit two blacks. The two students had been refused admission the preceding fall, but now here they were—like it or not. For the first time in the university's 175-year history, blacks had been given permission to be a part of the student body and to walk on the pristine campus.
All at the University of Georgia . . .
The University of Georgia—established in Athens, Georgia, in 1785, the oldest land-grant college in the United States, and the exemplar of the beliefs and values of the Old South.
The University of Georgia—whose sons fought and died in the Battle of Kennesaw Mountain, the Battle of Atlanta, the Battle of Jonesboro, and the March to Savannah, to save the southern tradition of slavery.

Separate Fountains

In spite of the mandates of the United States Supreme Court granting equal opportunities for all, education in the South continued to be served on separate plates—one black, one white.

The impossible was happening, and I was in the middle of it all. The *Atlanta Journal* reported the state of Georgia could do nothing to stop it. The United States Supreme Court ordered the integration of the University of Georgia based on its landmark decision in the case of *Linda Brown v. the Board of Education* in Topeka, Kansas, on May 17, 1954: Separate but equal schools were declared unconstitutional.

Through the media, voices across the state unfavorably responded.

"Why do these two niggers think they have the right to register for classes at a white people's university?"

"Who do they think they are?"

"I've never heard such a thing. Niggers going to school with whites!"

"Outrageous! What's this world coming to?"

"Dadgummit, I reckon the next thing you know there'll be black players on the Bulldogs' football team!"

"Did you hear the NAACP is threatening a lawsuit against the Dixie Redcoat Band if they don't stop playing 'Dixie' in Sanford Stadium?"

"Well, I guess if the Supreme Court has its way, we'll have to eat with niggers in restaurants, too."

"Or, sit with them in the back of the bus."

The black students' names were Charlayne Hunter and Hamilton Holmes. She entered as a journalism major, he registered in pre-med.

One of the first rules in the University of Georgia's 1961 Student Handbook stated that single women had to live on campus. But the dormitory assignments had already been made before Hunter's enrollment was accepted. Where would Charlayne Hunter live?

Although a sophomore, Charlayne was deliberately assigned—at the last minute—to the first floor of our freshman dormitory, Center Myers. This was no oversight. The first floor of our dormitory

Prologue

was the only women's dormitory on campus that had a whole floor of nonstudent rooms—the parlor, the housemother's living quarters, and the Women's Student Government offices. After Judge Bootle's court order, the office furniture was quickly removed to provide a place for Charlayne to live.

Charlayne Hunter now had a suite of rooms all to herself—with her own bath and water fountain. Segregation, ironically, still existed within the walls of the dormitory.

As I sat at my desk studying, I looked up and saw our housemother standing in our doorway. I turned to look directly at her, expecting her usual announcements or directions. Seeing her somber face, I quickly remembered what someone had told me about her: she hadn't smiled since her husband died fifteen years ago. I believed it.

She was the quintessential librarian type: gray hair in a bun and no makeup, except for ruby-red rouge on her cheeks. To complete the image, she wore granny glasses, a starched white blouse with a pleated black skirt, and God-awful clodhoppers.

It may have been her austere appearance that struck fear in me, but more likely it was my constant recollection of what she did to Mary Thompson at the beginning of fall quarter.

Mary lived in the room across the hall from my roommate, Rebecca, and me. Although Rebecca and I had only known her for a few days, Mary seemed to be a really sweet girl, devoid of any duplicity. We met Mary when she asked if she could borrow tacks to put up a Georgia banner. She was bubbly and very excited about attending her first football game that afternoon.

After she had gone, Rebecca and I laughed about Mary's overenthusiasm.

"The Georgia Bulldogs had better put her on the pep squad," Rebecca joked.

"Pep squad, phooey," I yelled out. "Put her on the team!"

On the third night of freshman orientation, at seven minutes after nine, our housemother called Mary's parents in Atlanta and demanded they come to get their daughter. She had broken the nine o'clock curfew.

From our room, we heard Mary crying while the housemother stood over her watching her pack. Mary was instructed to sit in her

Separate Fountains

room and wait for her parents. Our housemother's strict adherence to the rules included lights-out promptly at midnight, which forced Mary to sit in the dark until her parents arrived.

As Rebecca and I lay awake in our beds, we heard footsteps in the hall. We slipped out of our beds and tiptoed across the floor, opening the door just wide enough to see the unfolding drama.

Our housemother was leading the Thompsons down the hallway.

"Let me be direct, please, Reverend and Mrs. Thompson," she said in her precise, commanding manner. "The rules here in the dormitory have to be followed without exception if I am to have proper control. Young ladies who are mature enough to attend the university should have already been instructed to expect such guidelines."

"Excuse me, please," Reverend Thompson interrupted.

"No, excuse me, please, Reverend," our housemother continued brusquely. "I have already called Dean Tate and made my recommendation, which he supports 100 percent."

"But, please," Reverend Thompson tried to interrupt again.

"No, buts," our housemother continued with her fast-paced directions. "Mary is in her room. Perhaps she can attend the University next year when she might be more serious about her education."

Reverend Thompson's comment was loud enough for any to hear as he brushed past our housemother.

"The worst prison is a closed heart."

On that day of the 1960 fall quarter, I concluded that our housemother did, indeed, have a closed heart, or maybe no heart at all. Her rules were etched in stone and, no matter how outdated, were not to be broken.

On this evening of January 6, 1961, our housemother quietly opened our door wider and cleared her throat to get our attention. We instinctively slipped into our best behavior.

"Ladies, I'll get to the point," she began. "You know Charlayne Hunter's room is directly under yours?"

"Yes ma'am," Rebecca and I answered in unison.

"And you've no doubt seen the FBI agents standing outside her door?"

Prologue

"Yes ma'am."

"Well, one of the agents came to my parlor a few minutes ago. He said there might be some trouble here tonight."

"Trouble? What kind of trouble?" I asked.

"A demonstration march, against integration," she answered flatly.

"Who's marching?" Rebecca asked.

"I don't know," she answered, "but don't overreact—the cautious seldom err."

"Do you think they'll march all the way up to our dorm?" Rebecca questioned.

"Just stay in your room, girls. You'll be safe."

We listened to her heavy shoes clomping on the floor as she walked away, stopping at every room as she continued down the hallway. Rebecca jumped out of her seat and moved to the window. She jerked the venetian blind cord and lowered the blind. The last rays of light were shut out.

Rebecca plopped back down in her chair. "I guess we'd better study."

I bent over my books but could not concentrate.

BAM! Something hit our front window.

"What was that?" I jerked to attention.

The sound of people shouting swelled upward from the street. I leaped to the switch and turned off the overhead light.

Rushing to the window and peeping through the closed blinds, I saw something that I thought I'd left behind in Jonesboro—a white-robed and hooded crowd of Ku Klux Klan members. They carried flaming torches that lit up the sky. Students and other adults joined in, and all marched together up South Lumpkin Street under the one banner to which they all related—the Confederate Battle flag.

Suddenly the crowd spilled off the street and onto Center Myers's lawn. The lights of the torches added to the glow of the street lamps. In the common pool of light, we could see the uniformed police who were blocking the protesters from the front doors of the building. Using megaphones, the officers pleaded with the crowd to go home.

I heard rocks hit our building.

Separate Fountains

The angry crowd began a chant I had heard many times before:
"*Two, four, six, eight,
We don't want to integrate!
Eight, six, four, two,
We don't want no jigaboo!*"

Terrified, we watched as the crowd grew louder and more unruly.

"Katie Jane, what do you think's going on?" Rebecca asked nervously.

"It's hard to tell."

"Look over there, Katie Jane, see those people in the trees?"

"Yeah, they have cameras hanging around their necks."

"They must be news reporters. I wonder how they knew about the march?"

I had no time to answer.

A tomato crashed against our window, right in front of our faces. We both screamed and fell on the floor. Soon, however, curiosity drew us back to the window's edge.

We were in the direct line of fire. Angry people threw things at our dormitory, spewing their hate by pelting the building at every level. They didn't know which windows were Charlayne Hunter's, and they didn't care. The shower of debris continued to pelt Center Myers.

Rebecca jumped back, shrieking. "They're after us, too!"

"Get under the bed!" I shouted.

Fumbling in the dark, I found my pillow and scrambled under my bed. I don't know why I took my pillow since it certainly would be no protection against anything. I just knew my instincts were telling me to hold on to something.

My throat was dry and my skin felt clammy. The minutes crawled by, and my terror grew along with the noise outside. The angry mob might break down the doors. Or, what if they set the building on fire or started shooting in the windows?

What could I do? I lay there under the bed, willing myself to be somewhere else. The light from outside streaked in through the blinds, and the eerie sounds of people shouting and police sirens only added to my hysteria.

"Are you O.K.?" I asked Rebecca, trying to peer across the room in the darkness.

"I'm afraid," she whimpered.

"I hate this," I muttered.

"Me, too."

Prologue

Neither of us said what it was that we hated. Perhaps we didn't know. We just lay there, confused and afraid. Was everything so wrong in our society that a judge had to tell us how to live? Couldn't people find it in their hearts to offer justice to all? I knew for sure that it was wrong for the Ku Klux Klan to have any influence on justice for anyone, black or white.

I felt myself sinking into hopelessness. I was very alone, with no options. I prayed for an end to this madness.

The noise outside soared and the crowd grew louder.

One voice rose above the others.

"What would a nigger do with an education, anyway?"

Nigger.

Daddy called it a hate word.

I remembered back to the time when Josh said that word in childish innocence. Daddy's temper flared.

"I don't want to ever hear you say that word again, Josh!" Daddy flashed in a harsh voice that was out of character for our usually patient, easygoing father.

I remembered Daddy trying to explain his anger to us. Nigger, he had said, was a name that someone gave to coloreds even before the time of slavery. He said that it was a label used to degrade blacks and to separate them from other races.

Daddy told us that some plantation owners had grown rich using slave labor, and when the South lost the War Between the States, the slaves were left penniless and homeless. He explained that the slaves' descendants still live in the South, the one tangible reminder to deep-rooted Southerners of all that was lost.

As I continued to lie on the cold floor, my mind continued to wander. I could almost hear Reverend Wilcox's voice as he preached to us in church.

"Man is created in the image of God!"

I wanted to believe he meant all men.

I thought about Daddy again. What would be his advice if he were here with me?

Separate Fountains

I knew.

"Keep a cool head and use your wits, sugar lump," he would say. "Remember what President Roosevelt said, 'The only thing we have to fear is fear itself.'"

Perhaps President Roosevelt never encountered the Ku Klux Klan, I thought.

"Oh, God, help me," I prayed, as the tomatoes and other objects crashed against the dormitory walls.

Suddenly there was a loud crack.

Was that a gunshot?

A smell . . . what was that smell?

Is it tear gas? Would I recognize it if I smelled it?

Maybe it's the sulfur from the gunpowder.

The mob continued screaming their hate-filled words.

Weaker voices pleaded for sanity.

There seemed to be no end in sight.

Suddenly I thought of Charlayne Hunter alone in her room. She must be scared to death—more than we are. Maybe she's under her bed, too.

How long would this go on?

We could all die here.

Trembling and horrified, I wanted someone—someone who had cared for me since I was a little girl.

Not Mama.

Not Daddy.

I wanted Ardella.

She would wrap her big brown arms around me and heal my soul.

I closed my eyes tightly and felt the flow of tears run down my cheeks, over my ears, and into my hair. I couldn't blot out the image of the mob outside—images of white robes flowing in the dark. I knew that driven by hate and prejudice, the Klan didn't care who they hurt, or how many.

"Ardella," I whispered. "Now I know. Now I know how you must have felt."

Part One

Chapter One

Home

I first set my eyes on Ardella Sanders when she came through the front door of our one-room home at sunrise, on a cold winter day in 1946. I looked at her from my cot as she ambled across the floor with Daddy following right behind her.

"Mornin' Miz Taylor," Ardella said as she walked over to Mama's bed. "It's so nice to finally meet you, afta all Jake tole me 'bout you."

She extended her hand to Mama.

Mama's sleepy puzzlement gave way to a smile.

Without saying a word, I hopped off my cot and threw my quilt behind me as I raced toward Mama's bed and stood next to it. I noticed Mama's hair was tousled, and there was a crease across her cheek where she had slept on the fold of the pillowcase.

Surprised by Ardella's presence, I stood at Mama's bedside in my flannel nightgown waiting for her to put her arm around me. When Mama obliged by pulling me close to her, I looked over, and up, at the black woman looming over us.

She seemed huge in size and stature, and I felt very small. Tightly stretched across her body was a threadbare brown coat, larger than the quilt I had just thrown off. In her hands, she clutched an overstuffed pocketbook. A red wool scarf, tied in a single loop under her chin, framed her face. She wore white socks which marked a sharp contrast against her dark legs. Her loafers were worn and nearly bursting at the seams.

Mama reached up and took Ardella's hand.

"Welcome Ardella. I'm so glad you're here to help us," Mama said graciously.

Separate Fountains

I stood still. Only my eyes moved, darting between Mama and the stranger holding her hand. Who was this woman? Why did we need her to help us? Help us do what?

"You must be Miss Katie Jane," Ardella said, looking over at me. "I gots a girl 'bout yo' size."

Ardella stooped down, looking me squarely in the face. As I studied her face, I noticed her dazzling white teeth. Something about her broad, unassuming smile immediately put me at ease.

"What's your girl's name?" I asked meekly.

"Her name be Loula," she answered.

I held up four fingers. "Is Loula this old, like me?"

A laugh seemed to bubble up from Ardella's stomach.

"Dat's jes' how old Loula be," she said, as she stood up straight.

"But I'm almost five," I continued, trying to convince Ardella of my maturity. "Is Loula almost five, too?"

"Her birthday be coming up soon."

I watched Ardella as she pulled off her red scarf to reveal her shiny, slicked-back hair.

"Katie Jane, can you shows me a place to put my coat and pocketbook?" she asked.

"I have to go to work, Katherine," Daddy interrupted. He leaned over toward Mama and kissed her.

"Come here, my sugar lump," Daddy said, turning around and looking at me. "Run over here and give me a hug."

I skipped around the bed and into his hug, wrapping my arms around his neck as he bent down to pick me up. Then I asked a question I liked to ask him often . . . because I liked his answer.

"Daddy, why do you call me sugar lump?"

"Cause you're sweet as a lump of sugar," he said.

I gave him a kiss on the cheek in response to his answer.

"Help Ardella take care of your Mama today, you hear?" he whispered in my ear, as he put me back down on the floor.

"Yes, sir."

"See you gals tonight," he said as he left, closing the door behind him.

Suddenly, everything was silent—and different. Daddy had left Mama and me in the company of someone I did not know.

Mama's voice broke the silence.

"Katie Jane, show Ardella the coat-rack by the back door. She can put her things there."

Home

Reluctantly, I led the way.

When Ardella took off her coat, I noticed she wore a red-and-white checkered, knee-length cotton dress that stretched tightly over her ample bosom and stomach. The fit was so strained the buttons looked as if they might pop off at any minute if she sneezed. Short sleeves exposed her big, muscular arms and her hands obviously had never known dainty.

"Wat duz you think yo' mama wants for breakfast?" Ardella asked, ignoring the fact that our one-room house didn't allow for private conversations.

"I think she wants pancakes," I piped up.

Pancakes were certainly what I wanted. This was my chance to get a treat we usually had only on weekends.

"Pancakes sound good to me," Mama agreed. As she spoke, she fluffed her feather pillows and leaned against the headboard.

"Pancakes a-comin' up. Jes' tell me where de makins is, Miz Taylor."

"The flour and baking soda are in the right-hand side of the cupboard," Mama instructed. "There are eggs and milk in the refrigerator. Katie Jane, show Ardella where to find the bowl and sifter. And, don't forget the lard!"

Ardella pulled the ingredients out and lined them up on the counter. As she started mixing them together, she looked over at me.

"Loula heps me make pancakes at home," she said. "Would you likes to hep?"

"Yes ma'am!" I exclaimed.

Ardella pointed to the chair by the kitchen table.

"Git up on dis here chair," she said. "You can heps me stir."

I climbed up on the chair and waited. Ardella, bowl and spoon in hand, came over and stood beside me, placing the mixing bowl on the table. She gently took my hand and held onto it. Placing her hand over mine, she guided both our hands to the handle of the large wooden spoon. Our hands moved together as we began stirring.

I did not look in the bowl. I stared instead at Ardella's large brown hand covering my small white one, pushing the spoon around and around.

"That be jes' 'nough," she said, stopping the stirring motion of our hands. "But you such a good heper, Miss Katie Jane. Maybe we's can make cookies later."

Separate Fountains

She did not know it, but Ardella was quickly beginning to find a place in my heart.

Ardella, Mama, and I sat at the table together. Mama tried to eat her pancakes, but halfway through the meal, she had to jump up and run to the bathroom. I heard her throwing up. She had not been feeling well and was spending more and more time in bed. When Daddy was home at meal times, I noticed the worried look on his face as he watched Mama get sick every time she tried to eat.

"Don't you worries none, chile." Ardella reached over and patted my hand. "Everythang's gonna be all right."

"What's wrong with Mama?" I asked.

"She's jes' feelin' a little poorly with morning sickness. Go on and eats yo' breakfast."

When Mama came out of the bathroom, she went straight to bed. Ardella prepared a cold wet cloth and held it to Mama's forehead. Before long, Mama smiled and took the wash cloth from Ardella and held it to her own brow. I finished my pancakes in silence.

"Ardella, you better help Katie Jane get dressed," Mama instructed.

"Yes'm," Ardella answered as she ambled over to the chest of drawers and pulled out some clothing. "Come here, chile. Let's put dese thangs on."

Sliding a cotton shirt over my head, she pulled my arms through the long sleeves, then slid the shirt down over my body. Instructing me to sit on the edge of my cot, she held my jodhpurs in front of me.

Jodhpurs were the type of breeches I wore in the winter because I had only one pair of blue jeans. The jeans could only be worn on special occasions, like a trip to Atlanta. Mama had purchased several pairs of the jodhpurs for twenty-five cents each from one of Mr. Solomon's suitcase sales.

"Puts yo' leg in here," Ardella instructed as she guided my foot through the narrow ankle of the pant leg. She pulled up the riding-style breeches, cut full through the hips, and close-fitted from knee to ankle. She guided my pants over my hips, zipped them up, and snapped them shut. She crossed the straps over my back, brought them across my shoulders, and buttoned them to the front waistband.

"You puts on dese here socks, chile, then I heps you tie your Buster Browns."

I dutifully obeyed.

7

Home

After Ardella tied my shoes, she took my hand and led me to a chair at the kitchen table. Borrowing Mama's brush, she gently removed the tangles from my blond hair as she sang:

> *. . . Oh, when de Saints*
> *Go marchin' in,*
> *Oh Lord, I wants to be in dat number,*
> *When de saints go marchin' in . . ."*

As she sang and hummed, she braided my hair. With patience, she did one side and then the other, making pigtails and tying each at the end with a small rubber band. To keep the short, fine hair away from my face, she clipped a barrette on each side of my brushed-back hair.

"You be dressed for de day, Miss Katie Jane. Stays clean now, you hear?"

"Yes, ma'am."

For the rest of the day, Mama told Ardella what to do and where to find things while I followed my new friend around like a puppy. Asking for my help with the chores, she chatted with me about how Loula helped her at home.

As Ardella began ironing, I found the courage to ask a question.

"Ardella, do you live in a house?"

"Katie Jane! What a thing to ask!" Mama admonished me from her bed.

I did not know Mama was listening. I saw nothing rude about the question.

"We used to live in a trailer," I continued. "Have you ever lived in a trailer, Ardella?"

"No's, not me. But I heard 'bout yawl's trailer."

"It was only one room, a living room with a kitchen and bathroom," I carefully repeated the story as I knew it. "And Mama and Daddy turned the sofa into a bed at night."

Separate Fountains

Mama laughed. She knew I wanted to hear my favorite family story.

"That trailer was so small," Mama began, "the only place we had to put Katie Jane's bassinet was in the middle of the floor. Every time her daddy walked by, he had to pick her up and give her some attention. To this day, Ardella, Katie Jane is Daddy's girl."

"I knows wat you mean," Ardella nodded, still quickly and efficiently working her way through the pile of ironing. "Jake toles me how happy yawl waz to git dis house. You lucky to git all dem building supplies, it bein' so soon afta de war."

"Yes, luck and friends just seemed to drop out of heaven," Mama said.

"Dat dey did, Miz Taylor. Jake tole me how evey'body in town hepped yawl out."

A year earlier, Daddy, a civil engineer, had put an end to our traveling from one Army post to another by taking a job on an Army base in Atlanta. Reflecting back, I imagine it was probably Mama who put an end to the traveling. As she would say in her tell-it-like-it-is fashion, "I was sick of wandering around like a gypsy."

When Daddy bought land in Jonesboro, about thirty miles south of Atlanta, Mama did not complain about the fact that our home

Home

continued to be the one-room trailer we had hauled behind our Plymouth coupe. The trailer, sitting on a five-acre plot on Dixon Road, was parked there permanently until Daddy could find the time to build our present home.

"Katie Jane, that's enough about the trailer," Mama said. "Come here and I'll read to you."

Sitting next to Mama on her bed and propping my head against her shoulder, I tried to listen as she read. But, my mind wasn't on the story. I could not concentrate because of Ardella's singing.

Out of the corner of my eye, I watched Ardella at the ironing board, singing and humming as she worked. Ardella's talent displayed her personal musical style, filling in her own words and rhythms as she wanted.

> The Jordan river's deep and wide
> But soon I's be to the other side,
> I's gonna lay my burden down,
> de dum, de dum, . . . I's gonna lay my burden down . . ."

Holding the iron over one of Daddy's shirts with her right hand, she reached across with her left to dip her fingers into a bowl of water. Then she shook her dripping fingers over the shirt, dampening it. She smacked the iron down on the wet cloth, and the sizzling water created little puffs of steam. The air filled with the smell of hot, slightly scorched cotton.

My mind continued to wander from the story. As I watched Ardella and listened to her singing, I felt the easy peace her presence brought to the room. I wondered where Daddy had found her.

Somehow within those thoughts, I fell into a light sleep. Fuzzily aware of Ardella picking me up from Mama's bed, I felt her body against mine as she placed me gently on my cot.

I breathed deeply. Ardella smelled of lye soap, different from Mama who smelled of violets and lavender water.

As the years passed, I would get to know Ardella well, along with her husband, Jake, and their five children. But, at that time, as a young child in 1946, there was no way for me to know the hardships they felt

Separate Fountains

in a poverty-sticken Georgia. Work was scarce for whites, but work for coloreds was hard—sunup to sundown—with wages slim enough to put "poverty in yo' pocket" by the end of the week.

Ardella and Jake lived and worked on Colonel Bartlett's peach farm before they decided to move to Jonesboro's Colored Town. They had moved there so their children would have an opportunity to go to the Jonesboro Colored Elementary School, a chance Ardella and Jake never had.

Daddy said the peach farm had been a plantation during the War Between the States, and that it had been owned by Colonel Bartlett's grandfather. Daddy said Colonel Bartlett's first name was really Thomas, but everyone called him "Colonel" because he had served as an army colonel during World War I.

Ardella's and Jake's ancestors, originally slaves from Ebo, Africa, were brought to America by slave traders who smuggled them in along Georgia's coastal marshlands and barrier islands. Colonel Bartlett's grandfather bought the slaves for his cotton plantation from an Atlanta trader.

Ardella and Jake were born and raised in the shanty houses on the back side of the plantation. When they moved into town, Jake continued working on the old plantation. In a wooden wagon pulled by a mule, Jake made the five-mile trip back and forth every day.

Daddy said the boll weevil plague of the late 1930s devastated the Bartlett's cotton crop, causing the Bartletts to lose most of their fortune. Determined to find a new crop, the Colonel planted peach trees. Jake helped plant and nurture the trees, and in doing so, earned himself the position of overseer of the peach farm.

In the summer, Jake returned to Colonel Bartlett's peach packing plant at night and on weekends to work for additional wages. Ardella and their children worked there, too, on the assembly line packing the seasonal peaches for the Atlanta Farmer's Market.

When Daddy got home from work, he sat down beside me on my cot. He started his usual habit of waking me to one of his silly songs:
When I was a tiny sleepyhead,
Mama gently would tuck me into bed,
And sing of raisins and almonds,

Home

I rolled over and started laughing and singing with Daddy:
Raisins and almonds
Raisins and almonds . . .

"I'm home, Katie Jane," he said, as he scooped me up in his arms and took me to Mama's bedside. We stood there watching Ardella as she fluffed Mama's pillows.

"Ardella, did my little sugar lump talk your ears off today?" Daddy asked.

"No suh. She be a right smart chile, dat one. And Miz Taylor be as nice as Jake tole me."

"Thank you," Mama replied, with a warm smile. "I'm very pleased with your work today."

"Well, I guess we'd better get you home, Ardella," Daddy said. "Jake and the kids will be waiting."

From that day on, a new ritual in our daily lives began. When Daddy said he was ready to take Ardella home, I begged to go along.

At the car, when Daddy flipped the front seat forward for me to get in the back, Ardella insisted the backseat was for colored folks. Daddy insisted she sit in front with him. She protested. He insisted.

I quickly learned to help Daddy by jumping in the back before Ardella could, lying across the whole backseat so Ardella would not have room to get in. Daddy and Ardella would laugh at my clowning, and he'd settle Ardella in front with him for the ride to Jonesboro's Colored Town.

This friendly dispute over who was supposed to ride in the backseat was just the beginning of my observance of Daddy's integrity.

Riding to take Ardella home everyday led me to become Daddy's constant travel companion. Over the years, I was to travel many miles with him over Jonesboro's paved streets and Clayton County's dusty, red dirt roads.

Chapter Two

Jonesboro

Before I continue with my story, let me tell you about the town of Jonesboro and what it was like when I was growing up there in the late 1940s and early 1950s.

By outward appearance, Jonesboro seemed like a typical Southern town built along the railroad tracks. However, as I matured and became more observant of my surroundings, my perspective of Jonesboro changed. I realized a visitor driving through would not have any way of knowing what this town was really like. I knew for sure its underlying social structure was a well-kept secret—a side its good citizens did not want to admit. The sons and daughters of this old plantation community were in disguise, but they were still in control.

In Jonesboro, as in all the South, the black people had no human rights. No job opportunities—except for farm work, cleaning houses, or raking yards. No education—blacks could be arrested if they even set foot on the white elementary or high school grounds. No use of public facilities—blacks could not go to the bathroom nor drink from a water fountain unless they were marked "Colored." And for sure, blacks had no protection by the police—the police were afraid to protect them. Because of the Ku Klux Klan!

Like many towns in Georgia, Jonesboro's business district was a row of connected buildings on either side of the railroad tracks. Many of the one- and two-story buildings had been constructed before the

Jonesboro

War Between the States of handmade, Georgia red-clay bricks. A few of the buildings had cellars that had served as saloons during Prohibition, but now were used for storage or hiding places for hooky-playing children and the town drunks.

Directly in front of Jonesboro's stores, across the railroad tracks and up on a hill, was the Clayton County Courthouse. Jonesboro was the county seat for Clayton County, Georgia. When I went to the courthouse with Daddy where he had to pay taxes or take care of other business, he explained to me that the courthouse was a place where elected and appointed officials worked to run our county government. Daddy also explained it was a place where one could register to vote—if you were a landowner or if you could afford to pay Georgia's poll tax on voting.

Daddy explained to me that since very few black people owned land, the poll tax was a scheme the Georgia legislators developed to keep black people in the state from being qualified voters. All potential voters—white and black—had to purchase a "poll ticket" several weeks before voting time to prove they had paid Georgia's poll tax. Daddy said even if black people could afford to buy a poll ticket, white people were always trying to come up with ways to entice the blacks to forfeit their ticket—by putting up signs in stores offering free merchandise or food and by putting up signs in gas stations to offer free gas. I can remember every fall when the county fair came to the Jonesboro area, signs would be posted everywhere: One Poll Ticket = Free Entrance to the Fair.

14

Separate Fountains

Daddy said it was amazing to him how everybody put up such a fuss over the idea of black people voting in Clayton County—but nobody seemed to care if dead people voted on election day. He said we actually had a governor that was elected by dead people's votes. Clayton County's Courthouse must not have been the only courthouse in Georgia that had dead people on the voter's registration list.

Jonesboro

The beauty of Jonesboro was the scenery along the roadside before one entered the business district. On the outskirts of Jonesboro, a few antebellum homes still stood, having survived the War Between the States. For some reason, Sherman spared these stately homes, using some of them as headquarters for his troops on their march to Savannah. These houses were now the pride of Jonesboro.

The largest of the white-column homes was the Warren House. Daddy told me one time it was over a hundred years old, built somewhere around 1840. During and after the Battle of Jonesboro (August 31–September 1, 1864), Sherman ordered that the Warren House be used for the Union's headquarters and hospital for the Fifty-second Illinois Regiment.

Daddy said Union soldiers' diaries revealed some of the bloodiest fighting of the War Between the States took place at the Battle of Jonesboro. The Warren House was near the battlefield, and as a Union hospital, gruesome surgeries were said to have taken place upstairs in the operating rooms—turning the house into a horror chamber.

Doctors amputated limbs of wounded soldiers and threw them out the window. One diary stated there was a pile of arms and legs on the ground five or six feet deep. Another diary told of dead bodies stacked around the house—heaped like piles of cordwood. It was suspected that some of the Union soldiers may have even been buried on the property.

Separate Fountains

Roger Walker, a local house painter, told Daddy he once painted the Warren House, and that he would never paint it again—in this lifetime. He said he definitely felt the presence of supernatural beings in the house when he painted it. In the upstairs room where amputations were performed, Mr. Walker had to paint over signatures of the amputees who had etched their names on the walls with a knife.

To this day, some of Jonesboro's most respectable citizens tell of hearing footsteps on the staircase or seeing ghosts at the windows of the Warren House. All of the ghosts supposedly appear as white, shadowy figures dressed as Union soldiers. Several were seen sitting in the upstairs windows, staring across the street at the Confederate cemetery.

For some reason, as I got older, all these stories about the Warren House stayed in the back of my mind. I definitely felt the house had a mysterious ambiance about it, luring me to stare every time I passed by. I tried to imagine what it had been like when the Union Army occupied it.

One day I realized the irony of this location of the Union's medical headquarters. The place where Union soldiers received medical treatment was right across the street from the Jonesboro Confederate Cemetery. Southern boys were laid in the depths of the red-clay earth while wounded Union soldiers were laid on the white sheets of a plantation house—one symbol of Southern tradition for which the Southern soldiers died.

The Jonesboro Confederate Cemetery, for as far as the eye could see, contained white grave markers standing in straight, tight rows. In death as in life, the soldiers were lined up as if for inspection. Each plot was marked with one marker that bore no name. Hundreds of unknown soldiers, rebels in gray uniforms, had fought in the Battle of Jonesboro, which they lost, along with their lives.

Every time I passed the Warren House, I pondered over different thoughts that ran across my wandering mind. I wondered whether the struggle between

Jonesboro

Confederate and Union soldiers still went on even after death. Was there a South and a North in heaven?

Did the ghosts of these Confederate boys know that some of the blue-uniformed Union soldiers they fought were hospitalized in the Warren House? Did they know that Yankees—dirty, sweat-caked and bloody, many only identifiable by their Northern accents—occupied the Southern mansion?

When the Union soldiers were lying in the makeshift hospital, was even one aware that maybe a man lying in a grave across the street had died by his hand? As some of these Yankees lay at death's door, did they feel any sympathy for the Southern families who had lost their loved ones, never to hear their Southern accents again?

I even wondered if Sherman's overworked medical staff ever crossed the street in the middle of the night to the cemetery to quickly bury a Yankee. One time I asked one of Mama's friends, an active member of the United Daughters of the Confederacy, if she thought any Yankees were buried in Jonesboro's Confederate Cemetery by mistake. She got so upset with me for having such a thought she immediately pulled her smelling salts from her pocketbook.

The Warren House reflected not only mystery but beauty to me. I can still remember the loveliness of its manicured yard on a summer's day. During warm weather, the yards of all the houses on Jonesboro's Main Street mirrored nature's charm.

A variety of trees—pines, water oaks, and weeping willows—were scattered here and there. The beauty of the traditional Southern magnolia, with its waxy dark-green leaves and sweet-smelling white flowers, caught one's attention more than the other surrounding foliage. Plants bloomed with flowers—azaleas, crepe myrtle, day lilies, irises, and roses—to name a few, along with wild honeysuckle, of course.

The antebellum, white-columned homes, still a symbol of the wealth of the Old South, stood out, looking like a painted picture. The splendid mansions had wraparound porches, with rocking chairs ready for a lazy summer afternoon of sipping sweet lemonade, iced tea, or mint juleps with neighbors and friends. Behind the porches were ceiling-to-floor windows with forest green shutters against the dazzling white paint of the house. Sitting primly on their velvety green lawns, these two-story mansions seemed to mock the simple, wood-framed dwellings that lined the other side of the street.

Separate Fountains

Sprinkled between the mansions were modest wood-framed houses and brick houses. Daddy told me some people in Jonesboro thought a brick home was the new symbol of prosperity and a way to improve one's social status. Most of the brick homes were built of dark-red bricks, but some had a blending of multicolored bricks. Daddy explained the multicolored bricks were probably used because they could be bought at a discount at the Chattahoochee Brick Company in Atlanta. He said these bricks were a good deal even though they were slightly damaged, having been chipped or broken in the kilns. Daddy said even rich people like a good deal.

There was one other type of housing in our community, and some part of Jonesboro's society did not like to admit we had it. This was free public housing—clapboard shanties at the Poor Folks Farm. In these shanties, whites and blacks had to live side-by-side. But they weren't called whites and blacks—they were labeled as "poor white trash and niggers."

The Poor Folks Farm was located on a large tract of land called the County Farm. This property was owned by the Clayton County Government and was north of Jonesboro off a dirt road that ran parallel to the railroad tracks. The County Farm was a place where several government facilities were housed and was under the direction of three elected commissioners who ran the government from the courthouse.

When one first entered the County Farm, one saw a white wood-framed house which was the home of the overseer of this large complex. I had been to this house many times in my earlier years because our present neighbors, Clark and Eunice Elliott, had lived there when Clark worked as the overseer. Mr. Elliott and Daddy had been friends since they had worked together for Georgia's State Highway Department.

Whenever Mr. Elliott had a problem with any of the county's farm equipment, he called on Daddy to repair it. And of course, I tagged along with Daddy and roamed all over the County Farm. Often I walked down the short road to the Poor Folks Farm and played with my school classmates who lived there. One of them actually taught me to ride a bicycle.

Jonesboro

On the right side of the overseer's house was Clayton County's jail and a small garage for maintaining the county's school buses, police cars, and other county vehicles. The county garage also serviced the county vehicles with gas at its private pump.

On the left side of the overseer's house was a dirt road with an arrow-shaped sign posted by its entrance. This directional sign read: Poor Folks Farm. This one-lane dirt road went further north about five hundred feet, becoming a circular drive. The circular drive was surrounded by large water-oak trees and tall pines.

Around the outskirts of the circled drive were eight unpainted clapboard shanties with tin roofs and open windows. The windows had no screens, only wooden shutters to close for protection from rain and cold weather. Each shanty was like a duplex with a wall and fireplace separating the two families who shared the house. One chimney stack served the two fireplaces, one for each side of the house.

In the middle of the circle of shanties was a covered wooden well where all citizens of the Poor Folks Farm could draw buckets of water for bathing, cooking, and washing dishes or clothing. In the rear of each house was a small fenced-in yard that was sectioned off by tracts, giving each family an assigned garden plot. At the very back of each yard was a small outhouse that served as a bathroom for the occupants of that particular house.

The occupants of the shanties had to live up to the county government's rules and regulations. An assigned county official inspected the shanties every few days. To help the occupants remember the rules, the inspector had what he called the five finger rules. He would hold up his hand and repeat the following rules, flipping one finger at a time in front of the occupants' faces to stress each rule.

Starting by holding up his pinkie finger, then pointing one at a time to the other three fingers and the thumb as he went down the list of rules, the inspector would loudly announce: "Rule number one, take a bath every day with the Octogen soap furnished by the county.

Separate Fountains

Rule number two, clothing and living quarters must always be clean. Rule number three, no feuding, fighting, or drinking anywhere on the property. Rule number four, feed your own family by working your own garden plot. Rule number five, pray to God daily for employment and to get out of this God-forsaken place."

After the county official finished his speech about the five rules, he called on someone in the household group to repeat them, making sure everybody understood and obeyed the rules.

"God helps those who help themselves" was the motto at the Poor Folks Farm. All occupants of the shanties were expected to plant and harvest their own vegetables and fruits, with the county supplementing their diets with only a few staple items such as dried peas and beans, flour, and cornmeal. The county supplied seeds, plants, and fertilizer to the occupants, along with blue Ball glass jars for preserving some of their food for winter. In a side yard at the Poor Folks Farm was a fenced-in area for cattle. The county furnished several cows for the occupants to milk; therefore, they had milk to drink and cream to make butter.

The Poor Folks Farm was the only place in our community where whites and blacks lived side-by-side. Hard times had fallen on them: tuberculosis, pneumonia, loss of a job. These people didn't have the luxury of any choices. They lived one day at a time to survive until life offered them a way out, or until they gave up on life and died.

The only sunshine in these people's lives was when Jonesboro's church members and other caring citizens brought them food, clothing, or holiday baskets. Many of the townspeople helped these less fortunate souls by hiring them to work in their yards or clean their houses, and once some mutual trust was developed, usually helped the less fortunate citizens get a job.

Even today, I can still remember the names of my classmates from elementary school that were from the Poor Folks Farm. I was never aware of any social stigma against them because all students in our school were accustomed to having these children in our classrooms. I also remember when our teacher, on the first day of school, asked the children in the class to stand up and say their names and where they lived, a child from the Poor Folks Farm would stand up and say: "I'm _____ . I live at the Poor Folks Farm." None of my classmates ever giggled or laughed at their pronouncement.

Jonesboro

Maybe it was because back then materialism was not as much a part of our society as it is today. There were no credit cards; your family only bought the things they could afford. There was no health insurance, and some families could not even afford to go to the doctor or dentist.

All my classmates lived basically the same modest lifestyle I did. As children we each had limited material things—a few clothes, two pair of shoes (one for school and one for church), a lunch box with Roy Rogers or Dale Evans on it, a bicycle, a deck of Old Maid cards, jacks, a jump rope, and a few board games.

In the late 1940s and early 1950s, many families were struggling because of the effects of World War II on America's economy. In 1952 the average American's weekly wage for a forty-hour week was $58.32—$12.44 a day, or $1.43 an hour. That average weekly wage was based on wages up north where factory workers made more than people down south.

In my later years, Daddy told me he always made about the national average weekly wage since he worked on an army base. When he got a pay increase, he always increased Ardella's pay. By the time he paid Ardella, our living expenses, and Mama's doctor bills, Daddy said he hardly had a penny left in his pocket.

Mama somehow managed to save a little money now and then from our grocery budget, hiding the money, wrapped in wax paper, under the cookies in the bottom of the cookie jar. I can remember hearing Mama and Daddy counting that saved money as they scraped for extra dollars to help with emergency situations. As a family, we made do with what we had—and were thankful for that. Daddy and Mama consciously budgeted our money so we wouldn't have to go to the Poor Folks Farm.

I can still remember how the steeples of Jonesboro's churches could be seen across the town's skyline. The Methodist Church was on the south end of Main Street, and the Baptist Church was located on College Street, almost directly behind the Methodist Church.

Separate Fountains

The Presbyterian Church, which my family attended, was in the old Clayton County Courthouse on Stockbridge Street. Because our church's small congregation couldn't afford to maintain this large building, the Presbyterians and the Fraternal Order of Masons decided to purchase the building together. The Presbyterians used the lower floor, which furnished a sanctuary and several classrooms, and the Masons used the second floor for their meetings. In 1947, the Presbyterians started the building of a new church on the corner of Spring and Lee Streets. A new sanctuary was erected in 1953.

Only white people were allowed to worship in these three churches. The black people had their church in Colored Town.

There were three public schools within the city limits of Jonesboro. On Lee Street, the elementary and high schools for white students were located next to each other. The high school even boasted a football stadium next to it—for whites only, of course.

The elementary school for black children was on Smith Street, almost directly across the street from the west side of the football stadium. When I got older, I realized the black children did not have a high school to attend in our community. They were bused about ten miles away to a black high school, Fountain High, in Forest Park.

When I questioned Daddy about why the black children in Jonesboro did not have a high school, he said the black children in Clayton County got shortchanged on education all the way around. The Clayton County Board of Education even refused to buy them new textbooks. The black children used the old, outdated texts discarded by the white schools.

The black students also had to ride on the county's oldest school buses. When I was in high school, one of the buses carrying the black students broke down. The black bus driver had to walk several miles to the nearest house and ask to use the telephone so he could get help. He called the school bus supervisor at the bus maintenance facility at the County Farm.

The white school bus supervisor told the black driver that one of the white drivers had just brought a white-student school bus back to the maintenance facility, having finished his route of taking white students home. The supervisor sent the white driver with his bus to pick up the black students and take them home.

Jonesboro

That night the Ku Klux Klan burned three crosses in Jonesboro. One in front of the black school bus driver's home, one in front of the white school bus driver's home—and one in front of the bus supervisor's home.

Near the football stadium was the city of Jonesboro's swimming pool. Although it was supposed to be a public facility, only whites were allowed to use the pool. To make sure everyone in town understood, five "White Only" signs were posted on the chain-link fence around the enclosed pool—one sign at the shower house and entrance area—and one sign on each side of the pool. The city fathers kept the blacks out by requiring individual and family membership—preapproved, of course—and a seasonal membership fee.

One night after the pool was closed some black children climbed over the high fence and went swimming in the pool. The Ku Klux Klan heard about it and threatened to fill the pool with truck loads of Georgia red clay to keep the black children out of the pool. To quickly suppress the potential Klan involvement, the city fathers put padlocks on the pool entrance and barbed wire around the top of the chain-link fence. The city fathers also had the water from the pool drained and closed the pool for the rest of that summer. Now no child—white or black—could swim in the public pool.

Chapter Three

Taking Ardella Home to Colored Town

On this cold winter day in 1946, as Daddy, Ardella, and I continued our ride toward Ardella's house, we passed a few of Jonesboro's stores and then took a quick left to cross the railroad tracks. After crossing the tracks, we drove up a hill toward the Clayton County Courthouse. I looked up at the two-story brick structure and wondered if Mama's friend, Mrs. Watson, was looking out the window. No, I thought, it is getting dark so she's probably gone home by now.

"Ardella, are we almost to your house?" I asked.

"Jes' over de hill, chile. We almost be dere."

Behind the courthouse was a dirt road that we followed down the hill until we came to a fork in the road. As we took the right road that led through the woods, I looked back at the road to the left.

"What is that way, Daddy?" I asked.

"The city cemetery, don't you remember?" he answered.

"Oh, is that where Aunt Ruth . . ."

"Watch out fer dat hole, Mistuh Taylor!" Ardella interrupted. "When it rain, dis here red clay be a muddy mess. If it be a-rainin' when you come to git me, I be out on de main road a-waitin.'"

I forgot my question about the cemetery as Colored Town came into view. In the middle of the woods was a residential area with several blocks of red clay streets. Some of the streets were of loosened clay, and other streets were of hardened clay. The red dirt had become as hard as concrete, being compressed from years of use.

Daddy knew just where to turn to go to Ardella's house, since he had been there many times to pick up Jake when they were building

Taking Ardella Home to Colored Town

our house. As we continued down the street, Ardella pointed out the colored Baptist church.

Looking over Ardella's shoulder, I eagerly absorbed the sights and sounds of Colored Town. I saw small clapboard houses, some so dilapidated they looked as they would sink into the ground at any minute. Others, painted and well kept, had rocking chairs on the front porches. There was not much grass, but the yards were swept clean of debris.

"This be my house coming up next," Ardella said, as she pointed to her place with pride.

Ardella's house was white with a yellow front door. It appeared larger than the other houses, probably because Jake used his carpentry skills to build on extra rooms. Her house was one of the few houses with screens on the windows.

Jake was drawing water from the well in their side yard as we arrived. He paused to wave at us.

"Thank you for your help, Ardella," Daddy said. He reached into his pocket and handed her two dollars. "I'll pick you up at 5:30 tomorrow morning."

"Yessuh, I be ready," she answered, as she opened the car door and climbed out.

"Bye, Ardella," I said.

"Bye, chile."

Daddy and I watched Ardella as she walked across her yard, entered her home, and closed the door behind her.

"Why doesn't Ardella have any lights on?" I asked. "It's getting dark."

"She uses candlelight." Daddy said, as he backed the car out of the driveway.

"Can't she use light bulbs like we do?"

"No, Georgia Power won't run electrical lines to Colored Town."

"Is that why there are no street lights?"

"Yes, sugar lump."

I tumbled over into the front seat with Daddy as we started back to Jonesboro.

"Why don't we have a yellow front door, Daddy?" I said. "I wish our house wasn't blue all over, inside and out."

"I've told you all about that. Blue was the only color Smith's Hardware could get right after the war."

Separate Fountains

"Tell me again, Daddy," I pleaded, wanting to hear one of my favorite family stories.

I moved closer, snuggling against him on the car's bench seat.

"Well, World War II had just ended when we moved to Jonesboro," Daddy started. "There was a shortage of building materials, making it impossible to buy supplies unless you could prove they were needed for an emergency."

"Or, if you had the right friend," I prompted, knowing the story well.

"Right. And we were lucky to have a friend in the building supply business."

"Mr. M. C. Jernigan!" I exclaimed.

"Yes, Mama and I met the Jernigans at church, and I frequently saw M. C. at his store. When I'd run in to buy items needed to start our house's foundation, I'd hear him explaining to his customers how hard it was to get building materials."

"Because of rationing," I piped up again, using the big word I had heard Daddy and Mama say often. They explained to me that it meant we could not always have the things we needed. We had to share equally with others in the community.

"Right again," Daddy answered, then continued. "Well, one Sunday after church, M. C. came up to me and said he and Mrs. Jernigan were worried about us living in a one-room trailer. He insisted on giving me enough supplies to finish the house before your mother had the baby."

"But later you found out it was Mrs. Jernigan who insisted he give you the supplies," I added, having heard Mama tell this truth.

"Yes, she was your mama's friend, and she wanted Mr. Jernigan to help us."

"Why didn't Mr. Jernigan just sell you the supplies?"

"Because of the rules of rationing. If he sold to me, he had to sell to everyone. But he could give the supplies to us without anyone knowing. Mrs. Jernigan nagged and pestered him, insisting supplies for our house be his top priority."

"Did you ever pay Mr. Jernigan back?" I asked.

"Yes, but it took me almost a year. I had told Mr. Jernigan that the only way I would accept his offer would be with the understanding that I'd pay him as soon as I had the money."

Daddy went on to explain to me that Mr. Jernigan never mentioned the amount of supplies used or their value. As he talked, I thought of the times I had seen Daddy writing in his journal. One time, when I questioned him about his task, Daddy told me he was keeping a record of all the materials used so that one day he could pay off his debt to Mr. Jernigan.

"The ox was in the ditch," I quickly said, not sure of the meaning but sure that Daddy said it often when he had to do any kind of work on Sunday.

"Yes, Katie Jane, the ox was in the ditch. Our family needed larger living quarters because of a new baby. So, I met M. C. night after night behind his store. He and I loaded my car with concrete blocks and bags of cement. I'd drive home, unload the car in the dark, then the next morning go about my usual routine. After work and on weekends, Jake and I built our house."

"I remember some of the things you told me you and Jake had to do. You said you used a pick and a hoe to dig the foundation. You mixed the cement in a wooden trough and carried it by wheelbarrow to where it was needed."

"Are you sure you need me to tell this story?" Daddy joked.

"Oh, yes, Daddy," I said. "Because sometimes I come up with new questions."

"Like what?"

"Well . . . can you tell me why you made our house like a big box, with one little box inside for the bathroom."

"Because it was the quickest way to get a roof over our heads, Katie Jane."

"I have another question," I continued. "Do you know why Mama calls our house 'our blue heaven'?"

Daddy laughed.

"Oh, your mama's just joshing. She came up with that name because our house is blue, and because she feels all the people who helped us build it dropped out of heaven."

"What do you mean?"

"Oh, it's just a old saying that when people help you unexpectedly, you say they must have dropped out of heaven."

Daddy continued his story by telling me how Sue Watson, who worked at the courthouse, found two discarded sinks and a commode. The courthouse's public bathroom for whites had been remodeled, and someone threw the bathroom fixtures in the ditch behind the building. She hid them in the bushes until she could go home and get her husband to pick them up in his truck and deliver them to Daddy.

George Smith gave Daddy used plumbing supplies from his hardware store, and his brother, Charlie, who was a plumber, helped

Separate Fountains

Daddy with our house's plumbing. David Cummings, a farmer, gave us three windows and their frames—after a part of one of his tenant houses was destroyed by fire. Lamar Johnson, an electrician, did the electrical wiring in our house in exchange for Daddy's mechanical talent to repair his tractor.

"We even have a blue door, Daddy," I sighed as we walked up the front steps. "Why can't we have a yellow door like Ardella?"

"We have to keep it blue because your mama's blue heaven is really famous."

"What do you mean?" I asked.

"They've even written a song about it."

"Really?"

As Daddy opened the front door, he started singing:
>When whippoorwills call,
>When evening is nigh,
>I'll hurry home . . . to my blue heaven.

Mama started laughing.

"What's going on?" she asked, seated in a rocking chair in the center of the room.

"Oh, I was just telling Katie Jane our blue house is so famous they'd written a song about it."

Mama cackled with laughter.

Daddy and I crossed the room to Mama. As he bent down to kiss her, she reached out to me, pulling me up into her lap. Tired, I curled up and looked around the room.

All the walls were a soft sky blue. The back of the kitchen cabinets was even blue, forming a dividing wall between the kitchen and living area. In the living area, along the side of one wall, was Mama and Daddy's bed, and beside it was a chest of drawers with a mirror. Against the opposite wall was my cot, a thin mattress supported by a metal frame.

During the day, my cot became our sofa, with pillows propped against the wall behind it. Next to the cot was a small bookshelf and a floor lamp. In the corner was a built-in closet with a curtain hanging in front of it. The tiny bathroom with its block shower opened into the kitchen side of the room.

Yes, my family had everything we needed. And, now we had someone to share "our blue heaven"—Ardella.

Chapter Four

God Works in Mysterious Ways

One spring morning, Daddy woke me up by gently rubbing my cheek, urging me to get dressed. I looked toward Mama, who was already sitting on the side of her bed fully dressed. I knew immediately something was wrong.

"What's Mama doing?" I asked sleepily.

"She needs to go to the doctor, sugar lump," he answered. "Please get up and get dressed quickly."

"What's wrong with her?" I questioned.

"She's not feeling well," he said as he guided me to the clothes he had put out for me to wear.

"You can't go with us today," Daddy continued as he helped me dress. "You'll have to stay with Eunice and Clark Elliott next door."

"But Daddy . . ."

"Eunice is making pancakes for breakfast," he interrupted. "She knows how you love them."

"But Daddy, I wanna go with you and Mama," I whined.

"Not today, Katie Jane," Daddy answered sternly. By the tone of his voice, I knew there was no chance for discussion.

Although the Elliotts were kind and attentive, the hours dragged by slowly. I was restless and curious about where my parents were. I kept asking when they would be back to get me, looking out their living room window often for our Plymouth coupe. Finally, in midafternoon, Daddy drove up the driveway. When Daddy stepped out of the car and I saw that Mama wasn't with him, my initial joy turned to apprehension.

I ran to meet Daddy as he opened the front door.

Separate Fountains

"Where's Mama?" I asked, as Daddy picked me up in his arms and turned toward Eunice and Clark Elliott who joined us in the foyer.

As Eunice helped me put on my coat, Daddy informed us Mama was still at the hospital. I listened, but I didn't understand when Daddy told them that Mama had given birth to a stillborn baby. From the looks on their faces, though, I knew it was serious.

As soon as Daddy and I got into the car, I started asking questions. "Where's Mama?"

"She's in the hospital in Atlanta," Daddy answered solemnly.

"Why is she there?"

"She went there to have our new baby she told you about."

"A baby boy or a baby girl?"

"A baby girl," he answered. "But . . ." he hesitated. "I have some bad news. Our baby was not born alive."

"You mean she was sick and died like Aunt Ruth?" I asked trying to understand.

"Well, not exactly sick, sugar lump. . . . But yes, something was wrong. The doctors couldn't get her to breathe."

"Why couldn't she breathe?"

"I don't know. The doctors worked with her, but they couldn't get her to take even one breath."

All of a sudden, I remembered Mama.

"What about Mama?" I cried out.

"Mama's fine." Daddy said as he pulled me close to him on the car seat. "She just has to stay in the hospital for a few days so the doctors can watch over her."

Mama was in the hospital for a week. I stayed with Ardella during the day and with the Elliotts for a few hours in the evenings while Daddy went to visit Mama. I worried about her, even though Miss Eunice told me not to be a "worry-wart." I wondered why Mama was staying away from us so long.

No one talked about the baby who was named Alice, after my grandmother, so I turned to Ardella to try to understand what was happening. I knew I could talk to her because she never hesitated to answer my countless questions.

"Ardella, Alice died at the hospital, and I never got to see her. Where is she?"

God Works in Mysterious Ways

"Sweet Jesus got yo' baby sister up in heaven wif Him," Ardella said.

"Why didn't Jesus let us keep her?"

"I don't know, chile," she said. "We can't know the mind of God. Maybe He jes' thinks He needs her wif Him."

"Couldn't we ask God to change His mind?"

"Well, no," she continued, shaking her head. "But we can ask Him to hep us do without her."

The day after Daddy brought Mama home from the hospital, Ardella helped me put on my Sunday dress and black, patent-leather shoes. She told me we were going to Alice's funeral.

Neighbors and friends gathered at our house. All wore black clothing, the visible Southern tradition of showing respect for the dead. Women even wore black hats with black veils, and of course, black gloves. Some men who hadn't worn black suits wore black arm bands on the sleeves of their coats.

When the black hearse carrying Alice's body arrived, the mourners proceeded from our living room and front yard to the driveway where all the cars were parked behind our Plymouth. Daddy, Mama, Ardella, and I got into our car, followed by the mourners in their cars. The stream of vehicles followed us in a line, behind the hearse that carried my baby sister to the cemetery.

The black, shiny hearse drove slowly down the dirt road to Jonesboro. A thin cloud of red dust blew in the window as we followed. I turned around and looked at the cars behind us. A veil of fine red dust covered their cars, too.

"Daddy, where're they taking Alice?" I asked.

"To the Jonesboro Cemetery," he answered softly.

"Where Aunt Ruth's buried?"

"Yes, near there."

"Why does Alice have to ride by herself in that big black car?"

"That's just the custom, Katie Jane."

When the hearse entered the cemetery, I saw other people I knew gathered there, ready to join the procession of mourners. I

recognized a few of our family's friends, and some of Daddy's co-workers.

Jake was there, too. He had used his pick-up truck to provide transportation for some of the colored people who worked with Daddy at night at the peach packing plant. I noticed that the colored men and women stood near Jake's truck, back away from the graveside.

Quietly singing or humming, the colored people's voices harmonized, providing soothing music for the procession of mourners.

I looked over Jordan, and what did I see?
Coming for to carry me home.
A band of angels coming after me . . .
Coming for to carry me home . . .

Jake walked over to the graveside and stood by Ardella. I held Ardella's hand tightly as we stood by Mama and Daddy. All of us, in the presence of one who had no chance in life, stood puzzled and grief-stricken. Our friends and neighbors surrounded us, and all eyes were directed toward the small casket that lay by a hole in the ground. I studied the red dirt piled up beside the deep hole.

I had only been to one other funeral, Aunt Ruth's, last year. Knowing something of the ritual of burial, I understood my sister was in the casket. I also knew the casket would be put into the ground and covered with red dirt forever.

As Daddy held Mama, I squeezed Ardella's hand and stared at the casket, wondering what my baby sister looked like and if she could hear Mama crying. I heard Reverend Wilcox say something about dust to dust, and that Alice had gone to be with Jesus, and we'd all see her in heaven some day. As the minister spoke, strains of "In the Sweet By and By" filled the air behind us, sung by the colored friends Jake had brought with him.

As they sang, I looked up at the sky and wondered what Alice was doing with Aunt Ruth and Jesus up in heaven.

In the sweet by and by,
We shall meet at that beautiful shore . . .

That night Mama sat in the rocking chair with tears streaming down her cheeks. I climbed into her lap and put my arms around her neck.

"Don't cry, Mama. Ardella said Alice is with Jesus now," I said, trying to console her.

God Works in Mysterious Ways

Mama's arms tightened around me, as tears streamed down her face. "I know, sweetheart."

"Ardella said maybe Jesus needed Alice more than we did."

"Maybe so," she answered.

Mama's body shook with sobs. She held me tightly as grief overtook her.

Long after, as I lay on my cot, I heard the rocker creaking as it moved back and forth in the dark.

I knew Mama couldn't sleep.

After the funeral, Mama, Daddy, and I went to the cemetery once a week to put flowers on Alice's grave and to clean up around the site. Soon, grass covered the harsh red dirt.

Late one afternoon, I wandered from the grave over to a big marble structure gleaming white in the sun. I hesitated at the edge of the marble floor, which extended several feet beyond the columns that supported the roof.

Daddy walked up behind me and took my hand. Together we strolled past one of the columns into the strange building. I felt the coolness surround me as we stepped inside.

What is this place?" I asked.

"It's called a mausoleum, Katie Jane. Someone is buried here."

"Who?"

"Jimmy Bartlett, the son of Colonel Bartlett, who owns the peach orchard and the packing plant," Daddy said. "Jimmy was the Bartlett's only son."

As I got older Daddy told me the story behind the mausoleum. Jimmy Bartlett had been killed in Germany in World War II. When they shipped his body home, Mrs. Bartlett would not let the Colonel bury him. She insisted on keeping Jimmy's body on the bed that had been his since he was a boy.

Daddy explained how Mrs. Bartlett nearly died of a broken heart, and it was her wish to bury Jimmy in a mausoleum, above the ground. They kept Jimmy's body wrapped in blankets until the Atlanta Stone Company could build the private mausoleum. The

Separate Fountains

Bartlett's were the only family to have such a structure at the Jonesboro City Cemetery.

Mrs. Bartlett knew how afraid of the dark Jimmy had been as a child, so she had the builders of the mausoleum install a light fixture inside his tomb. Mr. Bartlett has maintained the light fixture through the years, changing the bulb often to keep Jimmy's private tomb illuminated.

As the years went by, Daddy also explained to me why people visit the graves of their loved ones. "Love for a person goes beyond death, Katie Jane," he once said to me. "The spirit of someone we love is always in our hearts—so that is why we visit their graves."

"Daddy, why didn't we build a mausoleum for Alice?"

"People like us don't have that kind of money," Daddy said. "Mr. Bartlett paid a lot of money to get the Atlanta Stone Company to build this."

"But remember, Katie Jane," he added. "Alice's spirit is with Jesus in heaven now."

"Will anybody else be put in this mausoleum?" I continued to question.

"Mr. and Mrs. Bartlett will be put to rest in two of the places."

As Daddy spoke, he looked away, toward Mama who was seated on the ground next to Alice's grave.

"I'm going back to be with your Mama," he said. "If you like, you can stay here for a few more minutes."

"I'd like that."

After my father left, I began to move slowly around the mausoleum, aware of the tapping echoes of my footsteps. I slid my fingers along the marble walls and wondered if Jimmy Bartlett knew I was here, in his private place. I wondered what he had been like when he was alive. What did he look like? Did he like ice cream? Did he like to ride a bicycle?

I came to a marble bench that had been placed directly in front of Jimmy's tomb. I sat down on it and sighed peacefully as I looked at the beautiful surroundings.

At the end of each bench were decorative stone scrolls that swept upward to serve as arms for the bench. I had seen similar pictures of scrolls in Mama's Bible, and I ran my fingers over the smooth surface of one of the bench's arms.

God Works in Mysterious Ways

On each side of the bench stood marble angel statues. I leaned over to admire one of them and timidly stretched my fingers out to feel the curls on her head. From there, my fingers slid down over the angel's stone-cold face, to her eyes, her nose, and her mouth. My fingers continued moving over the curves of her shoulders, finally resting on the stringed harp she held in her hands.

Sighing again, I was sure the angel statue was the most beautiful thing I had ever seen. I tried to imagine how rich Colonel Bartlett must be to be able to build such a fancy place to bury his son.

I looked up again at the tombs. I counted them—one for Jimmy, one for his mother, and one for his daddy. There were four tombs—who would be buried in the extra space?

I wished my sister could rest there.

After that, Mama slept a lot and complained of being too tired to play with me. I even noticed she didn't laugh at Daddy's jokes anymore.

Ardella must have noticed the change in Mama, too, because she was overly kind to her, patiently helping her with any request. She constantly tried to cheer Mama by baking her favorite pecan pie or by telling her funny gossip from town.

Consolation, however, apparently was not all Mama needed to recover. Her health deteriorated, and Ardella took increased responsibility for the household. As the weeks passed, Dr. Green's visits became more frequent. Finally, he diagnosed Mama's condition as phlebitis, the inflammation of vein tissue that could cause clots to form in the blood.

Separate Fountains

To this day, I remember clearly a conversation I heard between Daddy and Dr. Green one night on our front porch.

"B. J., I'm doing my best to help Katherine get well," Dr. Green said. "But the problem is, the medical profession doesn't know how to treat phlebitis. At this point, aspirin and warm-water massage are all we know to prescribe for pain, followed by a soft gauze wrap to support the injured veins."

"But she screams in her sleep from pain in her legs." Daddy responded.

"I understand your frustration. If we can get Katherine on a schedule of massage treatments twice a day, followed by a leg wrap, I think she will feel better soon."

"Can't you prescribe something for her besides aspirin?" Daddy pleaded.

"No, there's no specific medication for phlebitis. All I can give her is a few painkiller tablets for you to keep on hand. They are addictive, so promise me you make sure she only takes them when she needs them."

"Yes, I understand." Daddy said, pausing and then continuing. "Dr. Green, can you tell me when you expect Katherine will be over phlebitis?"

Dr. Green cleared his throat.

"B. J., I'm going to be truthful with you," he began. "Phlebitis is a very serious illness. We'll have to see how Katherine's body responds to rest and massage treatments. Phlebitis will affect her health for the rest of her life if she survives it."

"What do you mean?" Daddy quickly shot back, his voice reflecting concern. "Katherine couldn't die from this, could she?"

"I don't want to scare you," the doctor continued. "But with phlebitis, there's always a chance of death because of its unpredictability. There's a constant threat of a blood clot forming and moving to her heart or brain, killing her instantly."

That night, and for many nights after, I lay on my cot begging God not to let my Mama die.

As the months passed, Mama didn't show much progress. She hobbled along, trying to play with me and feeling guilty because of her confinement to bed. Determined to give me as much attention as

God Works in Mysterious Ways

possible, a picnic lunch became a daily outing just for the two of us. Ardella, after fixing our lunch, helped Mama as she struggled with each step to our picnic spot by the big oak tree.

Mama heard an old wives' tale from one of her friends that if phlebitis started after a pregnancy, it could be cured with another one. Mama consulted with Dr. Green about this belief, and he admitted there was no scientific support for such a remedy, but there was no evidence to dispute it.

When I was going on seven, my little brother Josh was born. So glad was I that Jesus let us keep him, I immediately became his protector, teacher, and friend.

Mama's condition didn't improve, and in fact, the birth of the baby actually made her phlebitis worse. She walked very little, and then only when holding onto something or someone. I often watched Mama's face, wondering how she could smile so sweetly when her days were filled with pain. She even managed to laugh at Dr. Green's silly jokes when he visited our house to check on her. I often wondered if he thought making her laugh was the only thing he could really do for her.

While medical research provided no cure for phlebitis, Dr. Green's instructions for Mama's treatment were specific. She was to stay in bed at all times with her legs bound in gauze from ankles to hips. Twice each day, she was to sit in a warm water bath for an hour to stimulate her circulation.

I worried that Josh would never get to run and play with Mama like I had. The memories of our family before Mama's illness flashed through my mind often. The grass had been greener, the sky bluer, the birds' songs sweeter when Daddy, Mama, and I laughed and played in happiness.

Chapter Five

Down the Red Dirt Road

Ardella participated in every decision concerning Josh and me. Although Mama's word was the law, she and Ardella rarely disagreed. We dutifully obeyed Ardella—well, most of the time.

It was a sweltering day in the summer of 1953. I was twelve and Josh was six, and exercising our imagination was just about all there was to do. All morning, we had been imagining what we were going to do that afternoon and awaited our opportunity during lunch for permission.

"Mama, after our chores are done, can Josh and I walk to town?" I asked.

"I just can't understand why you want to walk to Jonesboro every afternoon," Mama answered. "I do declare! I think you two just like to see how much red dust you can kick up."

"Dat's right," Ardella chimed in. She frowned at us and tried to sound stern: "And I has a devil of a time washin' dat red dirt out of Josh's overalls."

Josh stuffed a fork full of butter beans into his mouth. His eyes darted back and forth between Mama and Ardella while he waited for me to make the next move.

I swallowed my last bite of cornbread and took a long drink of iced tea.

"We just like to look in the store windows," I said, knowing what was coming next from Ardella.

"Well, you best not be watchin' dem folks in Cletus Jones's store," she stated emphatically in her I-mean-business voice. She crossed her

Down the Red Dirt Road

arms and held them in front of her. "Dere's a jillion no-gooders hangs out in dere."

"You just walked to town yesterday, Katie Jane," Mama interrupted. "I don't understand what's so exciting about Jonesboro."

"Oh, we just like to see what's going on, Mama," I answered innocently, staying shut-mouth about my plans for the afternoon.

"I like to go to the library to see Miss Ada Belle," Josh offered in his charming way. He often used his charm to work Mama. "She has a lot of new books for us to read."

Ardella, finishing her last slice of tomato, continued to look at us skeptically.

"Well, I says it again," she lectured, her eyes piercing through us as she spoke. "You chil'len best not be meddlin' in Cletus Jones's drugstore. De devil done picked dat place to be his home in dis here town. You hear me?"

"Yes ma'am, Ardella," we answered obediently, knowing that she wasn't finished with us yet.

"I tells you now, Miz Katie Jane and Mistuh Josh, if I ever hears you two done ben in dat place, dere be a whippin' in store fer you when you gits home—dat's for sure. Sure as a dog will bark at the moon."

"And you'll get another whipping from me," Mama chimed in. "Your daddy and I have told you a hundred times it's not a respectable place for children."

"Yes ma'am, Mama," we replied in unison.

Josh and I demurely sat at the table with our hands folded, avoiding eye contact as much as we could with either Mama or Ardella while they finished their iced tea. Neither had given us a direct answer about going to Jonesboro, so I assumed the answer was yes.

Ardella turned her attention to Mama.

"Miz Taylor, you best git back in dat bed and rest like Doctor Green done tole you. Chil'len, clean off de table and put dem dishes in de sink. I got to git yo' Mama settled."

"Yes, ma'am, Ardella," we answered, again in unison.

Although it had been seven years since Mama had developed phlebitis, her mobile activity continued to be limited. When she was up and about in the daytime, Dr. Green still insisted that her legs be wrapped in gauze for support.

To walk, Mama had to stabilize her gait by holding onto something or someone. Her infirmity, however, did not keep her from trying to help Daddy and Ardella with our day-to-day living. Mama helped with household responsibilities by doing what she called sitting chores—sitting in the rocking chair to sew, crochet, or knit, sitting on the bedside to fold the laundry, sitting at the table to cut up vegetables and fruits for Ardella to cook for our meals, sitting at the table to work on a household project or to help Josh and me with a special activity.

Although Mama couldn't walk around in the yard, she still loved working in her flower garden. She sat—with legs wrapped in gauze—on a small wooden stool, dragging it all over the yard as she sat pulling weeds, dividing her day lily and iris bulbs and then replanting them, fertilizing her roses and other plants. She also slid the stool up and down the rows of our vegetable garden, pulling the weeds out between the plants.

Whatever Mama chose for her morning chores, by afternoon she fell exhausted into her bed—ready for a nap.

Still seated at the table, Josh and I watched the routine we had seen many times in our lives: Ardella bent over toward Mama, who reached out with her frail arms. Ardella helped Mama out of the chair and helped her walk toward her bed. I could see Mama's legs below her cotton dress, each leg completely covered with white gauze.

As Ardella walked holding on to Mama, Ardella's singing voice filled the air:
> *Not my bruthers nor my sisters,*
> *But me, Oh Lord,*
> *Standin' in the need of prayer . . .*

Looking back, I now wonder if Ardella's soothing voice had a purpose in our lives. Constantly singing while she worked, Ardella's spiritual songs became a part of our household. Hearing her repetitious singing, I learned the words of many spirituals that had been

Down the Red Dirt Road

passed down to blacks from generation to generation by rote.

Did she use her singing to keep hope alive? Did her singing give hope of a higher power watching over us? Did Ardella sing for her own hope or was she singing to give Mama hope as she lay on the bed with useless limbs?

Placing Mama gently near the head of the bed, Ardella arranged two pillows behind her back then put two more pillows under her legs to elevate them.

"Dr. Green says you got to keep dose legs up so de blood will circulate," Ardella said, repeating what she had heard Daddy say to Mama many times.

As Mama settled in for her afternoon nap, Josh and I cleaned off the table and stacked the dishes in the sink. Our house offered no privacy for Mama as she rested, but she seemed adjusted to all the household activity, including our running in and out with screen doors banging.

Mama never complained. It was Ardella who quietly admonished us for our noisy games. I often thought Mama and Ardella probably enjoyed the quiet house when we walked to town, but they would never admit it.

Separate Fountains

"Have a good nap, Mama!" Josh yelled over his shoulder. We ran out the kitchen door, letting the screen door bang again.

We paused a moment on the back porch to discuss the afternoon's plan. It was nearly half-past noon. We would finish our chores as fast as possible and meet at the driveway gate at 1:00. That would give us plenty of time before the Greyhound bus got to Cletus Jones's drugstore.

Josh looked down fondly at his Mickey Mouse watch. He was proud to be able to tell time all by himself now, after much coaching from me.

"I gotcha," he said with a nod. "The little hand will be on the one and the big hand on the twelve. Right, Katie Jane?"

"Right."

He ran down the porch steps toward the henhouse. Josh had to feed and water the chickens and collect their eggs in Grandma's old straw basket.

My remaining chore for the day was to shell butter beans. I hated doing it, but I was resigned to it. I picked up the pot of unshelled beans Ardella had put out on the porch for me. Backing up to one of the big rocking chairs, I sat first on the edge, then scooted back to get comfortable. I sat the pot of beans on the folds of my dress.

Shelling butter beans was tedious and slow, and it took forever to fill the pot as full as Ardella demanded. She always gave me the same instructions when I tried to shell only a few beans: "Now don't you brings me dem beans 'til you gits a full pot. You know dey cooks down once dey gits to boilin' wif dat fatback."

As I sat there, I thought to myself, "I'm sick and tired of butter beans anyway." Ardella had cooked them two days in a row. So what if they were fresh picked from the garden?

Some of the shells popped open easily while others defied my prying fingernails. The tough shells sometimes cut my cuticles and fingers, making them bleed. Georgia's red dust covered every shell and stained my fingers. I hated the red stain almost as much as the sore fingers I got from shelling beans. Most of all, I hated the thought of the next pot of beans that needed to be shelled.

The kitchen door swung open and to my surprise, Ardella came out with a big empty pot in her hands. She dragged another rocking chair over beside me. I smiled at her with a sigh of relief.

"Since yo' Mama's nappin', I heps you wif dese beans while I cools off," she said, as she wiped the perspiration from her brow with her arm. "Dat house do git hot afta my cookin' in dere."

Down the Red Dirt Road

I watched Ardella as she reached down and unbuckled her sandals. She slid them off her feet and wiggled her toes.

"Oh," she groaned. "My feets is so tired."

Ardella reached over and took a handful of beans from the basket. She began to shell them into the pot she'd brought with her.

"Daddy told me about people like you," I said. "You're like an angel."

"Wat do you mean, chile?"

"Daddy says when somebody comes along and helps you unexpectedly, they're like an angel dropping out of heaven."

Ardella laughed her deep, bubbly laugh.

"You jes' keep poppin' dem butter beans outta dere," she instructed, with a twinkle in her eye. "You know dey cooks down, so we needs plenty to start wif if you's spectin' enough for supper."

"Yes, ma'am," I answered.

"You white folks is all alike," Ardella continued. "When you want som'pin, you wants it right now. You gotta learn to be patient and realize life jes' gits tedious sometimes."

"What does tedious mean, Ardella?" I asked.

"Oh, it jes' means dat life gits tiresome at times," she explained. "You git weary from doin' de same thang agin and agin but you jes' haf to keep doin' it to keep alive. Dat's when life gits tedious."

She paused for a moment and gave her undivided attention to a particularly tough butter bean. She then continued. "It's important, Katie Jane, to 'member all God's chil'len feel life gits tedious at times, but we's jes' gotta trust in de good Lord and keep on a-goin'."

"Yes, ma'am," I answered mournfully. "Life sure do git tedious for me when I'm shelling butter beans."

"Jes' thanks de Lord you got all yo' senses and can be shellin'," Ardella added with a laugh.

Seeing that she was in the mood to be philosophical, I decided not to pursue the subject any further.

We sat quietly under the tin roof, shelling beans and listening to the birds singing in nearby trees. An occasional summer breeze swept across the porch, giving us a brief moment of relief from the heat.

Separate Fountains

Our collie dog, Sherlock, walked up the wooden porch steps and curled up at the foot of my chair. As I shelled beans, I rubbed him with my bare feet.

Content with the quietness of the moment, Ardella and I continued our work. I looked over at her, and even in her freshly starched yellow dress, she looked tired. Her face was drawn with worry and the edges of her mouth drooped. I could tell something was troubling her. She seemed to be in deep thought.

As I struggled with the shells, I continued to watch her rocking back and forth. I admit, shamefully, that I never tired of examining her immense arms, legs, and feet. Josh and I often wondered why God gave Ardella black skin and us white. We marveled at the whiteness of the palms of her hands and the bottoms of her feet. As I sat there studying her, I noticed she had the butter beans' red-dust stain on the white part of her hands, too, just like I did.

Ardella did not seem to be aware of my stare. I finally asked, "Is something wrong, Ardella?"

"Nutin' white folks could undastand," she answered, getting up out of her chair and slipping her feet back into her white sandals. "But I thanks you fer askin' Miz Katie Jane."

As she walked toward the kitchen door, she announced, "I's finished wif my butter beans. Are you 'bout finished wif de ones you has dere?"

"Just a few more, Ardella," I answered. I sighed a big sigh, then with a dead-pan face, repeated her philosophy. "Life sure do git tedious to me when I'm shellin' butter beans."

Ardella laughed.

"Honey chile, let me tell you som'pin," she said, "yore jes' a young'un. One of dese days yore gonna look back and wish you wuz shellin' butter beans wif Ardella. You'll think life tweren't so tedious den after all."

"You're probably right," I agreed with a grin.

"I'm goin' in to wash dese here beans. When you finished wif yores, bring dem in," she instructed as she opened the screen door.

"I'm finished!" I yelled as I popped open the last shell and let the beans drop into my pot. Jumping out of my chair, I stumbled over Sherlock but didn't spill

Down the Red Dirt Road

any of my beans. I managed to catch the screen door before it banged shut behind Ardella.

I stood at the sink with Ardella while she filled it with cold water and dumped in both pots of beans. She washed them, swishing them around and squeezing them through her fingers. When the beans were clean enough to suit her, she scooped up bunches of beans and held them in the air letting the water drip from them. She plunged each handful of clean beans into a big pot of fresh water.

Ardella walked over to the refrigerator and pulled out a large slab of fatback—a strip of fat from the back of a hog that had been cured by drying and salting. She smacked the fatback down on the counter hard and using a sharp knife, she sliced some of it into long thin pieces. She put them into the pot with the beans.

Ardella turned to the stove and placed the pot on a front burner. I knew her routine of bringing the beans to a high boil then turning the heat down for simmering the rest of the afternoon.

Ardella looked over at me as she wiped her hands on her apron.

"A watched pot don't boil," she said. "So look de other way."

I turned around to wash my hands.

The lye soap was harsh, but I scrubbed my hands as hard as I could to try to remove the red stains from them. I would have to hurry to meet Josh on time.

"When Mama wakes up, tell her Josh and I finished our chores, and we're walking to town," I requested.

"Jes' be back here by five, chile," Ardella answered. "And don't you forget to carry yo' book satchel wif yo' library books in it."

Separate Fountains

Even though she paused, I knew Ardella wasn't finished. I waited for her usual list of directions. "Minds yo' manners," she began. "Don't you git into no trouble. Don't you speak to no strangers. Say 'Yes ma'am' and 'No ma'am' to Miss Ada Belle at the library. Don't forget yo' 'pleases' and 'thank-you's' when Miss Ada Belle gives you yo' books. And don't you dare go into Mr. Cletus Jones's drugstore!"

As always, Ardella then took a dramatic pause, ending with a statement meant to arouse guilt:

"And pleaze be careful. Yo' Mama been through so much wif dis phlebitis, and she would jes' die if you or Josh got hurt or som'pin."

"Yes, ma'am, Ardella," I answered politely, picking up my book satchel and grabbing Sherlock's chain off the nail beside the back door as I exited the house.

As I walked up the driveway, I enjoyed my freedom from my chores by kicking up some red dust with my bare feet. There was something about the feel of the warm ground that made summer so enjoyable.

Sherlock followed right along, zigzagging from behind me to each side of the driveway, sniffing the roadside foliage or chasing a butterfly. He was a typical dog with wanderlust when he followed me anywhere.

We had named our collie dog Sherlock Holmes because when we got him as a young puppy, he investigated everything in sight. Sherlock loved to roam, following Josh and me everywhere, even to town. We never fastened his chain to his collar except when we entered Jonesboro's business district.

As I neared the henhouse, I shouted, "Hurry Josh, we don't want to miss anything!"

"I'm almost finished, wait for me!" he yelled back.

"I'll meet you at the gate."

I felt tired as I walked toward the gate. By noon, I'd hung out the clothes to dry, fed and watered the livestock, weeded the garden, and picked butter beans. And then after lunch, I shelled those same damn butter beans!

Oh, dear Jesus, I thought, please forgive me for even thinking that word *damn!*

I walked slowly, looking down at the little clouds of red dust my feet kicked up. When I got to the end of the driveway, I put my satchel

Down the Red Dirt Road

down and hung Sherlock's chain over the gatepost. I climbed up to the top rung of the wooden gate and sat down, careful to fold my pink-flowered cotton dress in front of me so the folds wouldn't get caught on the nails.

As I sat there on the gate, I leaned with my back against the fence post, which smelled of sweet Georgia Pine. A breeze stirred, and I caught the heavy scent of summer clover. I could have fallen asleep, but Sherlock kept me awake with his restless motion. He continued to sniff and investigate the area, looking over my way often checking to see if I was still there. I surmised he kept glancing my way to make sure he didn't get left out of a trip to town.

I looked down the driveway at our blue cinder-block house. The dogwood trees reached up to the sky, and I remembered back to when Daddy and I planted them, before Josh even learned to walk. I recalled the brimming buckets of water we carried to the seedlings every day to keep them alive during the hot summer months.

Fields of grass bordered the dirt driveway. I watched as our cows walked lazily around looking for some fresh green sprigs near the gate. The carpets of grass flowed from the gate downward to the front of the house, stopping at Mama's carefully placed rose bushes, daffodils, and iris. There were pots of geraniums and impatiens on the porch.

Speaking of impatiens . . .

Where is Josh anyway? What's taking him so long?

I liked having Josh tag along with me wherever I went because I could convince him to do things I was afraid to do. My little brother thought I was the smartest and most clever person around, and, of course, I saw no reason to discourage his opinion.

Josh burst out the front screen door of the house and let it fly to crash behind him. His yellow hair bobbed up and down as he ran barefoot up the driveway. I knew Josh's overalls would be dusty red at his ankles by the time he raced to me. Josh, "the barefoot boy with cheeks of tan!"

Sherlock left my side and ran to greet Josh. I watched Sherlock's golden-haired body as he bounded swiftly toward Josh. He jumped up on my brother, showing affection by licking his face. Josh immediately returned Sherlock's affection by pausing to pet him.

As Josh and Sherlock reached me, Josh held out his hand.

Separate Fountains

"Look what Mama gave me!" he said excitedly. He held up two dimes. "We can buy a treat in Jonesboro!"

I jumped down from the gate. Josh put one of the shiny coins in my hand, and I carefully placed it in my dress pocket.

"I thought Mama was asleep," I said.

"She was," Josh answered. "Ardella actually gave me the money. She said Mama gave it to her to give to us."

Josh and I now faced the challenge of the homemade lock-contraption that Daddy had made for the gate. This so-called lock was a short piece of rope with one end attached to the gate and the other tied to a large steel nail. The nail fit into a curved metal slot on the fencepost when the gate was locked. Using the slack in the rope, I had to jerk the nail back and forth in the slot to either lock or unlock the gate.

To save time, Josh and I had discovered a special way to get through the gate without having to open it. If we pushed against the gate hard enough, we could make an opening between the gate and the fencepost that was just big enough for us to squeeze through—along with Sherlock, of course.

Daddy had stressed the importance of keeping the gate closed and firmly locked so the cows wouldn't stray. We were always careful not to open the gate too far, and with this method, we didn't have to unlock it at all.

We were free!

Josh and I looked at each other and started laughing. Passing through that gate always gave us a feeling of exhilaration and freedom. Mischief and curiosity settled in as we set off down the red dirt road toward town.

"Did you remember to get Sherlock's chain off the gatepost?" Josh asked as he carried my book satchel.

"Uh-huh, got it right here in my hand."

Chapter Six

Walking to Jonesboro

Josh and I sang at the tops of our voices as we walked enthusiastically with Sherlock down the red dirt road.

Mares eat oats and does eat oats, and little lambs eat ivey.
Oh! Mairzy doats and dozey doats and liddle lamzy divey,
A kiddley divey too, wouldn't you?

Singing, talking, and laughing were part of our travel routine. The dimes bounced in our pockets, stimulating our imagination of the treats we could buy with them. Would it be a double-dipped ice cream cone, or a cherry Coke with peanut-butter crackers, or maybe a banana split with two cherries—if we pooled our money together.

"School starts in a few months," I commented. "Are you excited about first grade, Josh?"

"I reckon," he answered, shuffling his bare feet through the powdery, red-tinted soil. He was always searching the dirt for anything of interest to a little boy.

"What grade will you be in?" Josh asked.

"Seventh."

Josh paused to pick up a stone. Throwing the stone at a tree, he yelled, "Wham, bam, ala-kazam!"

I laughed at his ability to even have fun with a rock, but then I noticed his mood suddenly changed.

"Katie Jane," he said, "I'm kinda scared of school. Were you afraid when you started first grade?"

"Scared to death. I didn't know anybody at that school."

"Will you go with me on the first day and show me what I'm supposed to do?" he asked seriously.

Walking to Jonesboro

"Sure, Josh. I know all the teachers."

"Will the teachers whup me if I'm bad?"

"Uh-huh, they sure will. But don't worry, Josh, you're so smart. The teachers are gonna love you."

"You really think so?" he asked.

"I've taught you your ABC's and numbers and how to tell time and how to count money. The teachers are really gonna be impressed."

"I sure hope so," Josh said, and a smile spread over his face.

We walked a little farther in silence.

"Will I get a Blue Horse tablet and two red Coca-Cola pencils like you did last year?"

"Sure, Josh. All the kids get them at the beginning of the school year. The Coca-Cola Company in Atlanta gives out free pencils and tablets to everyone. And Mama will give you a nickel to buy extra notebook paper when you need it, too."

"How come you always buy the Blue Horse kind, Katie Jane?"

"Because all the kids cut the blue horses off and collect them to try to win prizes for the classroom. One year our class got a set of the Bobbsey Twins books from the Blue Horse Company. Last year we got a Monopoly game."

"Oh boy," Josh galloped ahead, then galloped back.

"And fat crayons, Katie Jane, I'm gonna get fat crayons."

I laughed, surprised at the things that impressed little brothers. I had not taken fat crayons to school for many years, although pieces of them still showed up in our household from time to time.

"I can hardly wait for school to start," Josh exclaimed. "What grade were you in when you got to ride on the Nancy Hank train?"

"Now, Josh, you couldn't remember when I did that," I answered. "I was in the third grade."

"Well I musta heard you talking about it then," he said. "Tell me about it again, Katie Jane."

"Mrs. Dean always takes her class to Savannah for a trip on the Nancy Hank train," I explained. "Before the trip, though, she teaches about Nancy Hank. Nancy Hank was a nurse who helped Confederate soldiers during the War Between the States. The train is named after her."

"Does it cost a lot to go on the train?" Josh asked.

"About four dollars for the ride, a sandwich and milk, and an apple for dessert. Our family had the money, but in my class that year were three kids who lived on the Poor Folks Farm who couldn't pay for the tickets. Mrs. Dean asked the other parents to help out."

Separate Fountains

"I bet Daddy helped, didn't he?" Josh said.

"Of course he did."

Josh hopped, first on one foot then the other. He pulled his dime out of his pocket.

"Remember when you brought home the card with the picture of the crippled child?" Josh asked.

"You mean for the March of Dimes? Sure I remember."

"Maybe I'll get to do that, too," Josh said. "I'll save my dimes and put them in the circles on the card, just like you did, Katie Jane."

"Well, sure. First graders do that. Everybody gives money to the March of Dimes."

I wasn't exactly sure how dimes actually helped polio-stricken youngsters, but the campaign had captured my imagination, just as it had of children all across America. Apparently children not even old enough to be in school were inspired.

"If you collect enough dimes, does that mean you won't get that disease?" Josh asked.

"It's called polio, Josh, and giving dimes doesn't keep you from getting it."

Nodding he understood, Josh put the dime back in his pocket.

"I guess it's alright for me to spend this dime today," he concluded.

"Sure. The March of Dimes drive isn't until later this year."

We walked on.

I could tell Josh was still in deep thought, and after a few minutes, he looked over at me.

"Katie Jane, I was just thinking. Since Daddy works all day and Mama can't walk, who took you to school on your first day?"

"Ardella did," I answered. "She walked me as far as the big oak tree near the playground."

"Why there?" he asked.

"Because Ardella can't go in our school building, it's for white people only."

"What happened when you and Ardella got to the oak tree?"

"Well," I said, "Ardella stooped down beside me and pulled an envelope out of her pocket. She said Mama had put my birth certificate and a piece of paper with my name and address on it in the envelope. I was to take it inside and give it to my teacher."

"Gee, I bet you were scared," Josh said in an sympathetic tone.

"Scared to death. Especially after Ardella told me what I had to do. She told me to tell the teacher I wanted my birth certificate back since it was the only copy."

"Oh, that's a lot to remember," he moaned.

"Yeah, but Ardella hugged me and told me I had to do it. She said I was a big girl, and she wanted me to learn to read and write so I could teach her."

"Then what happened?" Josh asked, fascinated with the story.

Separate Fountains

"Ardella told me she would walk back to the school at three o'clock and wait for me by the tree. She stood under the oak tree and watched me as I went in the school's front door. Then she went home to take care of you and Mama. You were just a little baby then, Josh."

"You mean Ardella walked you to and from school every day?" Josh asked in disbelief.

"Every day until I got in the third grade."

"How far is it from our house to the school?"

"Almost a mile, if you use the shortcut through the meadow."

"Boy! Ardella walked a lot of miles for you. She must really love you."

"She loves both of us, Josh, just like we love her."

"Did she walk you to school even when it was raining or snowing?"

"Yes, she used Mama's big yellow umbrella to protect us when it rained. Daddy even bought Ardella and me yellow raincoats with matching galoshes so we wouldn't get wet. We must have looked like a pair of yellow birds!"

Walking to Jonesboro

"Ardella still loves those yellow galoshes," Josh replied. "She says they keep her feets warm."

We both laughed.

"If it started to snow when I was at school," I continued, "Ardella would be waiting for me with a wool blanket. She carried me in her arms with the blanket wrapped around both of us. Sometimes on real cold days, Mama let me stay home from school so we wouldn't have to walk in the cold."

"I think it'll be fun to walk to school in the rain and snow," Josh said.

We stopped to rest for a few minutes, moving into the shade of a stand of pine trees. This was a special place for us, a place we always stopped on our way to town. Our place for a pause from our journey—and a place for refreshment, thanks to nature!

There were scuppernong vines growing on the trees, and we both loved the cool wetness of the scuppernong's taste on a hot day like today. We pulled off some of the yellowish green plum-flavored fruit, and popped them into our mouths.

Sherlock even liked scuppernongs. He stood there wagging his tail and looking up at us pitifully while we ate. Josh finally held out a fist full of scuppernongs, letting the dog gobble them right out of the palm of his hand.

I started laughing out loud.

"What's so funny?" Josh asked.

"Do you remember when Daddy tried to make scuppernong wine?" I asked, as I chewed on the scuppernong pulp.

"Yes," Josh answered. "It tasted awful."

"Remember what Daddy did with it?" I continued, taking time to spit the fruit's small seeds from my mouth.

"Of course. Daddy threw it out the back door, and without knowing it the wine landed in Sherlock's bowl."

"And we had a drunk, staggering dog!" I interrupted.

We both howled with laughter.

As we continued eating our scuppernongs, Sherlock suddenly started barking and sniffing at the bushes beside us.

"What's wrong with Sherlock?" Josh asked.

Separate Fountains

"I hope its not a snake. Get away from those bushes until we can see what's going on."

Just as Josh stepped back, a small turtle emerged from the bushes and headed across the road. Josh bent over, picked up the turtle, and put it into the chest pocket of his overalls.

We resumed our journey.

Still curious about school, Josh began to question me again.

"Katie Jane," he said, "Ardella knows how to read and write. Did you teach her?"

"I sure did," I said proudly. "When I started bringing my work home from school, she would sit at the kitchen table with me. She asked me to teach her to write her name. Then I started teaching her the ABC's and numbers."

"What did Mama say about you teaching Ardella?"

"Oh, Mama was glad. She wanted Ardella to learn to read and write. It upset Mama that Ardella could only sign her name with a big X."

"I bet that was embarrassing for Ardella," Josh said.

"Well, yes, I guess so," I replied. "Mama said Ardella was probably embarrassed to admit she couldn't read or write, but she could learn from me, though, when we played school. We would sit at the kitchen table, and I pretended I was her teacher. I taught her words from my book, and she learned to read about Dick and Jane. After I finished my homework assignments, Ardella would take them home with her to copy at night, returning them the next morning for me to take to school."

"How long did you and Ardella play school?" Josh asked.

"Until she could read the *Atlanta Journal!*" I said with a giggle.

Our conversation brought us to the edge of Jonesboro. We slapped our dusty, red feet on the hot, concrete sidewalk that ran alongside U.S. Route 41. The highway, which was paved and smooth, ran south from Atlanta, through Jonesboro, and on to Macon.

Route 41 paralleled the railroad tracks. The first thing we saw on this day as we looked across the highway was the chain gang.

Walking to Jonesboro

Every time we came to town, we saw Georgia prisoners wearing black-and-white-striped uniforms working along the railroad tracks. Chained together at the ankle, these prisoners were used to maintain the tracks and the right-of-way on either side. Uniformed guards with rifles stood by supervising their work. Daddy had told us the guards would shoot if any of the prisoners tried to escape.

I could smell the creosote used to coat the railroad ties. The acrid smell was unpleasant, and I knew it could burn the skin of anyone who touched it.

I couldn't help but feel some sympathy for the prisoners, but I was also afraid of them. I wondered what crimes had put them there. Silently, I pondered over the chilling stories I'd heard from Daddy about the chain-gang runaways and what they did to innocent folk like us.

"Come on Josh, let's get away from here," I whispered.

We walked quickly away, leaving the sounds of leg irons and pounding sledgehammers behind.

We soon came into Jonesboro's residential area along Route 41, which became Main Street at the edge of town. Looking at the yards and houses as we passed, we saw a rather round woman sweeping the sidewalk in front of her home.

"There's Mrs. Solomon, Josh," I said as I nodded toward her. "She must be getting ready for one of Mr. Solomon's sales."

"Oh boy," Josh said. "They're so much fun. Do you think Mr. Solomon will have any toys this time?"

"Maybe, but remember, we never know what's in the boxes and suitcases he sells."

A true entrepreneur, Mr. Solomon had created a business out of unclaimed luggage and mismarked parcels he got at Atlanta's train station or post office. Twice a month, he went to Atlanta for auctions—one day at the Atlanta post office, another day at the Southern Railroad station. Mr. Solomon placed bids on unclaimed suitcases, trunks, boxes, and cartons, or literally any items needing to be removed from the site. Once purchased, he would bring the items back to Jonesboro and lay them out on his front porch and lawn for people to buy.

Separate Fountains

On the days when people knew Mr. Solomon would be returning with new goods, some would stand in his yard begging him to sell a suitcase even before he had examined it. As soon as his truck pulled into the driveway, would-be customers eagerly volunteered to help him unload.

Josh and I loved to come to the sales with Daddy. Whites and coloreds of all ages made their way to Mr. Solomon's house during the weeks following his trip to Atlanta, although most of the goods would be sold in the first few days after he returned. An afternoon of walking around the porch and yard, surrounded by clothing and other items—some common, some grand—felt to me like a day at the county fair.

Josh and I waved to Mrs. Solomon, and she waved back.
"Where did you tell me they go every Friday night?" Josh asked.
"To synagogue, in Atlanta. It's something like church."
"Why don't they go to church in Jonesboro?"
"'Cause the Solomons are Jewish, and Jonesboro doesn't have a synagogue."
"Why not?" Josh persisted.
"'Cause they're the only Jews in town."
"Is that why the Klan burned a cross in their yard?" he asked innocently.
"Well, I guess so," I said. "Don't you remember Daddy telling Mama how angry some of the people in town were after the cross burning? I remember Daddy said Mr. Solomon's friends decided to stand up for him and let the Klan know they didn't like their actions. These friends helped Mr. Solomon by word of mouth— stopping in a different store or business every day and talking loudly about how nice Mr. and Mrs. Solomon were."
"Why'd they do that?"
"They hoped Klan members would hear and would leave the Solomons alone."
"Did it work?" Josh asked.
"I guess. Daddy said the Solomons' friends knew our town needed his wares. Since that one cross burning, the Klan has left them alone."

Walking to Jonesboro

I wondered if my friend Julie's father, Mr. Parsons, had anything to do with persuading the Klan not to burn another cross in Mr. Solomon's yard. After all, he was a captain in the Klan's ranks and must have influence.

I had learned about Mr. Parson's status in the Ku Klux Klan on Julie's twelfth birthday. I had been invited to attend her birthday party and to spend the night along with six other girls. The excitement over presents, cake, and singing had the noise level to a mild roar, so Julie's parents intervened with a suggestion we go to Julie's room and play a game or something a little less rowdy.

We decided to play dress-up, using makeup and old clothing we could find around the house.

"Come on Katie Jane," Julie said, "Help me bring some of Mama's clothes and stuff over to my room."

I tagged happily behind her to her parents' room. When we opened their closet door, we got down on our hands and knees, poking through the closet, to find anything fun to dress up in. Mrs. Parsons had a whole collection of old high heels, and we gathered them up in our arms.

Julie stood up and started sliding the clothes hangers aside, giving full disclosure of everything in the closet while she decided which ones she could take for the girls to play dress-up. She parted her father's shirts, divulging a long white robe and pointed hood to match.

Looking quickly at me, she explained, "My daddy's in the Ku Klux Klan."

My mouth made no sound, but remained open for a minute in disbelief.

"Is your daddy in the Klan?" Julie questioned me.

"No," I answered quickly.

I had never seen a Klan robe hanging in a closet. I had only seen them on Klansmen when they were a shouting angry mob, ready for faceless violence and trying to seek the control of other men—black men, or the one Jew in our community, Mr. Solomon.

I cleared my throat. I stared at the robe. My unsinkable curiosity rose to the occasion as I heard myself ask, "Why is the small red cross on the shoulder of your daddy's robe?"

"Daddy's a captain in the Klan," Julie proudly answered. Suddenly her face reflected anguish. We both knew immediately we were passing the limits on something we neither one should be discussing.

Separate Fountains

"Katie Jane, you really shouldn't know about this," Julie stated. "It's a family secret."

"I understand," I answered softly. "I won't tell, Julie . . . I promise."

We heard the bedroom door open. There stood Charlie Parsons.

"What are you two girls doing in my closet?" he asked sternly, closing the door to the closet as we quickly scrambled out.

"We're just looking for some of Mama's old dresses and shoes to play with, Daddy," Julie answered, showing him the shoes and some old print dresses we had gathered.

I stood stone still . . . afraid to say a word.

"Take those things and go play," Mr. Parsons angrily responded. "And this had better be the last time I have to get on to you girls for noise or snooping—or there ain't gonna be no more party. Understand?"

"Yes, sir," Julie and I answered in unison, ready to run for our lives.

"And, Julie," Mr. Parsons yelled out. "I'm telling you for the last time. Stay out of my closet."

"Yes sir, Daddy," Julie answered meekly as we ran out of the room.

Walking to Jonesboro

As Josh and I continued walking toward the town's business district, we passed the Warren House, glancing up at it sitting majestically on the hill.

"Do you believe all those stories Daddy tells about people seeing ghosts in the Warren House?" Josh asked.

"I didn't until I heard Mama's friend, Mrs. Harrison, swear she felt a ghost push her down the steps when she was visiting there. She is thankful a kindhearted ghost at the foot of the stairs broke her fall."

"Katie Jane, do you really believe in ghosts?"

"Sometimes."

We kept looking into the yards of the houses as we walked past them. When we saw kids we knew playing, we would usually stop and invite them to walk with us. On this particular day, though, we didn't see anyone we wanted to invite along.

We especially wanted someone—anyone—to walk with us as we got close to the last house on Main Street before Jonesboro's business district. Before we could get to the stores on Main Street, we had to walk past a ramshackle house with cobwebs hanging all over it—from the porch ceiling, the railings, the bushes, and even on the big vines crawling up the sides of the place.

Mrs. Tribble lived there alone, and we just knew she had to be a witch. Everytime we saw her she was wearing black clothing and was sitting on her front porch holding a broom.

Daddy said everyone had called her a crazy woman for years. He said he heard she had gone mad when a rabid dog bit her. Now she spent her days yelling at people who walked or rode by her house. Sometimes she even chased children up and down the sidewalk in front of her property.

Josh and I slowed as we neared the edge of her yard.

We stopped.

We both knew, out of habit, what was coming next. Even Sherlock stood dead still.

Taking a runner's stance, I stretched my right foot in front of my left.

Josh did likewise.

I whispered, "Go!"

We ran as fast as we could, scared to death that Mrs. Tribble would chase us with her broom. Her capturing us and eating us, like Hansel and Gretel, was one of Josh's worst nightmares.

Separate Fountains

Sitting in her rocking chair on the porch, Mrs. Tribble got up and grabbed her broom. She walked to the edge of her porch and yelled at us as we ran by: "The devil's gonna gitcha! The devil's gonna gitcha!"

"Don't worry about her, Josh," I gasped, out of breath as we slowed back to a walk. "Everybody knows Mrs. Tribble's crazier than a bed bug. Daddy, who says good things about everybody, even says she's wacky."

"You mean Daddy really thinks Mrs. Tribble's wacky, just like Superman?"

"Just like Superman," I laughed, knowing Josh was referring to the man who rode his bicycle all over town, wearing a red Superman cape wherever he went. No one knew his actual name because he insisted his name was "Superman."

"Daddy said he heard Superman even tries to fly," Josh said, a big grin spreading across his face.

"That's right. Ardella told me Jake saw him try to fly off the barn at the peach packing plant."

"Did Superman get hurt?" Josh asked.

Walking to Jonesboro

"Not that time, but Ardella says one of these days he's gonna break his neck."

"Boy, Superman *is* wacky," Josh said.

"Yeah, and Daddy says that for some reason, the good Lord takes care of wacky people and drunks."

Once past Mrs. Tribble's house, we slowed down so we could look into the windows of the dime store, the hardware store, and the barber shop. After we passed the barber shop, we came to Jonesboro's public library.

"Let's get our library books first, Josh," I said. "Then we'll go to the drugstore for some refreshment."

Sherlock was accustomed to stopping with us at the library. As soon as we got to the library's front door, he plopped himself down on the sidewalk. I reached over and snapped Sherlock's chain on his collar and hooked it to a post beside the library's door. Sherlock knew he had to wait on us.

Separate Fountains

Looking back now, I realize going to Jonesboro's public library was one of the highlights of our simple lifestyle. The library was located between the barber shop and Thornton's grocery store, a convenient site for us to run in often and borrow books. Daddy started taking me to the library at an early age, and as Josh matured, he tagged along. As Josh and I got older, we went to the library alone while Daddy ran errands or when we walked to town on a summer afternoon.

Reading at the library not only opened up my mind to the outside world, but its environment stimulated my awareness of how one can learn when one ventures into new experiences and new surroundings. As I stood outside the library's doors to enter its vast room, a feeling of anticipation always engulfed me.

The library's double doors were so weathered that a few paint chips fell off every time Josh and I entered. When I turned the door handle, it made a creaky, ghostly sound—a secret invitation to step inside onto the library's wooden floor. Warped floorboards of Georgia pine told their own story of countless shoes—wet, muddy, or dry—tracking across them through the years, leaving a trail of wear up and down the wide aisle.

Walking to Jonesboro

The intrigue of the poorly lit high-ceiling room was heightened by its dimness and the pervasive odor of mildew which filled my nostrils. It was hard to determine whether the damp smell seeped up from the cellar through the uneven planks on the floor or if it came from some of the yellow-paged archaic books the librarian, Miss Ada Belle, carefully tended.

Across the length of the open room, individual lightbulbs hung on long cords from the ceiling. Each bulb swayed back and forth when caught by a breeze from the front door, or a drafty window, or when shaken by the vibration of the ground from a passing train on the railroad tracks across the street.

Though there were plenty of bulbs, the room was dark as the result of Miss Ada Belle's frugal ways. She had the habit of turning on only one bulb at a time in an area where she needed to see. To turn on the light bulb, Miss Ada Belle stretched her hand high up into the air and pulled a dangling white string attached to the bulb's light socket. The only bulb that stayed on permanently was over her desk.

As soon as Josh and I entered, we walked straight to Miss Ada Belle's desk to return the books we had read. We stood there silently as she checked each book for forbidden pencil marks or juice stains. After our returned books passed her inspection, she gave us permission to look for new books to check out. Often she helped us, but sometimes she had to sit at her desk to attend to other librarian duties. Sometimes she had to help other patrons check out their books. Pencil in hand, she was always ready to write the due date of the borrowed book.

A tall, thin woman, Miss Ada Belle wore her gray hair pulled back in a tight bun like all older women I knew. Her face, entrenched with wrinkles, was devoid of makeup except for circles of rouge on her cheeks. Though she was known as Jonesboro's old maid, to us she did not fit the stereotype of a stern-faced spinster. She talked to Josh and me a lot, and once she told us her full name was Miss Ada Belle Turner, but we could just call her Miss Ada Belle.

Miss Ada Belle graciously shared her enthusiasm for the printed word with us. She loved to tell us about the library's books, especially the newest ones the county library board had allowed her to purchase. She saved some of the new books for us if she thought a certain title would be appropriate for one of our family members, especially Mama. Josh and I were thrilled when Miss Ada Belle let us be the first ones to take a new book home.

After I put our selected library books securely in my book satchel, Josh and I went outside to the sidewalk where Sherlock was waiting. Josh grabbed Sherlock's chain. "Come on Katie Jane, let's go on down the street to the drugstore."

We passed Thornton's grocery store and stopped in front of Dr. White's drugstore. I gazed at our reflections in the window.

"Are you ready for an ice cream or Coca-Cola?" I asked, looking at Josh's image in the glass.

Knowing what I wanted him to say, he replied to my reflection.

"Nope, not yet, Katie Jane. Let's look in some more windows first."

"That's alright with me," I said, knowing if we walked a little further, we would come to Cletus Jones's drugstore.

Although the drugstores of Dr. White and Cletus Jones looked about the same—with black and white floor tiles in a checkerboard pattern, a soda fountain, and heart-shaped wireback chairs clustered

around small marble-topped tables—there was a world of difference between these two places of business.

Dr. White never smiled at children when they walked into his store. Always stern and serious, he seemed unfriendly, staying behind the pharmacy window in the back. A graduate of the University of Georgia Pharmacy School, he was a certified pharmacist and only interested in mixing expensive medicines that Dr. Green prescribed.

Cletus Jones, on the other hand, was not a certified pharmacist. He was a businessman with a store that he called a drugstore. He had a soda fountain and shelves of over-the-counter drugs like Witch Hazel, Smith Brothers Cough Drops, Lydia Pinkum's Pills, and other potions and ointments. He also stocked perfumes, makeup, body powders, and shaving items.

Cletus Jones's store was alive and noisy. Cletus, with his jovial personality, constantly interacted with the colorful characters who came in. The biggest difference between the two stores, though, was that Cletus loved children. He made them feel important and welcomed.

Separate Fountains

Josh and I continued to amble down the street, stopping for a few moments in front of all the stores to window shop. As we approached Cletus's store, we kept looking around, watching the people in front and behind us. We wanted to make sure nobody we knew saw us enter.

We were now close enough to Cletus's store to hear the other irresistible attraction that drew us there. The tune of "The Yellow Rose of Texas" floated through the air, played on a music box organ by a gray monkey named Tex. As we got closer, we saw Tex standing in front of the store. Tex was dressed up like a cowboy from top to bottom—cowboy hat, red silk shirt, suede vest, jeans, boots, and a belt with two holsters and toy guns slung on his hips.

We were afraid of Tex because Daddy warned us he would bite, scratch, and maybe give us rabies. I knew for sure Tex had jumped on little Buddy Watts and scratched him so bad he almost bled to death before they could get him to a hospital in Atlanta. Cletus ended up having to pay Buddy's hospital bills.

Tex still fascinated us, though, and we stopped a few feet away to watch Tex charm people passing by. I reached over and grabbed Sherlock's chain from Josh so I could prevent Sherlock from getting too near the monkey.

The monkey never failed to attract attention, and this sidewalk show gave Cletus a way to promote his business and his home state of Texas at the same time. Just as Cletus had taught him, Tex turned the handle on the side of the music box with one hand and held a small tin cup for donations in the other. Cletus got money from customers even before they set foot inside his store.

Enthralled for a few minutes, Josh finally spoke.

"Katie Jane, I'm so hot and thirsty."

"Me, too," I replied with a grin. "Help me get Sherlock inside."

Darting past Tex and his organ, we pushed open the screened swinging doors with no second thoughts, pulling Sherlock inside with us. Any intention of obeying Mama and Ardella was overridden by our desire for the excitement and adventure of this forbidden place.

Chapter Seven

Cletus Jones's Drugstore

As soon as we entered, the intrigue began. Compared to the glare of the sun outside, the store was dark and cool. We could hear the large paddle fans humming softly overhead, and I shivered at the sudden, delicious feeling of disorientation while my eyes adjusted to the low light.

The odor of Cletus's new batch of Georgia home brew wafted up from the cellar, overpowering the heavy scent of cheap perfume. I stood still as I was tantalized with a potpourri of smells—moonshine, perfumes, and medicines. It was supposed to be a secret, but everybody in town, including the police, knew what business Cletus was in after closing time.

"How's the Taylors today?" asked Cletus from behind the soda fountain.

"Fine, thank you," Josh and I answered at the same time.

"And Mr. Sherlock Holmes?"

"He's fine, too," Josh said, with a grin on his face, as I held Sherlock on his chain.

Baldheaded, skinny Cletus looked at us through black, horn-rimmed glasses, which were covered with spots of the vanilla, chocolate, and strawberry ice cream from the sodas he had made earlier in the day. His smile revealed wide gaps between a few crooked, tobacco-stained teeth. The skin on the right side of his jaw stuck out in a little pouch—the place where he stored his cud of tobacco.

"How about your Mama and Daddy, Katie Jane?" Cletus continued to question.

Separate Fountains

"Oh they're O. K.," I answered.
"Have you and your daddy been fishing lately, Josh?"
"Yes sir. Daddy and I went fishing Saturday."
"Where'd you go?"
"To Mundy's Mill Pond."
"Catch anything?"
"No sir. Daddy says the weather's too hot for the fish to bite. He says they stay at the bottom of the pond where the water's cool."
"Your daddy's probably right about that."
We all laughed.
"So what can I do for you kids today?" Cletus asked.
"We haven't decided what we want yet," Josh answered.
"You wanna sit up here at the fountain with me, or you wanna go to your booth?"
"We'll go to our booth," I said.
We turned and walked toward our booth, with its red, plastic, tufted seats. Afraid that Mama and Daddy's friends might see us at the soda fountain, we thought we were safe in the corner booth. There, hidden by the propped-open front door, was our special hiding place where we could still see everything going on. The screen doors

Cletus Jones's Drugstore

swung back and forth freely as people came and went. Josh and I quickly slid into our booth, Josh on one side, me on the other. Sherlock spread his large body out on the floor beside Josh.

Over the hum of the big paddle fans, Cletus yelled to us from across the room. "Give me a minute! I'll bring you ice water to sip while you decide what you want."

Josh rested his head back against the soft seat and watched the ceiling fan, its paddles spinning slowly around and around in a smooth continuous motion.

"Josh, what do you want?" I asked, breaking into his thoughts. "A Coca-Cola or an ice cream cone?"

"I want a banana split, with cherries on top," he replied with a grin. "I can already taste that banana and chocolate syrup."

"O.K. with me," I replied. I wanted that sweet treat as much as Josh did. If we pooled our money, we could afford one of Cletus's banana split specialties.

Cletus approached our table, balancing a tray of glassware high in the air with one of his hands. His white butcher's apron was wrapped tightly around his waist, and like his eyeglasses, spots of ice cream were splattered all over it. His apron was like a picture of his day, reflecting all the different flavors of ice cream he had served his customers.

As he moved closer, he switched his cud of tobacco to his cheek pocket.

"Here's your ice water," he said with a smile, as he placed a pitcher of ice water and two glasses and a bowl on our table.

"The bowl's for Sherlock—he needs water, too," Cletus instructed.

"Thank you, Mr. Cletus," we chimed, sure that we were getting special service for ourselves and our dog to boot.

"You decided what you want yet?"

"Yes sir," Josh piped up. "Your specialty."

"One banana split, coming right up!" Cletus replied with a twinkle in his eyes. He added with a smile: "And two spoons."

"Yes sir!"

"Give me a minute, and I'll have you all fixed up," Cletus said as he turned and hurried back to the soda fountain.

Cletus Jones claimed he was a distant relative of Colonel Samuel Goode Jones for whom Jonesboro was named in 1845. Colonel Jones

Separate Fountains

was a civil engineer who had supervised the building of the Central of Georgia railroad system between Forsyth and Atlanta. However, Jonesboro townsfolk were not convinced of Cletus's claim to fame. In fact, people usually didn't put much stock in many of Cletus's far-fetched tales.

As Josh and I waited for our banana split, I had time to again absorb the ambiance of the large room that surrounded us. To the left of the front door was the soda fountain, with evenly spaced stools. To the right, on the side wall, were cozy booths, including ours. Between the soda fountain and the booths were marble-topped tables and black, wire-backed chairs.

On the wall behind Josh's seat was a telephone booth with a door that closed for privacy. It didn't shut completely though, since a large customer damaged it while trying to force himself into the booth.

Beyond the telephone booth was a plywood enclosure Cletus had built. Over the door of this homemade, man-sized box was a sign that read Kodak Film. With mirrors on the outside and a sliding curtain for

Cletus Jones's Drugstore

privacy, this was a place to sit so people could have their picture taken. Cletus would stand behind his big tripod camera with his head under a black cloth and take pictures for fifty cents each.

In the back of the store, on one side, was a medicine corner with many shelves of bottles. Next to that was a cabinet of perfumed body products. On the opposite side, at the back wall, was a ticket counter where Cletus sold Greyhound bus tickets. By the back stairs was a desk, upon which laid an opened, leather-bound book that was used to register guests for Cletus's six-room hotel upstairs.

Through a doorway in the back of the store, Cletus's wife, Ginny, had a beauty parlor. Her customers had to walk through the front of the store to get to the shop, and Josh and I noticed all the ladies who came out of there had bright red hair.

What amazed me about this soda fountain/drugstore/bus station/hotel/photography shop/beauty parlor/monkey show was that Cletus worked and coordinated all of it himself, with his wife in charge of only the beauty shop.

I looked at Josh. He was again resting his head on the back of the seat watching the paddle fan as though hypnotized. However, as soon as Cletus started back toward our table with tray in hand, Josh snapped out of his trance and sat up.

Our banana split, arranged in a long, green dish that Mama called Depression glass, sat in the middle of the tray. Atop the split banana were three scoops of vanilla ice cream, pecans, two animal crackers, and two red cherries. Chocolate syrup oozed over everything like lava flowing down the side of a volcano.

"Just for Josh and Katie Jane," Cletus announced as he proudly presented his specialty to us, setting it in the middle of our table.

Then, taking two white cloth napkins from his apron pocket, Cletus held them up over our heads like he was about to perform magic. With showy fanfare and a sweeping motion, he brought the napkins down and placed one in front of each of us. Using the same motions again, he followed with a silver spoon on each napkin.

"Thank you, Mr. Cletus."

We could hardly speak for laughing.

"You're welcome, kids!" he said as he turned to go back to the soda fountain.

Separate Fountains

Scooting the banana split closer to Josh so he could reach it, I noticed his eyes getting bigger and bigger as he slid closer to the edge of his seat. I watched with a smile as he slid his spoon across the length of the sundae, trying to scoop up a little of all its goodies in one bite. I liked watching Josh eat his share as much as I enjoyed eating mine.

Sharing the banana split and sipping our ice water through a straw, Josh and I sat there without a care in the world. We felt as though we owned the whole universe. Without saying a word to each other, we watched Cletus at work, amazed at his ability to do so many things at one time. We ate our banana split as slowly as ice cream on a summer day would allow, savoring the scrumptious flavors. Of course eating it in a place we knew was off-limits only added excitement to the pleasure.

The delightful sounds inside the store were so familiar that we didn't really even have to look at Cletus to know what he was doing. As he worked behind the counter, he whistled and hummed. He swished water in the sink to clean glasses and other containers. When the glasses clanged together, we knew they were in his hands. He pivoted around quickly, gently placing the dripping glasses on the shelves behind him to dry.

A customer we did not know came in and took a seat at the fountain. We heard Cletus call the man Frank, and at times, they talked softly. Occasionally they laughed loudly. I decided they were telling dirty jokes, but I didn't mention this to Josh.

I could tell Frank ordered a shake, because I saw Cletus begin making one. I knew the routine almost as well as Cletus did.

First, I heard the snapping of the ice cream lids as Cletus popped them open. He then plunked several scoops of ice cream into the glass-shaped, stainless steel container. He closed the lids with a pop. A stomp on the floor signaled he had hit the floor pedal that opened the refrigerator door behind him. He reached for a glass bottle of milk and poured it into the container with the ice cream. It was three easy motions—take out the milk, pour some over the ice cream, and return the bottle to the refrigerator.

Cletus clipped the stainless container onto the electric beater and hit the start switch. The beater's high-pitched whirr drowned out all other sounds in the room for a few seconds. He turned off the beater, poured the sweet batter into a tall glass, and served it with a flourish to Frank.

Cletus Jones's Drugstore

After Frank talked to Cletus for a few more minutes, he finished his shake and left. We were alone again, for the moment, with Cletus.

I saw him look at his radio, which sat on a mirrored shelf directly behind the fountain. I had been in his store enough to know he could pick up only one Atlanta station, WSB, for the news, weather, sports, and music. Turning on the radio, Cletus began to sing along.

Hank Williams's voice poured from the box, and Cletus stopped working for a moment and stood still. He switched to a singer's stage presence and began to sing along with Hank in a deep baritone voice:

Your cheating heart
will tell on you . . .

Cletus sang louder and louder, forgetting we were there watching him. Josh and I got the giggles but Cletus didn't notice.

Above the radio and the singing, we heard the train go by on the tracks across the street. The vibrations from the fast train caused the soda fountain shelves to tremble, and the tinkling glasses brought Cletus back to reality.

A few glasses, perched too close to the edge of the shelves, fell and shattered on the floor. Cletus stopped singing, grabbed his broom, and forcefully swept up the broken pieces. As the last sounds of the train faded, we heard him mumbling and cussing to himself.

"Damn Southern Railroad," he muttered. "I'm gonna send them a bill for my glasses!"

Josh and I snickered at his cussing.

Looking our way, he yelled, "Hey, kids, you finished with my dish yet?"

"Yes sir," Josh answered, "but not with the ice water."

"Tell you what, Josh. Bring me the dish, and I'll let you borrow my checkerboard and checkers."

"That's a deal. I'm not ready to go home yet," Josh said. "I want to stay and see the Greyhound Bus."

Taking the dish, Josh walked to the counter and handed it to Cletus. In return, Cletus handed Josh his prized checkerboard and a sack full of red and black wooden checkers.

"That bus oughta be here any minute now," Cletus said as he glanced at the big clock above the door.

Josh hurried back to the table. "I bet I can beat you at checkers today, Katie Jane," he said as he opened the checkerboard and pulled red and black checkers out of the brown paper sack.

Separate Fountains

"I bet you can, too, if Mr. Cletus helps you like he did yesterday!" I said loud enough for Cletus to hear.

Cletus laughed heartily from across the room. "I don't have time to help today, Josh," he responded. "You're on your own. I've got to get back to the ticket counter. People will be coming in soon to buy their tickets to Atlanta."

As Josh and I started our checker game, several people—white and colored—entered the front door. They walked past the soda fountain and on to the ticket counter.

I heard Cletus tell the colored people: "Remember, when you get on the bus, sit in the back behind the white line."

Josh whispered to me, "Katie Jane, why do colored people have to sit in the back of the bus?"

"Well, Josh, that's the law. But Daddy says it's not right."

"What if Ardella comes here with Mama to buy a ticket?" Josh questioned. "Would she still have to sit behind that white line?"

"Yeah, even with Mama being sick and needing Ardella close by, they still couldn't sit together," I answered. "Ardella would have to sit behind that white line."

"Could Mama sit back there, too?"

"Hmmm, well, Josh, I don't really know. But knowing Mama, I don't think she would try it. Anyway, the Klan might start up a fuss."

"It ain't fair that coloreds have to ride in the back," Josh stated emphatically.

"You're right, it's not fair. Daddy don't like the law either, but he says he can't do anything about it."

"But why can't Daddy do something about it?" Josh asked.

I leaned over closer.

"He's afraid of the Klan," I whispered.

"Shhhh Katie Jane!" Josh whispered back through clenched teeth. "Somebody might hear you!"

"Nobody heard me," I shot back. "We're over here in this corner by ourselves."

"But Katie Jane, I'm scared," Josh whined.

"Of what?"

"That somebody heard you say that word."

"Oh Josh, don't worry about it. Nobody heard me."

"Are you sure?"

"Yeah. Let's play checkers. Your move."

Josh interrupted the game. "Look out the window. There's the bus."

Cletus Jones's Drugstore

Jumping up, we ran to the window and pressed our faces against it. We'd never been on a bus, so the Greyhound was a mysterious monster that filled our imagination every time we came to town. To us, the bright silver bus with a Greyhound dog on the side was the prettiest thing we had ever seen.

"Look at them big tires, Katie Jane!" Josh squealed.

"Uh-huh, they're almost as tall as you."

"Silver sure is a pretty color."

"Uh-huh."

"Do you think the driver has to shine it?"

"Uh-huh."

"Do you think we'll ever ride a bus, Katie Jane?"

"Uh-huh, when I get big and get a job. I'll buy us a ticket."

Cletus helped the new passengers with their luggage, carrying it out the front door toward the bus. A few travelers got off and quickly collected their bags from the compartment under the bus. Suitcases in hand, they headed for Cletus's store.

After Cletus helped the new passengers place their bags in the baggage compartment, he stood and talked to the bus driver for a few minutes. Then Cletus turned and walked briskly back to the store to serve the white passengers waiting for him at the soda fountain.

Josh and I moved away from the window and went back to our private booth. We didn't continue the checker game; we watched the activity around us.

Newly arrived passengers stood or sat at the fountain. As I gazed from one face to another, I wondered if any of these strangers would stay in our town, or were they only in the store for a few minutes to buy a treat before getting back on the bus? We began to play our usual game of trying to decide who the strangers were.

"Look at the man with the purple birthmark on his cheek," I said.

Josh looked closely at the man.

"Do you know who has a birthmark just like that?" I asked him.

"Joe Calhoun," he whispered. "The man who works behind the meat counter at Thornton's grocery store."

"Right. Maybe that's Joe's brother."

"Might be."

"Look over at that woman with the white suitcase, standing in the corner by herself," I directed. "She looks scared."

"I'd be scared, too, if I was traveling on that big bus by myself," Josh answered, looking her way.

"No, look at her. I bet she's running away from a mean husband who beats her."

"Probably so."

"Or maybe," I continued. "She's running away from her past and she doesn't want anybody to notice her."

"Uh-huh."

Still whispering, I asked, "If she stays here in Jonesboro, do you know what she can do so nobody will recognize her?"

"No, what?"

"She can get Miss Ginny to put some red dye on her hair."

"Yeah, good idea," Josh responded with a grin. "You're so smart, Katie Jane!"

One aspect of our game was to look for chain-gang runaways. Because of stories we'd heard about escapes, we were suspicious of any strangers in town, even those who came in on the bus.

"Do you think the man drinking coffee is a runaway convict?" Josh whispered.

"I don't know. He looks mighty clean shaven and dressed up in that brown suit and spit-polished shoes," I noted.

"But that could be part of his costume," Josh insisted.

"You mean disguise, Josh."

"Oh yeah, I have a hard time remembering that disguise word."

Josh and I laughed, muffling the sound with our hands clapped over our mouths.

Remaining quiet in our corner, we continued watching the passengers. We watched as some of the white customers went to the bathroom or water fountain. As soon as the colored people bought their tickets, they went back outside. They did not stay in the store to buy a soda or merchandise, or to go to the bathroom. We knew only white people could go to the inside bathroom in the back of the store. A big sign over it read, "White Only."

The colored passengers had to walk around to the back of the building to use the outside bathroom marked "Colored." Josh and I knew firsthand about this Colored bathroom. We had investigated it on our own one day after we left Cletus's store. Josh, using me as a lookout, even decided to use the Colored bathroom—more out of curiosity than of need.

Cletus Jones's Drugstore

Cletus's drugstore was the only business in Jonesboro, though, with two inside water fountains. He had modernized his store and had fountains installed on the wall near the ticket desk. Each fountain was marked—one said "White Only," the other said "Colored."

Cletus quickly waited on passengers who had to get back on the bus before it started for Atlanta. We watched as he quickly served ice cream and sodas, in awe of the speed he could work when he was making money.

Soon, everyone was gone except for one man, the man in the brown suit. He continued drinking his coffee.

"How long have you been in Jonesboro?" the stranger said, as he looked over toward Cletus.

Cletus, busily cleaning up after the rush of customers, answered nonchalantly, "About thirty years."

"So, are you the owner of this place?"

"Yes, sir," Cletus said, stopping his cleaning activity. After wiping his hands off on his apron, he extended his hand to the stranger in the brown suit. "Let me introduce myself. I'm Cletus Jones."

"Glad to meet you, Mr. Jones," the man said, clutching Cletus's hand to complete the handshake. "My name's Eric Pennington."

"Where you from?" Cletus asked.

"Upstate New York."

"What brings you to Jonesboro?"

"I'm here to hook up with an old friend."

Mr. Pennington sipped on his coffee, and Cletus started back to work.

"Well, if you been here thirty years, Mr. Jones, I guess you know just about everybody in town," Mr. Pennington said.

"I guess so," Cletus replied, with a smile.

"Do you know John Bethel?" the stranger asked.

"Yeah," Cletus paused, suddenly looking a little startled. "How do you know John?"

"John and I have been in the same organization for years," Mr. Pennington stated.

"Well, I-I d-don't really know John v-very well," Cletus said with a stutter I'd never heard before. "He hasn't b-been in m-my st-store for a long t-time."

"That's because he stays busy all over Georgia," Mr. Pennington answered matter-of-factly.

"I d-don't know n-nothing about that," Cletus said nervously. "And if y-you'll excuse m-me, mister, I g-gotta go in the back and help my wife with a ch-chore in her b-beau-ty parlor."

I saw Cletus walk hastily from behind the fountain, past the medicine counter, and into the beauty parlor. He gave a quick glance over his shoulder at Mr. Pennington, then closed the door sharply behind him.

Josh and I acted like we didn't notice anything. We resumed our checker game and sipped our last few drops of ice water. The stranger at the counter got up and headed toward our table.

Watching him uneasily out of the corner of my eye, I kept playing checkers as Mr. Pennington moved closer to us. As he walked by us toward the telephone booth, Sherlock raised his head and growled.

"Quiet, Sherlock," I commanded.

Josh looked at me with a frightened look in his eyes.

"I'm scared," Josh whispered.

"Shhhh." I put my finger to my lips.

We continued our game, even though it was clear I was going to win. I deliberately slowed down the game, stalling for time so we could listen to Mr. Pennington in the phone booth.

Over the back of Josh's seat, I saw Mr. Pennington's hand propped against the booth's door in an attempt to keep it closed. The booth was no longer soundproof, though, and we heard the rustling of the pages of the telephone book, the sound of the nickel dropping into the slot, and the spinning of the dial. Then, silence while he waited for someone to answer.

Josh and I had listened to conversations from the phone booth many times, so we both knew to be still and quiet if we wanted to hear.

"Hello, is this John Bethel's residence?" the stranger asked.

There was a brief pause.

"Is that you, John?" the stranger said. "This is your old buddy, Eric Pennington. I'm calling you to tell you I've arrived, and that I have pretty much stayed on our predicted schedule."

There was another pause.

"I will definitely be in Jonesboro to help you out for a few days," he continued. "I'll be waiting for you tonight at eight o'clock behind the train depot, just as we previously planned. You can pick me up on your way to Colored Town."

Another pause, then he spoke more softly.

Cletus Jones's Drugstore

"What did you say that nigger's name is?" the stranger asked. "Oh yeah, Sam Gilbert. Well, after tonight, Sam Gilbert will remember the Ku Klux Klan forever. See you at eight, John."

Josh's eyes reflected his uneasiness. I tried not to reveal my growing fear.

The telephone booth's door opened, and Mr. Pennington stepped out. I nodded my head toward the checkerboard so Josh would focus there instead of looking guilty or scared.

"Your move, Josh," I said confidently as the stranger walked by. Then, for effect, I added, "I'm gonna get that king of yours."

Mr. Pennington passed us. I watched as he walked to the front of the store, pushed open the screen door, and exited the building.

Josh collapsed limply against the back of his seat.

"Did you hear what he said?" Josh asked, wide-eyed.

"I did," I replied with concern. "You know which Sam he's talking about, don't you?"

"Ardella's brother Sam?" Josh guessed.

"I'm afraid so," I said. "I saw Sam working at the peach packing plant last night when I was out there with Daddy."

"What we gonna do?" Josh asked. "Should we tell Cletus?"

"No Josh! Don't you remember? Daddy said not to say that Klan word to nobody," I exclaimed. "Get hold of Sherlock, and let's get outta here."

I carefully picked up the checkers and the checkerboard and held them as I walked with Josh and Sherlock to the fountain. As I placed them on the countertop, Cletus came from the back of the store.

"You kids headed home?" he asked.

"Yes sir," Josh respectfully answered. "Thank you for letting us play with your checkers."

"Anytime, young man, anytime," Cletus said as he reached over and ruffled Josh's hair.

I couldn't help but notice—Cletus's stutter had completely vanished.

I walked toward the door, Josh and Sherlock following close behind. As I held the screen door open, Josh paused for a second and turned back. Looking fondly at the man behind the counter, he yelled, "Bye, Mr. Cletus!"

Once out the door, we started walking as fast as we could toward home. Sherlock's pace was almost a trot as he tried to keep up with us.

Separate Fountains

One short block later, I froze in my tracks.

"What's wrong, Katie Jane?" Josh asked, as he and Sherlock stopped beside me.

I couldn't believe my eyes.

Across the street, I saw the man in the brown suit who had just left the drugstore. Mr. Pennington was standing by Charlie Parson's red pickup truck. I knew what that meant. They were in the Klan together.

"Oh, nothin'," I answered, trying to protect my brother from further knowledge of the Klan. "We just need to take Sherlock's chain off."

After I unfastened Sherlock, I started walking again as fast as my legs would carry me.

"Don't walk so fast," Josh complained.

We didn't even change our pace when we passed Mrs. Tribble's house. We had much more important things on our minds than that crazy woman. We just heard her yelling her usual threat over and over: "The devil's gonna git cha. The devil's gonna git cha!"

"Walk faster, Josh," I commanded. "We gotta get home and tell Ardella what we heard."

"And Mama, too!" declared Josh.

I stopped again, thinking hard.

"What's wrong now?" Josh asked.

"We're just gonna tell Ardella," I told him firmly. "Mama doesn't need to get upset."

We started walking again.

"Will we tell Daddy when he gets home?" Josh asked.

"Of course."

"Katie Jane, how we gonna help Ardella's brother?" Josh whined.

"I don't know, but we gotta think of something."

Chapter Eight

Sometimes Secrets Have to Wait

We were winded and sweaty when we ran in the back door and found Ardella standing by the kitchen sink running water in a big pot. A long, galvanized aluminum bathtub sat in the middle of our kitchen. Because our bathroom only had a shower, Mama used the tub to sit in and soak her swollen legs. The tub was near the kitchen sink so it would be easier to fill. Ardella turned as we burst in, letting the screen door slam behind us.

"'Bout time you gots home," Ardella said. "I's beginnin' to worry 'bout you."

I went straight to Ardella, cupped my hands around her ear, and whispered. "I need to talk to you on the back porch. It's real important."

"Cain't stop fer you now, chile, don't you see I's busy wif yo' Mama? I almost got the tub full of water."

Josh put in his two-cents worth.

"But, Ardella, we have something real important to tell you," he pleaded.

"Nothin's as important as doin' for yo' Mama right now. Everythang else hast to wait."

"Yes ma'am, Ardella," we answered, standing beside her with the weight of worry on our shoulders.

For the moment, I gave up on communicating with Ardella. It was best not to push the issue so Mama wouldn't become involved and ask what was so important it couldn't wait. Besides, I knew that when Ardella made up her mind about something, nothing would change it.

Separate Fountains

"Can we have some lemonade, Ardella?" Josh asked. "I'm hot and thirsty."

"Yes, honey, but git Katie Jane to git it for you. I got to take care o' yo' Mama jes' now."

Ardella turned on the water again, intent on filling the tub.

Josh, exhausted from trying to keep up with me, had perspiration dripping off his forehead. He plopped down in a chair at the kitchen table.

"Please, Katie Jane," Josh pleaded. "Get me some lemonade."

I got the pitcher out of the refrigerator and two glasses from the cabinet shelf. I poured us both some lemonade and sat down next to Josh. We sat quietly, as we had many times, watching Ardella go through her daily ritual of caring for Mama.

Our silence this time though was anything but tranquil. We were fidgety and anxious about what we'd overheard in town.

When the tub was filled, Ardella walked to Mama's bedside and helped her sit up on the edge. Ardella unfastened the silver clamps that held the gauze wrapped around Mama's legs. After she carefully unwrapped each leg, she began to help Mama get out of her gown. With her back toward us, Ardella instructed, "You chil'len look de other way while yo' Mama undresses."

Respectfully, we turned our heads and looked out the window.

"Now, Miz Taylor, wrap this towel around you, and I'll tote you across de room," we heard Ardella say to Mama.

"You gotta promise you won't drop me," Mama teased.

"Don't you worry none, Miz Taylor. I gots you."

We heard the familiar shuffle of Ardella's feet across the floor, then the sound of rippling water as she lowered Mama into the tub. All the time Ardella is singing and humming one of her spirituals.

"You chil'len can look now," Ardella informed us. "I got yo' Mama in de water, hidin' all her privates."

We turned back around. As always, Ardella had turned Mama to face the wall so we saw only her back. Her hair was pinned up on her head.

We watched Ardella pull one of the kitchen chairs close to the tub. Sitting down, she reached into the water to massage Mama's legs, singing as she massaged. She worked each leg in turn, and after a few minutes, she got up and started toward the sink with the empty pot.

"Gotta keep de water warm," Ardella mumbled as she carried more hot water to the tub. "Dere's nothin' worse dan a summer cold."

Sometimes Secrets Have to Wait

Once I knowed a man don caught new-monia in de summer. Wouldn't think dat possible, but he did."

Ardella took a washcloth and rubbed it thick with Ivory soap.

"I scrubs yo' back fer you, Miz Taylor, but you got to take care o' those private parts yo'self."

Josh and I giggled. Mama laughed, too.

Because Dr. Green required Mama to soak her legs for an hour, Ardella—still humming and singing—continuously poured hot water into the tub. When the water was heated to the correct temperature again, she would sit back down by Mama, reach over into the water, and continue to massage Mama's legs.

As soon as Josh finished his lemonade, he went over to his cot in the corner, where he immediately fell asleep. I put the pitcher back in the refrigerator and our dirty glasses in the sink.

Going to the rocking chair by Mama's bed, I fell against the big cushion and started to rock. I was tired, too, and could have easily drifted off to sleep, but I was more worried than tired. I thought of poor Sam, and I wondered if anyone could help him. Surely, Daddy will find a way, I told myself.

"Katie Jane," Ardella said, interrupting my troubled thoughts. "You get dat extra towel off dat shelf, den spread it out on yo' Mama's bed. I'm fixen to lift her on over yonder to dry off."

I minded without reply. Ardella carried Mama's towel-wrapped body to the bed. She asked my help again.

"Katie Jane, you can dry off yo' Mama's legs and feets, ifen you would."

"Yes, ma'am," I answered.

I loved doing things for Mama.

Ardella helped Mama into a freshly washed house dress while I finished drying her feet. Ardella noted, "I irons dis blue dress so you looks pretty when Mistuh Taylor gits home. You always got to look pretty for yo' man."

Mama sat still as Ardella took two rolls of clean gauze from the chest of drawers. She pulled Mama to the edge of the bed and allowed her legs to hang freely over the side. With Mama's foot in her hand, Ardella began wrapping the gauze around Mama's ankle. She paused to fasten the wrap tightly with several silver clamps.

Continuing, she calmly circled the white gauze around and around Mama's outstretched leg, up the calf, over the knee, and up the thigh. Mama's leg was completely encased in gauze. Ardella

Separate Fountains

finished by snapping the silver clips onto the gauze, securing it tightly at the top of Mama's leg.

With one leg wrapped, Ardella patiently switched to Mama's other leg and began the same process. I continued to watch, and even though it was as much a part of the day as lunch or supper, it always made me feel sad for Mama, who was imprisoned in her own body. Mama's smiles were now fewer and farther between.

Ardella must have been aware of Mama's mood, because she stopped her humming and said, "Miz Taylor, I knows you's tired of bein' wrapped up like a mummy, but you's be better soon. Dr. Green said so."

"I hope he's right," Mama answered, her voice reflecting sadness.

Ardella pulled Mama's fragile body back up to the headboard of the bed and propped her against the pillows. Next, she brought Mama her beauty box, which contained a mirror, comb, brush, lipstick, powder, and rouge.

"It's 'bout time fer Mistuh Taylor," Ardella said, still trying to cheer up Mama. "Use dis stuff to git pretty. Show him how beautiful you is."

I continued to watch, and I agreed with Ardella. Mama was beautiful, with hazel-green eyes, fair complexion, and shiny black hair. Watching Mama as she brushed her own hair, I reflected back to when

Sometimes Secrets Have to Wait

I was small, and Mama would play beauty parlor with me. She would sit sideways on the edge of the bed, one leg tucked under her, something she could no longer do because of the pain in her legs.

She taught me how to place several spring-loaded clamps in her just-washed, wet hair. After her hair was dry, Mama would remove the clamps and brush back the curly waves. The curls enhanced her high cheeks and the delicate features of her oval face.

I sat there thinking Mama was the prettiest mother on earth, and I wondered if I would ever be that pretty. I remembered the many times Mama and I had run out the door together when we heard Daddy's car outside. Sometimes we even played jokes on Daddy, like hiding in the closet or in the shower. Josh had never really known Mama like that. I was sure no one was more sorry about it than she was.

Suddenly, I heard Daddy's car outside. Jumping out of the rocking chair, I ran over to Josh and tugged on his arm.

"Josh, wake up! Daddy's home."

I ran out the door and Josh followed, half asleep.

Standing by the Plymouth, Daddy watched us run to him. We flew into his arms. Without missing a beat, he swung us up and held us close to his chest. We smothered him with hugs and kisses.

"How's my two sugar lumps?" he asked affectionately. He kissed us both on the cheek.

"Fine," we answered together, laughing as he put us back down on the ground.

"Daddy, we gotta talk to you about a secret," Josh spurted out.

"Not just yet, Josh, I've gotta see about your Mama first," Daddy said. He reached out for one of our hands to hold as the three of us began to walk toward the porch.

"But Daddy," I pleaded tugging on his hand. "Josh is right, we need to talk to you about something real important."

"Later, sugar lump."

"Can we ride with you to take Ardella home then?" I continued, knowing that during the ride we could tell both Daddy and Ardella what we had heard in town.

"Please Daddy," Josh begged.

"Don't you always?" Daddy answered with a chuckle.

He walked up the steps of the house, opened the screen door, and immediately walked to Mama's bedside.

"Look what I found outside, Katherine. Our little sugar lumps," Daddy said. "Have they been good today?"

Separate Fountains

"Perfect, as always," Mama answered with a bright smile.

Stretching up toward Daddy, she prompted him for a kiss. Josh and I let go of his hand grasp.

He sat down on Mama's bed, taking her hand.

"My, you look pretty in that blue dress," Daddy said. "It makes your hazel eyes look blue."

Mama smiled, pleased with his compliment.

"B. J., you better go on and take Ardella home," Mama said. "Jake and the children are waiting on her."

"You're probably right," Daddy answered as he stood up. "I also need to run by the grocery store."

Daddy looked toward Ardella with mischief in his eyes.

"Ardella, are you ready to go home to that man of yours?" he asked.

"Yessuh!" Ardella answered excitedly. "Jes' let me git my pocketbook."

"Don't forget to take some of those tomatoes you picked from the garden this morning," Mama reminded her. "Get some beans, too, and take some of the eggs Josh got out of the henhouse."

"Thank you, Miz Taylor," Ardella replied as she filled up a large paper sack with some of the freshly picked vegetables and eggs. "We shore appreciates it."

"You know you're welcome to anything we have," Mama answered with compassion. "You're as much a part of this family as anyone here. Don't you ever forget that Ardella Sanders."

Ardella, with her face beaming, walked to Mama's bed and gave her a hug.

"Sees you in the mawnin'," she said as she headed for the door.

Daddy leaned over to kiss Mama one more time.

"We'll be back in about an hour, Katherine," he said.

As we were on our way out, he turned to Mama and added. "When I get back, I'll heat up leftovers for supper. Get some rest while we're gone."

At the car, Ardella started her daily speech.

"Lawds-a-mercy, Mistuh Taylor, you better let me ride in dat backseat. If de Klan sees an ole colored woman like me in de front seat o' yo' car, der gonna be some trouble fer shore."

"Now Ardella, you just let me worry about that," Daddy said calmly, opening the front passenger door for her. "You know the backseat is just the right size for my sugar lumps."

Sometimes Secrets Have to Wait

Smiling at us, he flipped the seat forward. Josh and I clambered in.

Continuing to hold the door open for Ardella, Daddy announced in a dramatic, clowning tone of voice: "And this front seat is for Miss Ardella Sanders, the best cook in Clayton County. Peach pie is her specialty."

Eating a piece of peach pie or chewing on a freshly-ripened peach was a symbol of a way of life in Jonesboro because of the many peach orchards in the area. Georgia's red soil seems to provide the perfect growing medium for peaches, therefore Georgia is known as the "Peach State."

The round Georgia peach has a fuzzy peeling. The peeling color ranges from touches of a yellow and pink blended together on a hard, newly developed peach to touches of a dark almost burgandy-red peeling on an overly-ripe peach. Because of the peach's high acid content, its puckery taste makes your mouth twinge with your first bite.

I watched Ardella many times as she made her specialty—peach pie. With her rolling pin, she rolled out a floury mixture into a thin and rounded dough piece on the kitchen countertop. Picking the rounded dough up, Ardella positioned it on the bottom of a tin pie pan. Next, she placed fresh sliced peaches on top of the dough and scattered small pieces of butter over them. With her thumb and fingers, she took pinches of sugar from the sugar canister and sprinkled it over the combination of peaches and butter.

She then rolled out another piece of dough, cutting it into long thin strips. With the strips, she interwove the dough into a lattice-top

Separate Fountains

design to make the crust of the pie. What was amazing about Ardella's peach pie and her other tasty dishes was she never used a recipe.

That seemed to be the way all Southerners cooked when I was growing up. A pinch of this! A pinch of that! Everyone had her own favorite recipe for making a peach pie—but not one person I ever knew wrote her recipe down. You see, everyone just seemed to know how to make one! Some enterprising cooks even discovered how to use peach juice to make schnapps and other peach drinks. And of course, peaches were used to make peach ice cream and other "peachy" desserts.

Ardella's grin spread widely across her face after Daddy's compliment about her peach pie.

"All right, Mistuh Taylor. I knows you must be taking actin' lessons from dat Milton Berle feller on de radio," she kidded back. "If you jes' stop dat foolishness and git in dis here car, I promise to makes you a peach pie tomorrow."

Turning to look at us, she continued, "If you can git yo' two sugar lumps to pick me some ripe peaches off dat tree."

"That's a deal," Daddy answered, winking at us in the backseat.

Closing Ardella's door, Daddy marched around the front of the car, still clowning by making faces at us. When he got in, he yelled, "Boo!"

Everyone laughed at his silliness.

After we got through the gate and started toward Jonesboro, Josh stood up on the floorboard of the backseat and leaned forward, putting his arms around Daddy's broad shoulders.

"Daddy, Katie Jane's got a secret she really needs to tell you and Ardella," he whispered loudly in Daddy's ear.

"Heaven forbid, Mistuh Taylor," Ardella stated. "Let dem chil'len tell der secret! Dey been pesterin' me all aft'noon."

Chapter Nine

The Klan

"All right, what's the big secret you've been dying to tell us?" Daddy asked, looking curiously at us in the rearview mirror.

From behind Ardella, I answered faintheartedly, "I need to tell you something Josh and I heard in Jonesboro today."

"Speak up, Katie Jane," Daddy said over the hum of the car's engine. "I can hardly hear you."

"She needs to tell you something we heard in town today!" Josh shouted.

"Well, then speak up Katie Jane," Daddy said again.

I could tell by the tone of his voice he was getting impatient.

"But, we're afraid to tell you, Daddy," Josh said shyly.

"All right, you two, what's going on here?"

Daddy's frustration was evident. He continued to watch us in the rearview mirror.

"Why is Josh afraid to tell me what you heard, Katie Jane?"

"Cause we heard it in a place we weren't supposed to be," I replied nervously.

Ardella snapped her head around, cutting her eyes toward us with that look we knew meant she was reading our minds.

"Has yawl been in Cletus Jones's drugstore?" she asked sternly.

"Yes, ma'am," we both answered at the same time in meek voices.

"But," I went on defensively, "we heard something about your brother while we were there."

Her expression of anger instantly changed to concern.

"Wat 'bout Sam?" Ardella asked.

Separate Fountains

"We heard a man in the telephone booth talking about him."

"What man?" Daddy said, joining the questioning.

"We didn't know him," Josh answered, still standing on the floorboard of the car so he could look through the front window, past Daddy's shoulder.

"Where did the man come from?" Daddy asked.

"He got off the Greyhound bus," Josh said.

"What in the world is Josh talking about, Katie Jane?" Daddy asked.

Words started rushing out of my mouth. I talked as fast as I could.

"This man in a brown suit got off the bus and made a phone call in Cletus's store. Josh and I were sitting by the telephone booth and heard everything he said."

"Lawds-a-mercy, chil'len!" Ardella interrupted. "Wait til yo' Mama hears 'bout dis!"

"Calm down, Ardella, let's see what else the children have to say," Daddy said.

He drove the car off the road onto the grass and stopped. When Daddy turned off the engine, Josh fell back on the seat beside me. He looked over at me, knowing we were in big trouble.

"All right, Katie Jane, what happened?" Daddy said, as he turned around to look at me.

"Well, when we walked to town today, we accidently ended up at Cletus Jones's drugstore."

"We'll discuss why you were at Cletus's later. Right now, I want to know what you heard about Sam."

"The man in the brown suit said that after tonight Sam Gilbert would remember the Ku Klux Klan forever," I stated.

"Lawds-a-mercy, wat's gonna happen to my brother!" Ardella moaned, wringing her hands, displaying her frustration. "Sam tole me and Jake a white man yelled at him on de street yestidy."

"What did he say to Sam?" Daddy asked.

"He yelled out, 'Yore next, Sam Gilbert.'"

"But why didn't you tell me about this Ardella?" Daddy asked.

"I hoped it don't mean nothin'," she said. "Anyways, dis be our family's trouble, Mistuh Taylor. We don't want to cause yawl no problem."

"Your problems are our problems, Ardella," Daddy reassured her.

Turning back toward me, Daddy said, "Katie Jane, tell me exactly what you heard the man say."

The Klan

"The man in the telephone booth told the man he was talking with that he had just gotten to Jonesboro, and he'd be waiting for him to pick him up behind the train depot tonight."

"Did he say where they were going?" Daddy asked.

"To Colored Town."

"What else did he say?" Daddy continued to question.

"He asked the man he was talking to, 'What's that nigger's name?' Then he said, 'That's right, Sam Gilbert.'"

"Anything else?" Daddy asked.

"Like I told you before, Daddy, he said that after tonight Sam would remember the Ku Klux Klan forever."

"Heaven help us," Ardella said. "Wat we gonna do, Mr. Taylor?"

"Calm down, Ardella," Daddy said as he reached over and patted her hand. "Katie Jane, do you by any chance know who the stranger was talking to?" Daddy continued.

"Yes, sir. I heard him ask for John Bethel."

"That's what I was afraid you were gonna say. John Bethel is an assistant to the Grand Dragon of the Ku Klux Klan of Georgia."

"Did you by any chance hear the stranger's name?"

"Yes, sir. Earlier when he was drinking coffee I heard him tell Cletus his name was Eric Pennington and that he was from New York."

"Eric Pennington. . . . That even sounds like a Yankee name to me. I bet he's come down from the North to hook up with the Klan."

Long ago, Daddy had explained to Josh and me about the Klan. He said it was an organization whose secret members thought it was their duty to scare or punish bad people to make them behave. Daddy said the Klan had its own definition of who was bad.

Even small children in Jonesboro knew the name John Bethel, from hearing their parents talk about him behind closed doors. His name represented fear to many people, both black and white. John Bethel was one of the few names ever publicly used when referring to the Klan; the other members' names were secret. Sometimes I even heard John Bethel's name on the Atlanta radio stations when we listened to the news.

Daddy also told us John Bethel traveled all over Georgia meeting with Klan members in other communities. He had an office in a place

Separate Fountains

the Klan members called the Imperial Palace, in Atlanta, the capital of their so-called "Invisible Empire."

Daddy said he never could understand why the Klan called themselves a secret organization because they had a network of members all over the United States. He said the Klan membership was so strong and powerful that they didn't have to be a secret.

Even when the Klan broke the law by doing something bad to a person or a group in the community, Daddy said it was amazing to him how all the witnesses went into the woodwork—afraid to testify. He said all Jonesboro citizens had the same answer when it came to Klan activities: "Don't ask me, I don't know nuthin'."

Although it was still early evening, clouds darkened the sky. I shuddered at the possibility that something bad might happen to Sam, or to Ardella, or to all of us.

"Let's get Ardella home," Daddy said as he started the car and reached over to turn on the headlights. "Boy, it sure has gotten dark and cloudy. I think it's going to rain."

We resumed our trip to Jonesboro and to Ardella's house in Colored Town.

Reaching over with his right hand, Daddy consoled Ardella by patting her folded hands.

"Ardella, don't you worry," he reassured her. "I'm gonna help Sam, but for now, we gotta get you home and talk to Jake about this."

At the edge of Jonesboro, Daddy suddenly slowed the car. Ahead on Main Street, we saw cloaked Klan members standing in the middle of the street, stopping traffic.

"Lawds-a-mercy, Mistuh Taylor. You in real trouble, hasin' me in dis front seat wif you," Ardella cried out.

Daddy quickly turned right, off the paved street and into the bank's parking lot. Moving our car slowly to the back of the lot, he took a left into a dirt alley behind the Jonesboro Furniture Store. As we moved slowly down the alley that paralleled Main Street behind the business section of town, Daddy turned off the car's headlights. Ardella, Josh, and I sat in silence wondering what he would do next.

"We gotta hide you, Ardella," Daddy said in a matter-of-fact way. "Don't you worry. Everything's gonna be all right."

The Klan

"Oh, Lawdy! Mistuh Taylor. Wat we gonna do?"

"I'll see if I can hide you in Smith's Hardware."

"Oh, no, Mistuh Taylor. I's scared," Ardella moaned.

"Me too," whined Josh. He began to sob as though his heart would break.

"Katie Jane, please take care of Josh," Daddy instructed. "We've all got to work together to help Ardella."

I was frightened too, but I slid over to Josh's side of the seat and bravely wrapped my arms around his small body. As I hugged him, I felt something hard in his overalls chest pocket. It was the turtle he had picked up earlier that day on our walk into town. How far away that time seemed now.

I pulled the turtle from Josh's pocket and held it up in front of him.

"Look Josh! This here is a genuine feel-good turtle," I announced. "If you rub his shell, he'll come out to see you and make you feel better. I promise."

Josh quit crying.

"Don't worry, Josh," I said. "Everything's gonna be alright. This feel-good turtle guarantees it."

Josh took the turtle in his hands and looked into the front of its shell. The turtle looked back at him with tiny, shiny black eyes.

"Sometimes," my brother said with a sniffle, "I wish I could live inside a shell. Then I wouldn't have to be scared of the Ku Klux Klan."

Ardella broke her silence.

"Mr. Taylor, how you knows Mr. Smith ain't one of de Klan?"

"I know George Smith well, Ardella," Daddy assured her. "We can trust him."

Separate Fountains

Pulling the car up as close as he could to the back of Smith's Hardware Store, Daddy stopped and jumped out. We saw him leap up on the loading dock, open the store's door, and disappear into the blackness. Ardella, Josh, and I sat quietly in the dark.

In a few seconds, Daddy hurried through the doorway and jumped off the loading dock to the ground. He opened Ardella's door.

"Come on, Ardella, up those steps at the end of the dock," Daddy instructed. "George says the coast is clear."

Pushing the seat forward, Daddy grabbed Josh and swung him up onto the dock. I climbed out of the car, and Daddy grabbed me and lifted me up beside Josh.

"Katie Jane, you three go inside to George," he said in a determined voice. "I need to move the car, then I'll be back."

"But, Daddy, I'm so scared!" I protested.

"Get inside!" he said sternly. "I'll be right back."

Josh and I stood there, side-by-side on the loading dock, and watched our father drive off. The car disappeared slowly down the alley.

We heard Ardella's shuffling footsteps as she came across the dock to where we stood. She silently took our hands.

We opened the store's door. The room we entered was dark with only shadows of light coming from the front of the store. We stood still. As our eyes adjusted to the dark, we saw Mr. Smith's silhouette, rifle in hand.

"Come this way, Ardella," he whispered. He used a small flashlight to point to a pantry where some of his personal items were kept. There was a chair in the room, and he directed Ardella to it.

"Just stay here for now," he said to her, "and be quiet. I'm gonna lock the pantry door from the outside so you'll be safe."

Ardella complied without a word, but, as the door closed, her face revealed the terror she felt.

All of a sudden, we heard Daddy fumbling at the store's door. He came in quickly, and we could hear his labored breathing. After his eyes adjusted, he saw all of us standing there.

"Jumpin' Jehoshaphat!" Daddy said to Mr. Smith. "We need cat eyes to get around back here."

"B. J., are you ever serious?" Mr. Smith laughed.

"Who wants to be serious?" Daddy answered, trying to make light of our situation.

"Where'd you put the car, Daddy?" Josh's voice chirped out of the darkness.

The Klan

"Don't worry, Josh, it's behind the Methodist Church," Daddy said reassuringly. He leaned over and picked up Josh. He reached his other hand out to me, including me in the circle of safety his presence represented to us.

"Let's go up front and see what's going on," Mr. Smith said. "Follow me."

Mr. Smith led us, shining the flashlight on the floor behind him so Daddy could see. We quietly made our way in single file. Daddy carried Josh and still held my hand, dragging me through the darkness between the crates and boxes stored in the back of the store. I kept glancing back at the pantry where Ardella hid, worried about her.

Before nearing the front window, Mr. Smith turned off his flashlight. The glow of the street lamps allowed enough light into the room for us to see.

Daddy placed Josh on the countertop, beside Mr. Smith's cash register. He lifted me, too, putting me up beside Josh. We were only a few feet away from the large display window, but hidden by the shelves holding Mr. Smith's inventory. From our vantage point, we could see into the street, but those in the street could not see us. We watched and waited.

"Where's your turtle, Josh?" I whispered. "You didn't drop him did you?"

"In my pocket," Josh whispered back. "I'm gonna keep him forever 'cause he makes me feel brave."

As he spoke, though, a slight tremor in his voice betrayed his true feelings.

Mr. Smith, rifle ready, moved to the front door to double-check the locks. Click, click. Click, click.

"Well, I guess we'll just have to see what happens," he whispered, as he sat down in a chair near us.

I looked out onto the main street of Jonesboro, a familiar place to me. But tonight, it seemed like a place on another planet. Almost afraid to breathe, I sat perfectly still by Josh on Mr. Smith's countertop. Daddy stood by Josh.

Several white-clad Klan members walked close by the store's window. As more Klansmen gathered, I noticed they seemed to organize themselves into small groups. I heard horns blasting and someone yelling to get into formation.

Separate Fountains

Several hooded knights on horseback led the parade, and each held a tall, flaming cross, mounted on the front of his saddle. Behind the leaders marched the Klansmen, six abreast, down Main Street.

All of the men were dressed in long white robes, or sheets, with only the bottom part of their pants legs and shoes showing. Their heads were covered with white hoods, eye slits cut so they could see. Some of the horses, too, were covered in white sheets, even their faces, and large round eye holes were cut out to permit full vision.

Many Klansmen carried torches that flamed high over their heads. Others blew long blasts on their bugles. Some had megaphones, shouting through them in booming voices:

"We are the white supremacists!"

"We are God's chosen race!"

"We're gonna get rid of all niggers!"

The street glowed with fire from the torches, lighting up the area so all could see. Daddy and Mr. Smith intently watched the men marching down the street.

I was transfixed by the procession. As I sat there looking out the window, I thought of what Daddy had told me: "If you ever come close to a Klansman, study his clothing and shoes that stand out from under his sheet."

In Jonesboro, shoes and pants cuffs were clues to the identities of the men who were neighbors and friends by day and vigilantes by

The Klan

night. Daddy always said that one needed to know which side of the fence one's neighbors were on.

As I continued to watch the Klansmen march, I thought of the many times I had gone with Daddy to the barber shop, and how he had taught me to observe the men's shoes and pants cuffs as we waited for Daddy's turn to get a haircut. We watched every customer as they got their shoes shined for a nickel by the colored shoe-shine boy in the back corner of the barber shop.

Daddy pointed out ways to help me identify men's shoes. "Katie Jane, you can look at the color, size, and shape, and for any unusual markings. Do the shoes have perforated toes? Do they have buckles or laces? Do they have rundown heels? You might even look for clay or cow manure on them."

I developed Daddy's habit even further by examining men's shoes at church and other social functions, trying to figure out who was in the Klan.

The mounted Klansmen turned their horses around and backtracked past the marchers. The leader signaled, and in unison, all of the riders jerked their reins to make the horses rear up on their hind legs. The horses whinied and snorted loudly.

"Why are they making such a show?" I whispered to Daddy.

"They want people to think the Klan's in control. They know people like us are watching from darkened rooms all up and down the street. They'll probably go to Colored Town next to put a scare into folks there."

"Are you afraid of the Klan, Daddy?" Josh asked.

"Yes," Daddy answered, as he pulled his car keys out of his pocket. "I'm scared of what they might do to some of our friends, or to us."

"Where you going, Daddy?" I asked.

"I think I'd better go see if I can find Sam," he replied.

"The children can stay here with me," Mr. Smith said, joining our conversation. "I'll take them and Ardella home after the Klan has gone."

Josh started sobbing.

"Don't leave me, Daddy," he sobbed pitifully. "I'm so scared."

Daddy picked up Josh to comfort him.

"George, I appreciate your offer," Daddy said, "but I believe we'll all stay together. I'll get Ardella and take her home."

"Are you sure that's what you want to do?" Mr. Smith asked.

"Yes, I'm sure, but will you please do me a favor, George?"

"Be glad to. What do you want?"

"Call Katherine for me, and tell her I'll be later than I thought," Daddy said. "And please, don't tell her anything about the Klan. She doesn't need to worry."

"O. K.," Mr. Smith replied.

"I so appreciate all you've done tonight," Daddy continued, "but I still have another favor to ask. Do you have a flashlight I can borrow, and maybe some peanuts for the children to snack on until I can get them home for supper?"

"Of course, B. J., my pleasure," Mr. Smith replied.

Reaching behind the counter, Mr. Smith pulled out several small cellophane bags of peanuts and gave us each two.

"Thank you, Mr. Smith," I whispered.

"Thanks," Josh whimpered with a sniffle.

Mr. Smith patted Josh's head as he handed Daddy the flashlight.

Reaching over to the counter, Daddy took my hand and guided me as I jumped off onto the floor beside him. "Come on, Katie Jane, follow me."

The Klan

With Daddy leading the way, we headed toward the safety of the back of the store. Surrounded by darkness, I peered ahead, following the bobbing flashlight beam on the floor.

Daddy walked over to the pantry where Ardella hid, unlocked the door, and opened it. He shined the flashlight inside. Ardella sat solemnly with tears in her eyes.

"Come on, Ardella," Daddy said. "Let's get outta here."

She was more than glad to oblige. She jumped up and quickly followed, not saying a word. When we got to the back door, Daddy turned off the flashlight and put it in his pocket.

"Be quiet and stay close together, " Daddy instructed. "The car's parked at the church. We just have to walk down the alley to the parking lot."

The alley wasn't as dark as it had been when we arrived. The cloud cover had cleared, and the night was brightly lit from the full

Separate Fountains

moon. The change brought me a feeling of hope. God would help us, I thought to myself. I could hear Ardella praying under her breath for His help as she shuffled along trying to keep up with Daddy's fast pace.

We hurried through the shadows of the buildings, moving as one down the narrow street. With one hand, I held onto Daddy tightly as he pulled me to keep up with his fast pace. With my other hand, I clutched my two bags of peanuts.

At the end of the alley, we came into the back of the church's parking lot. Parked behind the boxwood hedge was our car. When Daddy pulled the seat forward, Josh and I leaped in, relieved to be in a familiar place and confident again everything would work out.

"Make room for Ardella," Daddy instructed. "I think she'll be safer in the back where it will be harder for anyone to see her."

I slid over to the corner of the seat, pulling Josh close beside me. Ardella squeezed through the opening and plopped down on the seat with a groan.

"Oh, Mistuh Taylor, I's fills up this backseat," Ardella said.

We all laughed—a laugh much needed to relieve some of the tension.

Daddy quickly started the car and moved it slowly ahead with the lights off. He drove away from the church, across the back of the parking lot, toward an open field.

"Daddy, why don't you have the lights on?" Josh asked.

"I don't want the Klan to see us," Daddy answered. "Don't worry, Josh. The moon's bright now and I can see clearly."

Tired, hungry, and frightened, Josh softly cried against my shoulder.

"Don't worry, Josh, Daddy will take care of us," I whispered in his ear.

Ardella, too, tried to comfort Josh. "Come on over here, baby, and sits by yo' Ardella," she said. "Everythang's gonna be jes' fine, jes' fine."

Josh slid over, and Ardella put her arms around him as Josh put his head on her lap. I watched Daddy at the wheel of the car and felt secure he knew exactly what to do.

I reached over and rubbed Josh's back as I had seen Mama do so many times, hoping it would help him drop off to sleep. To comfort Josh, Ardella softly sang his favorite song:

Jesus loves me this I know,
For the Bible tells me so . . .

The Klan

The windows of the car were down, and as we moved slowly across the parking lot, the wind stirred my hair. I looked out my side window and saw pine trees shrouded in shadows but highlighted by the moonlight. I breathed in the cool night air.

I felt our car hit a bump, and I sat up to see why. Daddy had driven up over the curb at the end of the parking lot. I could see we were now in an open field, a place familiar to me. I remembered back to when I was a little girl, when Mama could still walk, and we used to come to this field for picnics.

Beyond the field, there was a wide path cut through the trees. Daddy had once explained to me that under the ground of this path was a pipeline owned by the Southern Gas Company. The landowners in the area had given the company permission to put the pipeline across their land. The company used the pipeline to carry natural gas to Clayton County and to other communities in the state of Georgia. Daddy said the Southern Gas Company had to sign a legal document with each individual landowner stating the company would maintain this wide, grassy path.

Daddy knew the cleared area went right through Colored Town. He flipped on the car's lights, confident now that no one would see him in this thickly wooded pass. We moved slowly, bumping along the secret avenue to Ardella's house.

"You all O.K. back there?" Daddy asked over the seat.

"Yes sir," I answered. "Josh's about asleep, and Ardella and I are doing fine."

"You know where we are, don't you Katie Jane?" he continued.

"Yes, sir. On the pipeline right-of-way, on our way to Colored Town."

"Smart girl, Katie Jane."

As we continued to ride along, everyone remained silent in the seriousness of the moment. I continued my own thoughts about the Klan, watching out my window for their possible appearance.

Yes, even today I can still remember the Ku Klux Klan marching through Jonesboro unexpectedly on a Friday or Saturday night. Their

Separate Fountains

marches were a part of our community life.

Daddy said the Klan's marches were meant to instill fear and to remind the public of the group's power. If any citizens disagreed with the Klan's philosophy, they would be quickly targeted. Sometimes, people would be accused for no reason, especially if they were blacks, Jews, or whites sympathetic to minority causes.

Most Jonesboro folks just kept to themselves to avoid any conflict with the Klan. I remembered the time Daddy and I were walking on the sidewalk in the broad open daylight, and all of a sudden, we heard yelling and screaming coming from the south end of town. We turned and saw a truck full of hooded Klansmen, speeding forward, then driving by us, pulling a black man by a rope. The rope, attached to the bumper of the truck, was tied around the man's waist.

The black man struggled to run and keep up with the moving truck, but the driver would speed up, causing the black man to fall and to be dragged behind the vehicle. The driver would slow down, the black man would get back up on his feet and try desperately to keep up his running pace with the moving truck. Then the driver would speed up, causing the black man to fall again. The Klansman riding on the back of the truck laughed and yelled at the black man. One of the Klansmen yelled out: "Come on, nigger. Let's see how fast you can run."

The town policemen, usually on the streets, were nowhere in sight. Daddy felt helpless when he recognized the black man behind the car

The Klan

as Cecil, a worker on Colonel Barlett's peach farm. We watched as they dragged Cecil through the town and went on up Route 41, taking a side road and disappearing. A few days later Daddy heard that Cecil's mangled body was found floating in the Flint River.

The Klan had the practice of doing what they boasted as "Saturday night bottom-fishing." They looked for a black man to tie up with a rope, then tied him to a concrete block and threw him into a lake or a river to drown. Daddy felt like poor Cecil had been their target for bottom fishing.

"Ardella, do you think Jake will still be home when we get to your place?" Daddy asked.

"Yessuh, he should be. He tole me when I lef' this morning he had to work the late shift at de plant tonight."

When Daddy arrived in Colored Town, he drove straight to Ardella's house. Jake was waiting for her on their front porch, and as soon as he saw us, he ran to the car. He quickly opened her door.

"Ardella, honey, is you O.K.?" Jake asked. "I's worried 'bout you fer bein' so late."

"I's fine, but de Klan, dey be lookin' fer Sam right now," Ardella explained as she got out of the car. "Jake, you's gotta hep Mistuh Taylor find him quick."

"Lordy Ardella, you shore 'bout Sam?" Jake asked, his eyes appearing wide open with fright.

"Yes, Jake," Daddy joined in. "Jump in the car and let's go find Sam."

Ardella went in the house as we backed out the driveway.

"Sam be here a few minutes ago," Jake said. "He go home, so he sez, to git ready fer work at de peach packin' plant tonight. He wuz gonna come and ride in de truck wif me and Ardella, but when she ain't showed up, he sed he'd best go on without us."

As the car rolled along, Jake directed Daddy.

"Sam's house be on de next road, on de left."

All of a sudden Jake turned his head toward the backseat and saw me.

"Miss Katie Jane, wat in de world is you doin' back der?" Jake asked.

Separate Fountains

"I came with Daddy to bring Ardella home. Josh is back here, too, but he's asleep."

"Mistuh Taylor, yo' chil'len oughta be home in bed," Jake said, turning back toward Daddy.

"Well, you know I know that," Daddy laughed. "But when we left home we didn't have any idea tonight would turn out like this."

"Yessuh, Mistuh Taylor."

"I need you to listen carefully, Jake," Daddy instructed, turning to a serious tone. "After we find Sam, you need to show up at the packing plant, just like you always do. Tell Mr. Bill that Ardella and I won't be at work tonight. If he questions you, just tell him I said I'll explain things tomorrow."

"Yessuh, Mistuh Taylor," Jake answered as he pointed to Sam's shanty-type home, signaling Daddy to stop the car.

"Go see if Sam's in there," Daddy said. "If he is, bring him out so we can decide where to hide him."

"Yessuh."

"And Jake, while you're in there, grab a blanket. We'll need it before the night is over."

I watched Jake disappear through Sam's front door. A few minutes later, Sam emerged holding a blanket. His wife, Maude, and their children followed him. Jake slipped off the side of the porch, passed everyone, and quickly opened the car door for Sam.

"Here Sam be," Jake said, holding the door back. "Wat we gonna do now, Mistuh Taylor?"

"Put Sam in the back on the floor and throw the blanket over him. I'll take him across town to hide."

"Jes' git in here, Sammy," Jake instructed. "'Afore we run clear out o' time."

I thought it would be impossible to get a big man like Sam in the backseat on the floor, but somehow he managed to squeeze in. Daddy put the blanket over the top of Sam's head while I pulled it down over his feet. Between the dark and the blanket, Sam had disappeared.

Maude and the children couldn't hold back their tears as they stood beside the car. Maude clasped the baby who wailed in her arms. The other two children held fast to Maude's skirt.

"Jake, stay here for a few minutes and calm everyone down." Daddy said. "Tell Maude that if the Klan shows up, to tell them she doesn't know where Sam is."

The Klan

"Yessuh, Mistuh Taylor," Jake answered confidently.

"And, Jake . . . you go to work like we discussed," Daddy reminded him.

"Yessuh, Mistuh Taylor."

The baby's cries filled the night air.

Josh was fully awake now because of all the commotion. In sympathy for the baby, Josh reached in his overalls pocket and pulled out the turtle. Stroking the turtle fondly, he pushed it out the window toward Jake.

"Give this to the baby," Josh yelled out to Jake. "It's a genuine feel-good turtle."

Jake took the little creature from Josh.

As Daddy drove away from the house, Josh and I observed that the baby calmed down when Jake gave her the turtle.

Daddy headed back toward the pipeline. Once on the wide path, in the woods away from Colored Town, he spoke loudly over his shoulder.

"Katie Jane, are you and Josh all right?"

"We're fine, Daddy," I answered. "Josh's head is in my lap, and he's just about asleep again."

Sam didn't say a word.

Daddy turned back toward me as he drove with one hand and used his other hand to reach behind the seat, pulling at the blanket covering Sam.

"Hey, Sam, can you hear me under there?" Daddy asked him.

"Yessuh, Mistuh Taylor."

"I heard the Klan was after you Sam," Daddy said. "Do you know why?"

"Yessuh, Mistuh Taylor," Sam began. "Last week I caughted a white lady wif her arms full o' groceries when she come stumbling out de steps of Thornton's Store. She jes' fell out de door, and I happened to be a-standin' dere. I reached out and hepped her."

Sam took a deep breath and continued. "'Bout dat time, some white man goin' by de store yelled, 'Hey nigger, git yo' hands off dat white woman.' Den he sez, 'Yore next, Sam Gilbert.'"

Separate Fountains

"Did you go to the police and report what happened?" Daddy asked.

"Now, Mistuh Taylor, you know dat be jes' a waste o' time," Sam explained. "No policeman in Georgia gonna protect no colored man from de Klan."

"I'm afraid you're right about that, Sam."

"Mistuh Taylor, I be mightly obligin' what you doin', but you gots to think 'bout yo' own self and yo' chil'len. Don't stick yo' neck out too far."

"I've already stuck my neck way out," Daddy answered with a chuckle. "Right now, I must look like a longneck rooster."

"Aw, Mistuh Taylor, dat's what I likes 'bout you," Sam said. "You ain't never serious."

"Well, Sam, I'm getting serious right now. We're coming to the edge of Jonesboro, so stay under that blanket. I'm going to get back on the highway."

Daddy slowed the car, looking up and down the side streets as we drove past them.

"It looks like the Klan's gone," Daddy said. "Now I have to find a place to hide you."

"Yessuh, you shore has," Sam muttered from under the blanket. "You gotta decide wats to do wif me."

"Got any ideas where you can hide, Sam?"

"Yessuh, Mistuh Taylor. As we been ridin' along, I's be thinkin' of de hermit's place. You know where dat old black hermit Alfonso live?"

"Yeah, in the shack behind Bubba Scott's barn," Daddy stated, "but Sam, I think Bubba might be in the Klan. You think it's smart for you to go there?"

"Mistuh Scott don't never bothers Alfonso."

"I still think it's a bad idea," Daddy stated emphatically. "You know sometimes these Klan members even have colored people living on their property and working for them."

"So wat you thinks Mistuh Taylor?" Sam asked. "Where can I go?"

"I have an idea," Daddy responded. "Let's go to the north side of town, where the old tourist court burned. There are still some cabin structures holding up, and at least you'll have a roof over your head. You can stay there until the Klan stops looking for you."

The Klan

"But Mistuh Taylor, dat's where dem gypsies makes der camp when dey comes through," Sam protested.

"This is only July, Sam. The gypsies don't usually come until August, just in time to put their children in school."

"But sometimes dem gypsies come early, Mistuh Taylor," Sam said. "Dis year dey lef' in de spring 'afore school let out, so I be thinkin' dey might come back early."

"I still think you'd be safe there, even if it is with the gypsies," Daddy stated. "They're afraid of the Klan, too. You remember what the Klan did to one of them last year?"

"Yessuh, Mistuh Taylor," Sam answered. "Dey done tarred and feathered him fer stealin' veget'bles out of Mistuh Hunt's field. Dat's why de gypsies left 'afore school let out, dey be 'fraid of de Klan."

Sam's voice was high and filled with distress as he continued. "Mistuh Taylor, I be scared of dem gypsies. Dey has dat crystal ball and be entertainin' de devil some dark nights."

"Don't worry about the devil, Sam," Daddy laughed. "Worry about the Klan. I know the tourist court is the safest place for you."

Sam had no real choices. He fell silent. I could hear him breathing under the blanket, and I wondered how he must feel. He knew for sure that the Klan was hunting him, to possibly harm him, or even take him on one of their Saturday night "bottom-fishing" trips.

"Sam, the tourist camp is just ahead. And . . . I can see a campfire."

"It's dem gypsies, Mistuh Taylor. I's so 'fraid of dem. Dey sell der own mama for a piece o' silver."

"You might be right, Sam," Daddy agreed. "But their leader Don Rodriguez wanted to buy one of my horses last spring. I'll see if I can make a deal with him for the horse if he'll help me hide you."

"Yessuh, Mistuh Taylor," Sam replied in a dubious voice.

"Don't worry, Sam," I interrupted. "I go to school with the gypsy children. They're nice."

"Yes'm, Miss Katie Jane, if you sez so," he mumbled, without much conviction.

Josh was sleeping soundly as Daddy pulled into the circle driveway of the tourist camp. I could see a group of men sitting around a nearby campfire.

Separate Fountains

"Katie Jane, stay in the car and be quiet," Daddy directed as he turned off the car's motor. "Sam, you stay under the blanket. And don't worry, I'll be right back."

Every year, usually in late summer and always in the middle of the night, the gypsies came to Jonesboro in a convoy of horse-drawn wagons. Brightly painted in hues of red and orange, the coach's windows and door were trimmed in gold. Mr. Rodriguez had explained to Daddy that all of the wagons in the convoy were decorated alike to identify the family of gypsies to which this group belonged.

The gypsies came in time to enter their children in school, settling at the abandoned tourist court site with their wagons in a circle around a campfire.

As soon as people in Jonesboro realized the gypsies had arrived, the telephone party lines began to buzz with the news that the colorful gypsies had returned. There was something mysterious about this clan of people in their wagons, and they always created a stir when they came to town.

I watched Daddy walk over to the men sitting by the campfire. I rolled my window all the way down so I could hear what was being said.

The Klan

"Excuse me, fellows, I'm looking for Don Rodriguez," I heard Daddy ask. "Is he still with your troupe?"

One of the men spoke up. "Is he in trouble with the law?"

"Not that I know of," Daddy answered. "I'm not the law."

"Why do you want to see him?" another man asked.

"I have a horse for sale," Daddy said. "Last year Don came to my farm and showed an interest in buying it."

Then Daddy added a statement to get their trust.

"His son, Pepe, goes to school with my daughter, Katie Jane."

"Don's over there in the wagon closest to your car," another man said.

Daddy walked to the Rodriguez's wagon and knocked on the red door. The Rodriguez family, Don, his wife Carlita, and their two children Rosa and Pepe, were well known to us. They came to school functions.

I could see Pepe clearly when he opened the door, immediately recognizing Daddy.

I heard Pepe say, "Father, here's Mr. Taylor."

Mr. Rodriguez came to the door.

"B. J., what in the world are you doing out here in the middle of the night?" Mr. Rodriguez asked.

"I'm sorry to bother you, Don, but I need your help. Can you step outside for a minute?"

"Sure," Mr. Rodriguez replied.

Closing the door behind him, Mr. Rodriguez followed Daddy to our car, away from the campfire. They stood there by the front bumper in the shadows of the tall Georgia pines.

I sat there in silence, with Josh's head in my lap as he slept.

I listened for the two men to speak.

"Don, you remember that black horse you wanted to buy from me last fall?"

"Yes," Mr. Rodriguez answered. "And I'd still like to have him."

"That's what I hoped you'd say," Daddy responded with relief. "How would you like it if I offered to give you the horse if you will help me with a problem?"

"Well, I don't know," Mr. Rodriguez answered, doubt edging his voice. "Does it involve the law?"

"No, it involves the Ku Klux Klan," Daddy said.

"Oh, dammit, B. J.," Mr. Rodriguez sputtered. "That's worse than the law."

Separate Fountains

"I want you to help me hide a colored man for, maybe, two or three weeks," Daddy continued seriously. "The Klan might hurt him if they find him."

"How can I take this kind of chance?" Mr. Rodriguez asked. "I can't jeopardize my family."

"Don, no one will know but us," Daddy assured him. "I want to hide him on the back lot in one of those burned cabins. All you have to do is help me get food and water to him."

"I don't know about that, B. J.," Mr. Rodriguez said. "The Klan don't feel too kindly toward us gypsies. You know how they watch us when we're in Jonesboro . . . and, I personally had trouble with Charlie Parsons last year when he had some missing chickens. He even threatened to get the Klan after me."

"I remember," Daddy said. "I can imagine how frightened you must have been. I'm scared of the Klan, too, but I feel like I've got to help Sam. He's got a wife and children who need him."

"I don't know, B. J.," the gypsy said again, shrugging his shoulders.

"I'll give you the black horse tomorrow if you'll help me," Daddy pressed, anxiety in his voice. "The plan will be for me to get food for Sam to you, and at night, when everybody's asleep at the campsite, you can take it to him."

"Where's Sam now?" Mr. Rodriguez asked.

"Right here in the car, " Daddy said, as he smacked his hand on the bumper. "Let's go for a ride so you can meet him."

Mr. Rodriguez walked around to the passenger door. It was then that he saw Josh and me in the backseat.

"B. J., you didn't tell me you had your children," Mr. Rodriguez said, his voice reflecting surprise.

"Well, you know this night wasn't exactly planned, Don. We were just taking Ardella home when we got caught up in this mess."

Daddy started the car and headed out. Nobody spoke. The only sounds heard were the motor of the car and the whissing sound of the wind coming in the open windows.

After driving a few miles, Daddy pulled over and stopped on the shoulder of the highway. Turning off the lights, he and Mr. Rodriguez

The Klan

sat silently in the moonlit car, watching the road for approaching cars.

Daddy reached back and pulled the blanket off of Sam.

"You can sit up now, Sam," Daddy said quietly.

Sam struggled to sit up.

"Where is we, Mistuh Taylor?"

"It's all right, Sam," Daddy said calmly. "I want you to meet my friend, Mr. Rodriguez. He might help us."

Sam reached over the front seat with his long arm to shake Mr. Rodriguez's hand. "Pleazed to meet you."

Mr. Rodriguez returned the gesture.

Sam sat up on the car's floor, propped up against his blanket.

"I'll help Sam on one condition," Mr. Rodriguez said, obviously moved by Sam's situation.

"What's that?" Daddy inquired.

"If the Klan happens to find Sam at the tourist court, he'll never mention my name to them."

"Do you hear that, Sam?" Daddy asked.

"Yessuh, Mistuh Taylor."

"What do you think, Sam?" Daddy asked. "Do you think you could forget Mr. Rodriguez's name if the Klan found you?"

"Yessuh. I'd tell de Klan I's don't know nobody at dat gypsy camp, fer shore."

"It's a deal," Mr. Rodriguez agreed hastily. "Now let's move this car, B. J., before we're spotted by some roving Klan member."

Daddy turned around and headed toward the tourist court. Pulling off Route 41, he took the circle driveway, passed the gypsy wagons, and continued on a back road, where the empty, burned cabins stood. Pulling up to the last one, Daddy flashed the car lights on it.

"That looks like a good choice, Don," Daddy said. "Take this flashlight, and you and Sam check out the cabin."

Turning toward Sam, Daddy continued. "Take your blanket with you, Sam, in case the nights get cool. Stay here until I come back for you."

"Yessuh, Mistuh Taylor, and I thanks you."

Sam and Mr. Rodriguez hurried into the blackened cabin. Don re-emerged almost instantly, jumping back into the car as though nothing had happened.

"Let's get outta here," he said.

Separate Fountains

"Thank you, Don," Daddy said as we rode back to the front of the camp. "Tomorrow I'll bring the black horse and some food for Sam."

"I just hope we're not digging our own graves," Mr. Rodriguez stated. "The Klan's business is not to be meddled with."

"You're right," Daddy agreed. "But I know we're doing the right thing."

"Sam said he hadn't eaten anything all day," Mr. Rodriguez continued. "I'll take food and water to him now while everyone's in their wagons and settled for the night."

I knew then that Sam was in good hands.

Daddy reached over and tapped Mr. Rodriguez's shoulder as he exited the car.

"Thanks again, Don," Daddy said, leaning over the opposite side of the car to look out the window at him.

"Mr. Rodriguez," I interrupted. "Here's two packages of peanuts. Would you give them to Sam for me?"

"Sure, Katie Jane."

Daddy and I watched as Mr. Rodriguez walked toward his wagon.

As the gypsy disappeared behind his door, Daddy thrust the car forward, heading south toward town. Looking at his watch, he exclaimed, "Oh my goodness, Katie Jane, it's almost midnight. Your Mama's gonna be sick with worry over us."

Chapter Ten

Hot Water

"Cussed gate," Daddy mumbled.

He left the car running as he jumped out to open our gate. After driving through, he jumped back out to set the lock again.

Josh woke up when Daddy got back in the car. He had slept the entire time we were at the gypsy camp and all the way home.

"Where are we, Daddy?" Josh asked sleepily.

"We just got home, sugar lump," he answered.

As we drove toward the house, I noticed our porch light was on. In fact, I quickly realized all the lights in the house were on. I could see a truck parked near the front steps and the semblance of three people in the rocking chairs on the porch. When we got to the house, there were Mama, Ardella, and Mr. Smith waiting for us.

"Looks like we got company at midnight," Daddy commented as he stopped our car beside the truck. Stepping out of the car, Daddy pulled the back of the front seat forward so Josh and I could get out.

As Josh hopped out, he recognized the green truck with "Smith's Hardware" written on the door.

"What's Mr. Smith delivering this late at night?" Josh asked drowsily.

"Me!" Ardella shouted, running down the steps to meet us. "Lawds-a-mercy, Mistuh Taylor, where yawl been?"

She tried to gather us all three in her arms.

"How'd you get here, Ardella?" Daddy asked.

"I's worried to death 'bout you and de chil'len," Ardella started to explain, "and Miz Taylor up here in dis house all alone, so I got Jake to bring me up here 'afore he goes to work at de plant."

Separate Fountains

"Oh thank you, Ardella, thank you," Daddy exclaimed.

"Where's Sam?" she asked. "Is he all right?"

"Don't worry, he's in a good hiding place."

"Praise de Lord!" Ardella exclaimed, looking up at the night sky.

Mama sat quietly in her rocking chair, with her gauze-wrapped legs hanging freely from under her nightgown. Her white shawl was thrown around her shoulders, and she looked like an avenging angel. I saw the expression of fury on her face.

Daddy must have seen it too, because he quickly ran up the steps and fell to his knees in front of Mama.

"Katherine, I'm so sorry," Daddy said helplessly. "I didn't mean to worry you."

Mama angrily pushed him away from her.

"Get away from me, B. J. Taylor!" she said, her voice trembling with rage. "What do you mean endangering our children like this."

"B-but Katherine, let me explain."

"Explain! What is there to explain?" Mama yelled. "You think nothing of taking our babies on one of your wild adventures. Have you lost your mind!"

I rushed to the top of the steps to defend Daddy. He continued to kneel on the porch in front of Mama. Bewilderment was written all over his face.

"Mama, we're O.K.," Josh said as he ran past me. He climbed into her lap and wrapped his arms around her neck.

Smothering him with kisses, Mama began to sob. Her whole body trembled as she held Josh close to her, crying her heart out.

I stepped toward Daddy as he stood up. Reaching for his hand and holding on to him, I intervened on their conversation.

"But Mama, you didn't give Daddy a chance to explain what happened."

Mama snapped back at me with rage in her eyes.

"Young lady, you mind your place. You and Josh always take up for your daddy no matter what he does."

"Please, Katherine," Daddy said softly. "Let's not upset the children. It's been a long night for all of us."

By this time, Ardella had joined us at Mama's side. She leaned over to Mama and stroked her calmly on the top part of her shoulder, trying to soothe her.

"Miz Taylor, pleaze try to calm down," Ardella said. "I know you be upset all de evening. We jes' need to thanks de good Lord dey all got home safe."

Hot Water

"I guess you're right, Ardella," Mama sniffled, still holding Josh close to her.

"When I's got here, Mistuh Taylor," Ardella continued. "Miz Taylor be waitin' on de front porch. She sez she got so worried 'bout you and the chil'len she jes' couldn't stay in dat bed no longer. She walked from her bed to de porch by holding to de wall."

"Oh, Katherine," Daddy said, reaching to Mama and Josh in the rocking chair. "You shouldn't have walked with no one here to help you."

Mama nodded yes, responding to his embrace as he wrapped his arms around her.

"But, B. J., I was going crazy in this house alone, not knowing where you and the children were."

"Didn't George call and tell you we were going to be late?" Daddy asked.

Mr. Smith sat quietly in his rocking chair, staying clear of our family business.

"When I called," Mr. Smith spoke up, "no one answered. I assumed Katherine was asleep and didn't hear the telephone. When I kept calling and calling and no one answered, I decided to drive out here and check on her. When I got here, I found Katherine and Ardella sitting on the front porch waiting for you."

"I heard the telephone ringing several times before Ardella got here," Mama said, "but I was afraid to try to go back in the house to answer it."

"Oh my," Ardella interrupted, shaking her head. "We's all got upset wif each other 'cause of folks being at de wrong place at de wrong time. Ifen Sam hadn't been at Mistuh Thornton's store when de white lady fell out dat door, de Klan wouldn't be after him. Ifen I hadn't be ridin' in de front seat of Mistuh Taylor's car, I wouldn't had to hide at Mistuh Smith's store. Ifen Mistuh Taylor and dese chil'len hadn't been in Jonesboro when de Klan was marchin', dey wouldn't been trying to heps Sam, and ifen Miz Taylor hadn't been outs here on dis front porch, she coulda answered Mistuh Smith's call. You wanna knows the truth 'bout all dis mess we be in, we all be in trouble tonight 'cause we all be in de wrong place at de wrong time. And that be all I gots to say."

Everyone laughed at Ardella's ingenious explanation.

"Oh, no," she suddenly continued. "I thinks of one mo' thing so I guess I ain't through speakin' my piece, jes' yet. Praise God you good people wuz willing to hep my brother tonight. I knows fer shore a black man ain't worth white leather in de South."

Separate Fountains

Silence completely engulfed the moment.
Her words struck chords throughout our being.

"I'm afraid you're right, Ardella," Mr. Smith finally said. "A black man hasn't much of a chance around here."

"We definitely live in a society that judges people by their skin color," Daddy said. "But, Ardella, I want you to know I'll do everything in my power to change that."

"Yes, we will," Mama said, as she reached up toward Daddy.

Then, Mama started to sob again.

"I'm so sorry, B. J. for all those mean things I said to you," Mama sniffled. "Please forgive me."

Josh quickly hopped out of Mama's lap, sensing Mama needed Daddy. Daddy grabbed Mama and picked her up in his arms. As she looked up at him, he gave her a quick kiss on her lips.

"Look here, sugar lumps," Daddy said, his face beaming with love. "Your Mama still loves me!"

Josh and I stood looking at them.

"Mama," Josh pleaded. "Please don't get mad at my daddy ever again."

Reaching down to Josh, Mama shook his hand in agreement.

"That's a deal," she said, with a smile.

"Lawds-a-mercy, Mistuh and Miz Taylor," Ardella interrupted. "You folks be som'pin else! Fusses and makes up jes' likes two young'uns in love."

Daddy and Mama laughed.

"Come chil'len," Ardella said. "Let's leave yo' Mama and Daddy alone in dis moonlight. You need to git to bed anyhow."

As Josh and I followed Ardella to the door, she turned around and looked back toward Daddy and Mr. Smith.

"I won't ever forgit what you two done fer my brother dis night, Mistuh Taylor and Mistuh Smith. I'll be beholdin' to yawl for de rest of my days."

"Glad to help out," Mr. Smith responded.

Daddy nodded in agreement.

"See you tomorrow, B. J.," Mr. Smith said as he walked down the steps. We stood and watched as he got in his truck and drove away.

Hot Water

Ardella led Josh and me into the house, closing both the screen and wooden doors behind us.

"Why are you closing the wood door, Ardella?" Josh asked, knowing we usually left it open in the summer, only latching the screen for security.

"Cause yo' Mama and yo' Daddy needs some privacy, Mr. Josh," Ardella answered in her I-mean-business voice. "You young'uns shoulda be in bed long ago."

"But, I'm hungry," Josh whined.

"Ardella, can we have some Kellogg's Corn Flakes?" I quickly asked.

"I know you must be hungry, ridin' all over Jonesboro all evenin'," Ardella said sympathetically, sitting us down with bowls of cereal.

When we were finished eating, Ardella said "Forgits de baths. Gits yo' pajamas on, brush yo' teeth wif bakin' soda and gits in bed right now, you hear?"

"But, Miss Ardella, where're you gonna sleep?" Josh asked as he got up from the table.

"She can use my cot," I said. "I'll get Grandmama's quilt and make me a pallet on the floor, right by your cot, Josh."

"What fun!" Josh responded with mischief in his eyes. We'll pretend we're camping. I'll be the Lone Ranger, and you can be Tonto."

"Good idea," I answered, playing along with his game.

Ardella began to laugh.

"It's one o'clock in de mornin'," she said, "and here you be thinkin' 'bout playin' cowboys and Indians. Hasn't you had 'nough excitement for one day?"

We stood looking at Ardella, knowing we'd better do what she said.

"Gits yo' pajamas on right now," she ordered. "Then use the bathroom and git yo'self to sleep."

"But Miss Ardella," Josh whined. "You don't have any pajamas."

"Oh Josh, hush up and quit worryin' 'bout me," snapped an exasperated Ardella. "I's gonna sleep in my clothes and when de sun comes up, yo' daddy gonna take me home. Tomorrow's Saturday and I's got to work all day at de peach packin' plant."

Following her directions, Josh and I quickly settled in for the night. After she turned off the interior lights, the light from the front

Separate Fountains

porch shone through the thin cracks around the door frame. I heard Mama and Daddy's muffled voices and occasional laughter.

Knowing they were on the front porch holding each other, I felt contentment spread over me. I wasn't sure if the feeling came from my heart or my stomach, or maybe it came from my soul. Wherever it came from, though, it made me think about Reverend Wilcox. He was always preaching about feelings in our heart and soul.

I just knew the feeling I had was good—knowing my Mama and Daddy still loved each other and that we were still a family.

As I lay on the pallet beside Josh's cot, the moonlight coming through the windows lit up the room I knew so well. Looking over toward my cot, I could see the silhouette of Ardella's large body. Her shadow, synchronized with her heavy breathing, moved up and down on the wall.

Out of the darkness, Ardella said to us, "Chil'len, don't forgit to say yo' prayers. We has so much to be thankful fer."

Then, in a soft voice, I heard her pray. "Thank you, dear Lord, fer watchin' over us another day."

I said my prayers to myself, then turned on my side.

I fell asleep instantly.

When I awoke the next morning, the sun was shining right on my face. I looked up at Josh and saw he was still asleep. I glanced toward my cot, but Ardella was no longer there.

I turned my head toward Mama and Daddy's bed, and saw Mama was still asleep but Daddy's side of the bed was empty. I knew Daddy had taken Ardella home and would be back soon to make our special Saturday morning breakfast—pancakes and sorghum syrup.

I rolled over to go back to sleep until Daddy got home. It had been a long night, a night I wouldn't soon forget.

After breakfast and chores, Josh and I went into town with Daddy to Thornton's grocery store. The only grocery store in Jonesboro, it always buzzed with activity. Each trip there was like attending a

Hot Water

social event; people stood in the aisles and visited, sharing the town gossip or the latest political news.

Upon entering, I recognized the fresh smell of the oiled, wide-planked oak floors which Teddy, Mr. Thornton's son, was constantly sweeping. Teddy used a wintergreen-scented powder, sprinkling it in front of the broom as he made his way up and down the aisles.

Other familiar smells drifted around the store—the sweet smell of apples, oranges, and other fruits in the fruit bins, along with the strong, earthy aroma of turnips, sweet potatoes, and greens at the vegetable counter.

By the bakery, the essence of newly baked breads was so strong I could almost taste them, and the aroma of coffees, teas, and chocolates made my mouth water. By the front door, Miss Sally Thornton stood behind the checkout counter, beside the large, silver-plated cash register. To the side of the register was a weight-measuring pan hanging on a long cord from the ceiling. Miss Sally, as everyone fondly called her, measured the weight of the fresh fruits and vegetables and rang up the grocery prices.

Around the checkout counter, items Daddy called flim-flammers were displayed. He said merchants put flim-flammers out to make you spend extra money when you got ready to check out of the store. Josh and I loved the flim-flammers because they were always the things kids enjoyed—Cracker Jacks, fireballs, jawbreakers, Bazooka bubble gum, and suckers and candies of all kinds.

While Daddy and Josh pushed the cart, it was my job to hold Mama's grocery list and a pencil. As Daddy picked out each item, I marked them off the list. Josh's job was to be Daddy's helper and to fetch the items he could reach.

When Daddy and Josh pushed the cart around the corner of the first aisle, I stopped dead in my tracks. There in the aisle was Eric Pennington, holding a can of Vienna sausages and a box of saltine crackers.

Trying to figure out a way to alert Daddy to Mr. Pennington's presence, I fell behind Daddy and Josh as they proceeded along with the cart. Josh did not seem to recognize Mr. Pennington.

"What are you looking for, Katie Jane?" Daddy said, turning around to look back at me.

"Oh nothing, I'm just looking at the different canned goods," I answered, pretending to look at the shelves of food, but I was really watching Mr. Pennington.

Separate Fountains

As Mr. Pennington walked around the corner to the next aisle, I dashed to Daddy's side and reached over to stop his cart.

"What on earth is going on, Katie Jane?" Daddy asked with a puzzled expression.

"That's the man Josh and I saw in the telephone booth yesterday," I whispered, pointing to where Eric Pennington had just gone.

Josh's eyes got big, and he looked up at Daddy, waiting for his response.

Daddy acknowledged he understood by nodding his head. Then he put his fingers to his lips, indicating to us to be quiet.

Daddy pushed the cart forward again and continued around to the next aisle. There we saw Eric Pennington talking to Lester Collier, a man I knew Daddy thought was in the Klan. Daddy gave me a double wink, our secret signal when he wanted me to eavesdrop on someone's conversation.

As Daddy and Josh moved past, I pretended to look for a particular kind of Campbell's soup. Standing behind the men, I looked down to study their shoes.

"Yep, Eric, we're gonna ride over to the peach packing plant tonight," Mr. Collier said in a low voice. "We'll scare them niggers into telling us where Sam is."

"What you gonna threaten them with—bottom fishing?" Mr. Pennington laughed.

"Maybe so. After all, it is Saturday night," Mr. Collier said in a sarcastic tone.

"I'll be waiting behind the train station," Mr. Pennington continued.

"See you at nine o'clock sharp, Eric."

Mr. Collier walked to the front of the store.

I rushed on around the corner shelves and found Daddy and Josh standing at the meat counter. Daddy was talking to the butcher, Joe Calhoun. As usual, Josh was quiet and seemed to be afraid of Mr. Calhoun because of the blue-veined birthmark which stretched across the side of his face. Mr. Calhoun laughed and joked with Daddy every time we came to the store, but Josh never joined in the fun.

"I want some lean beef for a meat loaf, Joe. About two pounds," Daddy said.

We watched Joe open the back of the refrigerated meat counter. He reached in and grabbed a handful of ground beef. At the same time, he reached over with the other hand and tore a wide strip of white paper off of a big roll, which was conveniently mounted in a rack on

Hot Water

the counter's top. He placed the meat on the white strip of paper, then placed it on the scale for measuring.

"That's about two-and-a-half pounds, B. J.," Mr. Calhoun said, "but I think you'll need that much for a good meatloaf."

"That'll be fine," Daddy answered.

Joe wrapped the meat in a special way, which Daddy called the "drugstore wrap." First, after placing the meat on the center of the white paper, Joe brought two ends up together and then folded them down to make a tight seam. He then rolled the opposite end pieces into another seam, sealing the package with a piece of thin, white string wrapped around it several times. He tied the string tightly to hold the package together.

Joe used a red crayon to write twenty-three cents on top of the package, then handed the package of meat to Daddy.

"Thanks," Daddy said with a smile.

"You're welcome," Mr. Calhoun answered. "See you all in a few days."

Pushing the cart toward the front of the store, Daddy said, "Let's get Miss Sally to check us outta here. I've got to get you two sugar lumps home so I can go to work at the peach packing plant by six o'clock."

"Daddy," Josh said, pulling on Daddy's pants pocket, "can we buy a flim-flammer?"

"Sure, Josh," Daddy said, chuckling while he unloaded our groceries onto Miss Sally's checkout counter. "How about picking one out for me, too?"

Josh chose two packages of M&Ms, one for him and one for Daddy. I got a Baby Ruth.

As soon as we were in the car, Josh asked Daddy if he could open his candy.

"You'd better wait 'til after supper. We're still in trouble with your Mama for being late last night, and I don't want to get into hot water again."

Heading toward home, Daddy begin to question me about what I'd heard Eric Pennington and Lester Collier say. As I told him of their plan to try to find Sam at the peach packing plant, our attention quickly changed to the slow traffic ahead of us. Usually, everyone on

Separate Fountains

Route 41 drove at the speed limit, so we seldom had to pass any cars. Today, though, there was a long line of cars ahead of us, moving at what seemed to be a snail's pace. In a few minutes, cars began backing up behind us.

"I wonder what's wrong," Daddy asked.

Josh bounced up and down on the seat between Daddy and me.

"The Goat Man! The Goat Man!" my brother yelled with excitement. "I bet the Goat Man's ahead of us."

The mysterious, magical Goat Man, with his small covered wagon pulled by goats and followed by a caravan of more goats, came through Jonesboro twice a year. His visits always caused great excitement. He and his goats traveled on the highways, coming from Florida to pass through Georgia, then going on to Tennessee and Kentucky. In the winter, the Goat Man traveled south with his goats to Florida to give them a warmer climate and to have grass for them to graze. In the spring, he started traveling north with his goats to the mountains of Tennessee and Kentucky for a cooler climate.

Hot Water

"It's awfully early for him to be coming through Jonesboro," Daddy commented. "He usually spends the whole summer in the mountains."

Instead of looking ahead, I watched the people in the cars moving the opposite way, headed toward town. They had obviously seen what was slowing traffic on our side of the road.

"Look, Daddy," Josh said, pointing at all the cars going by. "All the people coming this way are laughing."

"The lady in that car has a handkerchief covering her nose," I said, knowing when the goats were near there was a stench in the air. "It has to be the goats."

"Well, I guess we can open up our candy," Daddy said, as he reached over for his M&M bag. "Unless the cars up ahead can figure out a way to get around the Goat Man and all his goats, we might be starved before we get home."

One by one, when there was enough visibility to see ahead, cars inched out onto the road's passing lane to go around the Goat Man's miniature covered wagon. No one could speed up while passing, though, because goats wandered all over the road. There were goats in front of and behind the wagon, and on both sides as well. Finally, our car was directly behind the goats that brought up the rear of the caravan.

Daddy pulled out into the left lane very slowly, carefully attempting to pass the goats and the wagon.

"Can you read the sign on the wagon, Katie Jane?" Josh asked. "Is it still a nickel to pet the goats?"

"Sure is, Josh," I answered, hanging my head out the car window. "And it says a dime for a cup of goat's milk."

"Can we stop and pet the goats, Daddy?" Josh begged. "Pleeese Daddy."

"Not today, Josh," Daddy said. "I have to get home so I can go to work at the peach packing plant tonight. Anyway, the Goat Man has already passed through Jonesboro and is heading north."

"Please slow down, Daddy," Josh whined, as he leaned across the seat in front of me and stuck his head out the window beside me. "I want to say hello to the Goat Man."

"Hi, Mr. Goat Man!" Josh yelled as loud as he could. "Where're you going?"

"To Atlanta," the Goat Man yelled back.

Looking toward us, the tall, thin man waved.

"I'll be coming back here in a few weeks," the Goat Man yelled again, "if you want to buy some goat's milk."

Separate Fountains

Even though Daddy was busy watching for oncoming traffic, he glanced over at the Goat Man and waved to him, acknowledging his message. Then, quickly speeding up, Daddy guided the car safely around the last stray goat and headed on up the road.

"Daddy, do you think the Goat Man ever takes a bath?" Josh asked innocently. "His clothes are always dirty and wrinkled, and sometimes he smells like goat's milk."

"Well, he may not get many chances to take a bath, and I'm sure he has only a few changes of clothing."

"The Goat Man must be really poor," I said. "I don't know how he can live in that small covered wagon."

"I don't either," Josh responded with sympathy. "It's not much bigger than my red wagon at home."

"The Goat Man doesn't have many material things, that's for sure," Daddy agreed.

"But he's always so happy," Josh said. "He loves his goats."

"Just goes to prove what Reverend Wilcox says is true," I said.

"What's that?" Josh asked.

"That material things don't make you happy."

"I think Reverend Wilcox is right about that, Katie Jane," Daddy agreed.

"Do you think the Goat Man has any family?" I asked.

"I wish I could be in his family," Josh said. "The Goat Man is my hero."

The Goat Man was like a folklore hero to many people who lived in towns along Route 41, some remembering the popular character from when they were children and now sharing him with their own children. He was also a hero to the people who needed his goat's milk for their health—people with stomach problems and bleeding ulcers.

Do you think the Goat Man ever gets a hair cut?" I asked.

"He sure has a lot of hair," Josh said. "I can never tell where his hair stops and his beard begins." The three of us laughed out loud.

I felt slightly guilty for laughing at the Goat Man, because I knew Mama would not approve of us laughing at someone. Yet, Daddy was laughing—so maybe it was all right to laugh this time. After all, the Goat Man and his goats were quite an amusing sight.

Hot Water

"I know it's not right to make fun of anyone," Daddy quickly commented, as though he were reading my mind. "But the Goat Man's such a character—and all those goats! I can't help but laugh when I see him."

"Do you know what Ardella said about laughter, Daddy?" I asked.

"No, what sugar lump?"

"Ardella said laughter is God's hand on the shoulder of a troubled world."

By the time we got to our gate, though, the laughter had faded. Foremost in my mind were the words I had overheard in Mr. Thornton's grocery store.

I wondered what would happen at the peach packing plant tonight? Would Daddy still let me go with him when it was possible the Klan might show up? But Daddy and I knew the Klan was unpredictable—we never knew when or where they were going to appear in our community.

Chapter Eleven

The Peach Packing Plant

Riding with Daddy to the peach packing plant was a special time for me, because it gave me a chance to be an only child again, even if it were short-lived. I had Daddy all to myself. Tonight could be different, though, and we both knew it. As we rode along, Daddy started questioning me.

"You sure about what you heard Eric Pennington and Lester Collier say about the Klan coming out to the plant tonight?" Daddy asked again.

"Yes, Daddy," I answered. "I heard them clearly."

"I don't think they will come," Daddy stated, "but if they do, you know what you have to do."

"Yes, sir, hide in the backseat of the car," I answered solemnly, sure of his instructions. These instructions had been drilled into my head for as long as I could remember. Hide from the Klan, as soon as you see or hear them coming. Hide in the house or the barn. Hide in a store if you're in town. Hide in a ditch or the bushes if you're walking on the road. Just hide!

I moved over close to Daddy and clutched his sleeve.

"Daddy, what are you gonna do if the Klan shows up?"

"I don't know, sugar lump, but no matter what, you must stay in our car. No matter what happens," he stressed again, saying the last four words one syllable at a time.

"I promise," I answered. The words stuck in my throat.

Daddy put his arm around me to soften my fear.

The Peach Packing Plant

"I know you carry the weight of an adult on your heart," he consoled. "But you can never let anyone know where Sam is, Katie Jane."

"I know," I answered.

Daddy parked at the back of the plant near the machines he maintained. As soon as Daddy stopped the car, we heard Mr. Bill's loud voice.

"Keep those peaches rolling! We gotta get'm crated."

White and colored workers stood, side by side, at the conveyor belt, sorting the good peaches from the spoiled ones. Hearing the car door slam, Mr. Bill looked toward us and waved. As we approached, he extended his hand to Daddy.

"B. J., where were you last night?" he asked. "Is Katherine all right?"

"Katherine's fine," Daddy answered. "Something important came up and I just couldn't get here. Did Jake give you the message?"

Mr. Bill nodded yes.

"Is the machinery running O.K.?" Daddy asked, quickly changing the subject.

"Thanks to you. The machines purr like a kitten," Mr. Bill said emphatically.

Daddy smiled.

"One thing's bothering me, though, B. J.," Mr. Bill continued. "Some of my most dependable workers have just disappeared. Sam Gilbert hasn't shown up for two nights."

Daddy didn't answer.

He looked over at me.

"Come, Katie Jane, let's get outta Mr. Bill's way," Daddy said. "We have work to do."

I followed Daddy toward the closet where he kept his tools.

"I hope I work late tonight," Daddy said, as he organized his tool box. "A few more wages, and I'll be able to pay off your mama's doctor bills for the month."

Several local mechanics had the responsibility of keeping the equipment at the peach packing plant in working condition. Each was "on call" all the time. Daddy was thankful Mr. Bill scheduled him to work the most. A self-taught mechanic, Daddy worked every

Separate Fountains

Friday and Saturday night at the plant until after midnight. He also put in extra hours during the week whenever he could. Making extra money to pay Mama's doctor and hospital bills was always on his mind.

Admirable, and not unusual in these times, people valued honesty, paying their bills, and staying as current with them as they could manage. Daddy said he didn't know anyone who wanted to be "obliged" to anyone else. Daddy, and others like him at the peach packing plant, were honest and dependable, living under the hardships of rough times and trying to make money to support their families.

At the plant, I knew to stay out of Daddy's way while he was working and to always mind my manners. I didn't want to lose the privilege of coming to work with him.

As I watched Daddy work, I also kept my eyes on the other workers. Under the tin roof, they worked in harmony sorting the peaches. The workers—white and black—were not interested in the differences between them other than the division of labor. Each concentrated on the task at hand.

The Peach Packing Plant

The peach harvest season began in June and lasted until late August. After the peaches were picked, they were carried to the packing plant on the south side of the farm. The plant was an open shed with no walls. The tin roof was supported by discarded, creosote telephone poles. The red clay floor was thick with pine sawdust.

Hiring day at the peach packing plant was a big event in Jonesboro. Who would be the lucky ones to make extra wages? The whites and coloreds from town mingled with those from the surrounding rural areas, all wishing to be hired. Others who hoped for work were people from the Poor Folks Farm.

On hiring day, where one lived or the color of one's skin was not important. Both white and black people stood in line in the hot Georgia sun outside Mr. Bill's office wanting the fifty-cents-an-hour seasonal job. Mr. Bill employed over one hundred workers each summer. He kept Jake at his side during hiring time, allowing Jake to help him decide which workers were dependable and productive.

The plant had two shifts, and operated from five-thirty in the morning until after midnight. Many people with other full-time jobs went home to eat supper, then worked at the peach packing plant every night. At the peak of harvest time, the plant stayed in operation until two in the morning, getting the peaches ready for shipment to Atlanta's Farmer's Market.

The plant was closed on Sundays since all workers were expected to go to church. A deacon at the Baptist Church, Colonel Bartlett believed the good Lord wanted everybody to rest on Sunday. Peaches packed on Saturday night were taken to Atlanta on Monday.

Inside the shed, the air, a smoldering one hundred degrees or higher, circulated only with a rare summer breeze. A break in the scorching temperatures came only with an unexpected afternoon or evening thunder storm.

The disciplined workers rushed with their individual job responsibilities. If a worker was careless, he or she might fall onto a conveyor belt and lose a hand or limb in the machinery. The workers knew that if they didn't work fast and efficiently, Mr. Bill would fire them. Cautious haste was the byword.

Ardella kept Mama and me up-to-date on the activities at the peach packing plant. Ardella came daily with stories about what

Separate Fountains

happened during her shift. After working one night, she came in our front door the next morning shaking her head and wringing her hands and talking as fast as she could.

"Lawds-a-mercy! Dat Mr. Bill wuz in a bad mood last night. He gots mad at Willie Brown for gittin' his shirt caughts in dem rollers. And he tuks it out on all us, coloreds and whites."

"Ardella, what did he do?" Mama asked from her bed.

"He wuz a-rantin' and a-ravin' and a-cussin'. He said he wuz gonna fires all us."

"Had Mr. Bill been drinking?" Mama questioned.

"As surely as de vine grew 'round de stump," Ardella stated. Not pausing for an answer, she continued, "You cain't do a thang wif dat man when he be drinkin'. You jes' hast to do wat he sez do. He mades us wuk fer two hours without no break. I's gots so hot I thoughts I jes' gonna die."

I stood there, sorry for Ardella as she wrung her hands together, telling her story. Distress, even fear, showed in her eyes and voice.

"Last night I wuz a-scared of Mr. Bill every time he walkt by me," Ardella continued. "He had anger on dat red-jowled face of his. His eyes so full o' hate I jes' prays to the good Lord not to let dat man hit me."

"Oh, Ardella, you know Mr. Bill wouldn't hit you or anybody else," Mama said. "Colonel Bartlett would fire him."

"You wrong 'bout dat, Miz Taylor," Ardella stated. "Why, I heards Mr. Bill hit workers wif his leather belt when he be drinkin'."

"Are you sure that's not a rumor?" Mama asked.

"Naw ma'am," Ardella replied. "Dat's de reason Jesse Mann has dat patch over his eye. Mr. Bill's belt buckle hit Jesse when strappin' him for workin' too slow."

Ardella sighed heavily. "I even heard Mr. Bill carries a gun," she continued. "I's 'fraid he gonna shoot somebody one night."

"Mr. Bill has a gun?" Mama exclaimed. "Don't tell me that!"

"Yes'm," Ardella answered. "Homer Dickson seez it strapped to Mr. Bill's chest jes' de other day, when Mr. Bill pulled off his shirt to shake water off afta de rain."

"Oh, Ardella," Mama said. "It worries me that Mr. Bill tries to work when he's intoxicated."

Mama's face showed concern.

"It worries us'sons, too," Ardella agreed. "We all watches Mr. Bill when he walks by our stations. He has hate and sadness in his eyes. He don't show nobody no kindness."

The Peach Packing Plant

Ardella breathed deeply and sighed again.
"I ain't never gonna forgit dat look Mr. Bill gave me yestidy."

After hearing Mama and Ardella's conversation about Mr. Bill's gun, I decided to discuss it with Daddy the next night on the way to the plant.

"What are you talking about?" Daddy asked.

"Ardella told me and Mama Mr. Bill carries a gun," I said. "She's afraid he's gonna kill somebody."

"What proof does Ardella have that he has a gun?"

"Homer Dickson saw it. He told Ardella that Mr. Bill wears it under his shirt."

"Well, if anybody tells the truth, it's Homer. He's like Jake. You can trust everything he says."

"What can you do about Mr. Bill and his gun, Daddy?" I asked, convinced in my mind that there was no problem my father couldn't fix.

Separate Fountains

"Nothing, sugar lump. That's his right, for his protection and for the protection of Colonel Bartlett's property. It's a right given to us by the United States Constitution. And, as for Mr. Bill's temper, I can't do anything about that, either."

After a pause, Daddy continued.

"Katie Jane, life's not always fair. I don't like the way Mr. Bill treats the workers when he's been drinking. I've seen him yell at them like they were dogs."

"Then, why don't you talk to him and tell him he's wrong?"

"I hate to admit this, Katie Jane, but when Mr. Bill's been drinking, I'm afraid of him, too."

Daddy glanced at me with a worried look, then continued. "And I'm afraid Mr. Bill might be connected to the Klan."

A shiver went down my spine and the anxiety in my father's eyes held my attention.

"Remember, you must not ever talk to anyone about the Klan," he instructed in a stern voice. "And I mean anyone."

"Yes sir," I responded.

"When I see Mr. Bill mistreating the workers, I'd like to step in and help," Daddy continued, "But there's nothing I can do. I have to keep my anger to myself, . . . and I feel helpless."

I nodded my head. I understood.

As I followed Daddy around the plant, my fear of the Klan was stirring. I kept remembering the night before and how we had hidden Ardella's brother. Would the Klan come looking for him tonight?

I refused to open my mind to the answer and instead, enjoyed the sights, smells, and sounds of the peach packing plant. It was especially hot for July, and I felt perspiration run down my face. The sweet scent of ripe peaches, the smell of the workers' perspiration, and the pine-scented sawdust beneath my feet all combined to create an odor I can still smell, even today, when I think of the plant.

All of a sudden, a pouring rain began. I loved the feeling of camaraderie that occurred during a thunderstorm. Everyone stopped working and huddled together in the middle of the shed, away from the rain and lightning. Excitement filled the air as the workers rested

The Peach Packing Plant

for a few minutes from their tedious jobs. The time clock kept ticking. The workers got paid for standing idle.

Whites and coloreds together—farmers and field hands, housewives and maids, teachers and students, mechanics and carpenters, office workers and salespeople, townsfolk and Poor Folks Farm residents—were all talking and laughing and wishing the thunderstorm would last a long time. I noticed Mr. Bill, too, seemed to enjoy the break from the monotonous routine. Sometimes his stone face broke into a smile at someone's funny story. At these moments, I saw a human side that wasn't evident when he was acting as a boss.

With the rain pouring down on the tin roof and the thunder and lightning all around us, there was no prejudice. All were as one, bound together in a bond of human experience.

Chapter Twelve

Trouble

The rain stopped as suddenly as it had started, and the brief break was over. Everybody went back to their stations and resumed work.

Suddenly, I saw Daddy running past me toward Mr. Bill.

Startled out of my peach-scented reverie, I knew something was wrong. I quickly followed him.

"Bill," Daddy yelled over the sound of the machinery, "there's a bunch of cars coming up the road to the plant. Looks like a lot of 'em."

Mr. Bill seemed surprised at Daddy's announcement.

Looking toward the road with curiosity, he asked, "It's almost midnight, I wonder what's going on?"

Suddenly, Homer Dickson came running out of nowhere. Nearly out of breath, Homer ran up to the foreman and blurted out, "Mr. Bill, de Klan's a-comin'! I be down de hill gettin' water at de well, and I sees 'em good. Mr. Bill, what's we gonna do?"

Immediately, silence fell over the entire plant. It was as though an electric shock had passed along the conveyor belt. Fear shone on every person's face. Hands mechanically continued to sort and pack peaches, but the chatter and laughter stopped, banished by the white-clad harbingers of hate speeding toward us.

Coming up the hill, I could see white-hooded men hanging out of the car windows as the car lights lit up the night. As the cars drew nearer to the plant, Daddy clasped my hand.

"Come with me, sugar lump," he said.

We walked hastily to the machine cages that housed the large motors responsible for operating the conveyor belts. It was dark there,

Trouble

since Daddy had shut down the lights as soon as he heard the cars. We were hidden in a shadow, away from the illuminated area where the workers stood. We could see Mr. Bill and the entire conveyor line from our hiding place.

"If any trouble starts, you know what to do," Daddy whispered.

"Yes, sir," I said, looking past a machine cage to our Plymouth coupe parked a few feet away. "I'll hide in the car's backseat."

"Good girl," Daddy answered, giving my hand an extra squeeze.

"But Daddy, what are you gonna do, if the Klan starts trouble?"

"I don't know," he said, nodding in disgust. "I'll just have to wait and see what happens. But no matter what I do, sugar lump, you must stay in the backseat until I can get you home."

"Yes, sir," I said with conviction.

With an air of authority, Mr. Bill walked quietly down the graveled path that flowed from the front of the plant's entrance to the circle driveway. I watched the outline of his tall-framed body and saw him stop about halfway down the path. He stood still in the shadows of the pines, waiting to see what the Klansmen were going to do.

"Don't you wish we were close enough to see their shoes?" I whispered.

Daddy just nodded slightly.

The Klansmen didn't notice Mr. Bill standing on the path when they stopped their cars on the driveway and got out. They talked quietly among themselves for a moment, helping each other light their homemade torches of sticks with kerosene-soaked rags tied to the ends.

I could faintly hear one man's voice louder than the others. He seemed to be giving orders. I wondered if it was the man who I knew for sure was in the Klan. Did he have a red cross on his shoulder to designate his leadership? Was this Julie Parsons's daddy, Charlie?

At the command of the leader, the Klansmen got in a line, two-by-two, and held up their flaming torches. As they walked up the path, I saw that many of them were also carrying rifles. Then, for some reason, the men abruptly stopped their slow march forward. The leaders of the parade had come face to face with Mr. Bill as he stepped out of the shadows in front of them.

Trouble

"We're looking for Sam Gilbert," I heard the leader yell out. I kept very still, trying to listen closely to the gruff voice. Was it Mr. Parsons?

"Sam Gilbert doesn't work here anymore," answered Mr. Bill in a calm, polite voice that I'd never heard before.

"I bet your niggers here know where he is. We want to talk to them . . . right now!" a Klansmen in the back demanded.

"My workers are at their stations getting peaches ready for the Atlanta market," Mr. Bill responded emphatically. "If you want to talk to them, you'll have to come back tonight after they get off work."

"What time will that be?" asked another white-hooded man.

"This shift works until two," Mr. Bill answered.

"You've got to be kidding, Bill," another responded sarcastically. "You think we're gonna come back here at two o'clock in the morning?"

"If you want to talk to my workers, that's when you can see them," Mr. Bill stated in a stronger voice. His body language reflected calmness as he tried to control the situation.

The Klansmen were silent.

Almost as an afterthought, Mr. Bill firmly insisted, "And I'll tell you this. If any of you set a foot on this property before that time, I'll call the sheriff and have you arrested for trespassing."

Silence.

Everyone standing in the plant's shed waited to take their next breath. Silent fear filled the air.

The Klansmen whispered between themselves. I hoped their sudden quietness meant withdrawal. I watched as they turned and slowly retreated down the hill, still talking quietly to each other as they moved along.

I sighed with relief.

"We'll see you at two o'clock, Bill!" the last Klansman yelled out angrily as he walked away. "We'll get your niggers to talk!"

When the Klansmen reached their parked cars, they rolled their flaming torches in the dirt to smother them. They pitched the blackened torches into the trunks and climbed into their cars. The cars backed down the long driveway to the main road.

Mr. Bill stood frozen on the path, still holding his ground. Everyone watched the caravan of cars as, one-by-one, they turned onto the main road, heading north toward Jonesboro. When the last tail-light was out of sight, Mr. Bill turned and walked toward the plant.

Separate Fountains

Suddenly, all the workers exploded with applause, shouts, and whistles.

"Hooray for Mr. Bill! He saved us from the Klan!" one worker shouted.

"Let's give Mr. Bill a hip-hip-hooray!" another yelled.

"Hip-hip-hooray! Hip-hip-hooray for Mr. Bill!"

The loud cheering continued, echoing under the pointed tin roof and smothering out the normal sounds of the plant's activities.

As Mr. Bill walked back under the lighted shed, his face reflected its usual stern demeanor. Without blinking an eye or showing any sign of acknowledgement for the cheers and whistles, he said in his controlling voice, "Get to work! We've got crates of peaches to pack!"

Turning away from the workers, Mr. Bill headed toward the back of the plant. As he walked past me, I was shocked to see tears running down his weathered face. I continued to watch as he retreated to his office, flipped on the lights, and shut the door behind him.

Daddy unlocked one of the machine cage doors and climbed inside. The cages were off limits to me, so I stood outside watching him use a spouted oil can to lubricate the motor. I would have to be on my own for the next few minutes.

I shuffled over to the corner of the shed and sat down on a soft pile of sawdust. I propped my back against the side of one of the wire cages. As I sat there in the shadows, I kept vigil over the roadway below, listening keenly for any unusual sounds in the night.

I knew the tricks of the Klan. I was afraid they might be moving slowly back up the hill with their lights turned off. Or perhaps they had parked their cars out of sight and were stealing through the woods to surprise us.

Suddenly, Mr. Bill ran out of his office toward the machine cages.

"B. J.," he yelled, "turn the machines off!"

"What did you say?" Daddy yelled back, touching his ear to indicate he could not hear him.

"Turn the machines off!" Mr. Bill shouted again. He continued to run toward Daddy.

"Did you say you wanted me to turn the machines off?" Daddy asked in disbelief.

Trouble

"Yes, I'm shutting down the plant for the night. I don't want any bloodshed on my hands."

Daddy nodded. Moving to the main electrical switch, he shut off every machine in the plant with one downward thrust of his hand. The unexpected stop of the conveyor belt happened so quickly that all heads turned at the same time toward Daddy, as the workers sought an explanation.

Mr. Bill jumped up on a wooden peach crate. Looking down the conveyor line, he started waving his arms in the air, signaling he wanted everyone's attention.

"The plant is now closed!" he yelled in a loud voice. "Go home to your families as quickly as you can."

Again, silence descended on the plant.

Without question or comment, the workers began to move quickly from under the shed, filing out like ghosts into the dark, still air. Some of them piled into their cars and trucks while others walked along the road. Few words were spoken. They just left.

I stood beside Daddy and Mr. Bill as pairs of red car tail-lights disappeared down the drive.

"Let's get outta here, before the Klan comes back," Mr. Bill said, turning to go to his car.

Daddy reached over and took my hand. He said nothing.

Hand in hand, we walked to the back side of the empty plant. Still holding on to me, Daddy reached up and opened the electric circuit-breaker box. At the main switch, with one downward stroke, he turned off all lights in the plant.

We stood in the darkness.

"Let's go home, sugar lump."

The storm clouds had cleared, and the moon shining through the trees lighted our way to the car. As we drove toward Jonesboro, I slid over by Daddy and put my head in his lap. He stroked my hair.

"I'm so tired, Daddy," I said, taking comfort in the soft rumbling of the car engine and the whooshing of the night air blowing in the windows. "But I'm happy."

"What makes you feel happy, sugar lump?" Daddy asked, "after everything that has happened in the last few days?"

Separate Fountains

"'Cause I found out two things tonight."
"And, what are those two things?"
"One, Mr. Bill has a heart. Two, he's not a member of the Klan."
"I think you're right, sugar lump."

Daddy continued to stroke my head as we rode along. As I was about to fall asleep, he suddenly stopped stroking me. I drowsily looked up at him and immediately saw a look of apprehension on his face. He now had both hands tightly clenched on the steering wheel.

"Listen, Katie Jane," Daddy said urgently. "Someone's coming! It sounds like cars coming toward us."

Quickly I sat up.

Looking out through the windshield, I saw reflections of lights approaching us on the pines along the road.

Quickly I got up on my knees on the seat and put my arms around Daddy's neck.

"What in the world are you doing?" Daddy asked.

"It might be the Klan. I want them to see me with you."

Somehow, I was completely aware of what I had to do. I felt outside myself, with a sudden acute awareness of danger and a need to protect my father. All my life, he had been my protector but now I must protect him. In that moment, I became an adult.

The line of cars came toward us. As the first car drew near, I tried to see who was in it. With one quick look, I saw a car full of Klansmen. I knew they would recognize our car, and I also knew they would not stop Daddy since I was with him.

"Well, it looks like the Klan's on their way back to the plant," Daddy said. "I'm glad Mr. Bill sent everybody home early."

"Me, too."

Daddy and I were quiet for awhile as we continued our drive home. As we rode along, I thought about everything that had happened.

Daddy broke the silence.

"Sugar lump," he said, "do you think that, for now, we can keep what happened tonight a secret from your Mama? You know how upset she got last night, and Dr. Green says she needs to stay calm and get well."

Trouble

"Whatever you think's best, Daddy," I answered, knowing he didn't always tell Mama everything because of her health. "But you know she'll hear the whole story from Ardella tomorrow."

Daddy laughed. "You're right. Keeping a secret in this town is impossible."

I was willing to cooperate with Daddy, afraid if I crossed him, I might lose my privilege of spending so much time with him. No other twelve-year-old girl in Jonesboro got to go with her daddy as much as I did.

I knew Daddy well. In fact, I probably understood his love of people and adventure better than Mama. But, I also knew Mama. Daddy was right. She would definitely be upset about the dangerous situation we had witnessed tonight. Yes, I was willing to keep the secret for a few days, to keep peace in our house. I didn't like seeing Mama upset with Daddy, and besides, Mama was calmer when she heard things from Ardella.

Dead tired, I fell into bed when we got home. I couldn't fall asleep, though—my mind kept wandering. Tonight, did Julie see her father, Charlie Parsons, sneak in their house and hang his Klan robe in the closet? And what about John Bethel—the man we'd heard so much about on the radio? Did his family see his hooded robe? Did the Klan members remember to pick up Eric Pennington at the train station? Where did he change clothes? Was he with the local Klansmen tonight at the peach packing plant? How was poor Sam Gilbert? Was he cold and hungry out there at the tourist camp? How did it feel to be colored and to know the Klan was after you? How could Sam sleep knowing the Klan might find him and drown him, just for the fun of it? What about Sam's children? Could they sleep, or were they also lying in bed wondering if their daddy would ever return? How many innocent people—just like me—were lying in their beds afraid of what the Klan might do tomorrow?

Daddy warned me never to talk to anybody about what happened at the packing plant that night, but I thought about it constantly. I became obsessed with watching people. Every Sunday, when I saw small groups of people huddled on the church lawn after the service,

Separate Fountains

I wondered if they were whispering about the Klan. When Daddy and I were in Jonesboro, and I saw people talking together on the street, I was sure they were discussing the whereabouts of Sam Gilbert or speculating about the Klan's next threat to our community.

As the days went by, I heard Daddy several times tell Mama he'd heard nothing but rumors about Sam's situation. Daddy said the story of the white woman falling out the grocery store door into a colored man's arms was still the town gossip. He also said that, to some of Jonesboro's citizens, Sam Gilbert's efforts to help the white woman were appreciated, and that he had become somewhat of a hero. This in itself was unusual because very few people in our town had colored heroes.

Several weeks passed before people felt secure there would be no repercussion from the Klan's threat on Sam or the other workers at the plant. I heard Daddy and Mr. Bill speculate that Colonel Bartlett may have paid somebody to call off the Klan, but I never really knew why the Klan gave up on Sam.

The next time I saw Sam he was at his assigned station at the peach packing plant.

Part Two

Chapter Thirteen

A Different Kind of Trouble

Josh and I had finished our morning chores, our lunch dishes were in the sink, and Ardella was helping Mama get settled for her nap. Josh and I sat together in Mama's big rocker, and I read to him. Reading was part of our afternoon ritual if we didn't walk to town. As usual, he wanted to hear his favorite story, *Mike Mulligan and His Steam Shovel*.

After I finished reading to Josh, we carefully returned his beloved book to the bookcase in the corner, our designated area for library books. Josh and I were very careful about where we stored our library books. We didn't want to take a chance on losing them.

We headed out to do the final chore of the day, which was gathering eggs from the henhouse.

"When I finish wif yo' Mama, I's gonna give dis house a good cleanin' from de top to de bottom," Ardella said as we were on our way out the back door. "I's gonna mop dis linoleum floor, and I don't want you trackin' 'cross it wif yo' bare feet. You chil'len has to play in de yard 'til I finish cleaning."

"But Miss Ardella," Josh whined, "it's so hot outside."

"You right 'bout dat. When you git done collecting dem eggs, I'll has a pitcher of Kool-Aid ready fer you to takes outside."

Later, after we had our raspberry Kool-Aid, Josh went to play in the sandbox. Daddy had built it in a perfect square, with small triangle seats in each corner.

Separate Fountains

Earlier in the spring, Jernigan's Building Supply had delivered a load of sand, dumping it beside the driveway out front. Some of the sand was used to mix with concrete for making stepping stones for Mama's rose garden, some was used for rooting azaleas, and some was shoveled into Josh's sandbox.

Josh had tagged on Daddy's heels, along with Sherlock, on every trip he made with the sand-laden wheelbarrow. He stood on one of the sandbox's triangle seats watching in fascination as each load was dumped into the new structure.

The sandbox quickly became Josh's favorite place to play. He had small plastic models of items one would find on a farm—a farmhouse, a barn complete with fence, chickens, pigs, horses, cows, and sheep. He even had a toy John Deere tractor, with attachments to plow through the sand. He had little plastic cowboys and Indians, with horses that had removable saddles. His favorite toy, though, was a reproduction of a yellow Caterpillar bulldozer, which he called Mike Mulligan's steam shovel.

When Josh played in the sandbox, he visited a fantasy world. He ran his own farm and had the Indians attack. Roy Rogers or Hopalong Cassidy, or some other popular movie cowboys always came to the rescue.

Even though in my mind I was too old to play in the sandbox, sometimes I played along with Josh to appease him. I didn't want to play with him today, though, because the afternoon heat was stifling. As I sat in the swing, I felt perspiration run down my face. I swung back and forth, hoping to make a breeze to cool myself.

As I continued to swing, I listened to the song of a mockingbird from a nearby tree. I watched Josh at play and listened to his make-believe conversations with his plastic cowboys.

Suddenly Josh stopped playing. He started heaving and throwing up all over his toys. He heaved again and began to cry.

I jumped out of the swing, screaming for Ardella as I ran toward him.

I embraced Josh, trying to hold him upright. I could feel his small body jerk back and forth with muscle spasms. Remembering what Ardella had done for me when I had the flu, I held my hand across his forehead, trying to steady him as he bent over and continued to throw up.

Ardella came running down the back steps.

"Lawds-a-mercy! Wat's de matter wif my baby?"

A Different Kind of Trouble

When she got to us, she pushed me out of the way and put her loving arms around Josh, holding his forehead as I had remembered to do. My brother continued to heave and cry in terror at what was happening to him.

Picking up Josh's limp body, Ardella placed him on her shoulder like a baby, rubbing and patting his back as she rocked him back and forth.

"Don't worry, Josh," she said in a quiet, soothing voice. "Yo' Ardella's gonna take care of you. Everythang's gonna be all right."

She rocked him until he finally dropped off to sleep. At intervals, his body would spasm and he would wake up, pitifully sobbing for help. Slowly, Ardella carried Josh toward the back porch, with me following close behind. I ran ahead and opened the screen door for her, then followed her to Mama's bed.

Ardella gently laid Josh beside Mama, who began to rub his back. Her sweet voice echoed Ardella's assurances he would be all right. As she reached over and felt Josh's forehead, I saw Mama's face instantly go pale.

"Katie Jane, run over to the Elliotts," Mama said, her eyes reflecting panic. "Mr. Elliott's working somewhere on the farm. Ask him to come help us get Josh to Dr. Green."

"Yes, ma'am," I answered, knowing immediately that Mama must have felt Josh was in danger if she wanted to ask a neighbor for help.

I ran out the front door like the house was on fire. I knew something was terribly wrong with my brother. At the top of the driveway, I pushed my body against the gate so I could slide through it without having to fumble with the lock. I took off running down the hill toward the Elliotts' farm.

I could see Mr. Elliott riding on his Farm-All tractor, plowing his field along the side of the road. I sprinted toward him waving my arms wildly.

"Mr. Elliott, Mr. Elliott!," I screamed. "Please stop! Josh is real sick!"

I realized he couldn't hear me; he didn't even look up. Turning at the far end of the row, he began to plow back in my direction. Slowly he guided the tractor, watching the plow behind him as it made a furrow in the ground. I continued running toward him, waving my arms, and shouting in the loudest voice I could.

Finally noticing me, he pulled up the plow, shifted gears, and drove the tractor over to where I had come to a halt in the dirt. He stopped and turned off the motor.

Separate Fountains

"What's the matter, Katie Jane?" he asked. "Is your Mama O.K.?"

"It's not Mama," I exclaimed, gasping for breath. "It's Josh! He's burning up with fever. Mama wants to know if you'll help us get him to Dr. Green, quick!"

"Yes, of course! Let me put the tractor in the barn, and I'll get the truck. I'll be there in a few minutes."

"Oh thank you, Mr. Elliott. I'll run ahead and open the gate for you."

"I'll hurry, Katie Jane!" he yelled as he turned away from me with the tractor.

"Meet you at the gate!" I shouted back at him as I started running up the road.

The next few minutes crawled by, feeling like hours as I worried about Josh. Finally, Mr. Elliott pulled up to our gate, and I swung it open to let his truck pass through. He knew to stop and wait for me while I relocked the gate. Then running to the passenger side, I opened the truck's door and jumped onto the seat beside him. We sped down the driveway to the house. As he stopped at the edge of our front porch, Ardella burst through the screen door.

"Come in here quick, Mistuh Elliott!" she yelled. "We got a real sick chile on our hands."

He hurried inside and gasped when he saw Josh's flushed face, covered with perspiration.

"Let's get him to Dr. Green," Mr. Elliott said. "Come on, Ardella, help me get Katherine and Josh into the truck."

"I's pick up Miz Taylor," Ardella answered. "You git Josh, Mistuh Elliott. Katie Jane, you git yo' Mama's pocketbook and close de door behind us'sons."

"Yes ma'am."

Ardella placed Mama in the front seat, and Mr. Elliott put Josh in her lap. Mama continually comforted Josh with her kind voice, reassuring him he would be all right. Josh just whimpered, delirious with fever.

"Hop in the back of the truck, Katie Jane," Ardella ordered. "You and me gonna go to Dr. Green's wif Josh."

As I tried to scramble over the back tailgate of the truck, Ardella caught me by the waist and boosted me over. Mr. Elliott had cut sugar cane earlier that day, and the bed of the truck was covered with a pile of long cane stalks. Shuffling through them, I crawled on my knees

A Different Kind of Trouble

toward the cab, pushing some of the canes aside to make a place for us to sit.

I have no idea how Ardella pulled her body up onto the bed of the truck, but the next thing I knew, she was scrambling on her hands and knees across the stalks. She plopped herself down on the spot I had cleared for her. She pulled me close to her and, as always, I felt comforted and protected by her presence.

Mr. Elliott started the engine and guided the truck up the hill. At the gate, I jumped off to open it, then, with Ardella's help, jumped back on the truck after fastening the lock.

As we rode along, Ardella and I could hear Josh crying. Both windows were rolled down, and we could hear what was going on. Mama continually consoled Josh, telling him Dr. Green would make him well.

I snuggled close to Ardella, needing the solace of her body. Suddenly, the chill of a new realization shook my insides. In the past, I had fervently believed that between them—Daddy, Mama, and Ardella—they could do anything or solve any problem. I had believed it in the face of Mama's illness, the threat of the Klan, and the injustices I saw around me. Now, though, when my little brother was burning with fever, I realized that life's circumstances really were beyond our control.

Tears began to run down my face.

"Wat's wrong, chile?" Ardella asked as one of my tears dropped onto her arm.

"Oh, Ardella," I sobbed. "I'm so worried about Josh."

"I's worried, too."

"I've never seen him so sick. His body's so red he looks like he's on fire."

"He gonna be all right, Katie Jane," she consoled me with a hug. "Dr. Green will hep him."

"But, Ardella, why Josh?"

"I don't know, chile. The good Lord says it rains on de innocent and guilty alike. We jes' has to have faith that He takes care o' our baby."

Ardella then started her usual habit of singing, when she didn't want to talk any more.

That mile to Jonesboro seemed like a hundred miles as we bumped along on the dusty road. As I sat next to Ardella and felt her arm around me, I dropped my head onto her lap and listened to her singing.

> *Nobody knows de trouble I's seen*
> *Nobody knows but my Jesus.*
> *Nobody knows . . .*

To this day I can still hear Ardella's singing voice. She had her own repertoire of songs with catchy melodies, sensitive and memorable lyrics, and haunting words that captured your imagination and your heart. And she loved her spirituals! Was singing them her way of sharing her faith?

When we drove into Dr. Green's driveway, Ardella and I slid to the end of the truck bed. Ardella hopped off first, then turned to help steady my jump to the ground. Mr. Elliott got out of his side of the truck, and he and Ardella got to Mama's door at the same time.

"You carry Josh, Mistuh Elliott," directed Ardella. She always surprised me with her self-directed authority. Sometimes, she even deemed it appropriate to be the decision maker for our family, and today was certainly one of those times.

"I's pick up Miz Taylor," Ardella said, "and Katie Jane, you run up on Dr. Green's porch and open de door."

The outside door was already open, propped back with a green, cast-iron frog. When I pulled open the screen door and stepped inside the foyer, the screen slammed behind me with a loud smack.

Weak rays of sun shone through the narrow, stained-glass windows on either side of the front door. The only other light came from a bulb attached to an electrical cord suspended from the high ceiling. The light bulb began to sway when I slammed the door, and the shadows it created waltzed lazily around the walls.

I had been in Dr. Green's office many times with Mama. As soon as I walked in the door, the stringent smell of alcohol filled my nose.

There were two doors that opened into the foyer where I stood, one on the right and one on the left. Dr. Green used these rooms to

A Different Kind of Trouble

examine his patients. He and his wife Louise lived in the back of the house with their daughter, Beth, who was the same age as Josh.

Both doors were closed, and I could hear Dr. Green's voice in the room on the right, where he was talking to a patient.

"Help! Dr. Green!" I yelled at the top of my voice. "Josh is sick!"

Seeing that Mr. Elliott and Ardella had reached the porch with Josh and Mama, I opened the screen door for them to enter. I continued yelling for the doctor. The interior door on the right opened quickly, and there stood Dr. Green in his white coat, glaring at us.

"What in the world is going on?" he asked in a voice that reflected aggravation.

Dr. Green took one look at Josh and grabbed him into his arms. He led us into the empty room on the left side of the foyer and laid Josh on the examining table. He quickly covered Josh with blankets while at the same time directing Ardella to put Mama in a chair nearby.

We all watched in silence as Dr. Green examined Josh.

"Josh is very ill," Dr. Green said, as he finished taking Josh's temperature. "We must get him to Grady Hospital. Clark, can you come with me to take Josh and Katherine to Atlanta?"

"Of course, I can," he answered.

"Good. I want you to drive my car. We'll go by the police station to get an escort," Dr. Green said, taking control of the situation. "We'll put Mrs. Taylor in the front seat, and I'll sit in the back with Josh. I have to watch his breathing as we travel."

Dr. Green turned to Ardella and me. "Go to the back of the house and tell Mrs. Green what happened. Have her call B. J. at work and tell him to meet us in the emergency room at Grady Hospital. She'll call one of our friends to take you two home."

Dr. Green grabbed his black bag and several blankets. "Follow me."

I held the screen door open as Mr. Elliott carried Josh and Ardella carried Mama. They followed Dr. Green around the side of his house to the garage. The doctor opened the front door of his car and directed Ardella to place Mama on the front seat.

Opening the back door and climbing in, the doctor placed his medical bag on the floor. "Give Josh to me, Clark, and help me wrap these blankets around him. He's having chills."

Mr. Elliott did as he was told, then got into the driver's seat.

"The keys are over the visor," Dr. Green instructed Mr. Elliott.

Ardella reached for my hand, and we stepped back together to let the car back out of the garage. We watched as the car pulled away, heading toward the police station.

Separate Fountains

"Come on, Katie Jane," Ardella said, "let's ask Miz Green to call yo' Daddy."

"What do you think is wrong with Josh, Ardella?"

"Lawdy, I don't rightly know," she answered. "I jes' know I didn't like de look in Dr. Green's eyes."

Mrs. Green answered our knock immediately. When we explained what had happened, she embraced us. "You poor dears," she said. "Come on in. The telephone's right here."

I dialed Daddy's office number but nobody answered. Noticing the clock on the Greens' fireplace mantle, I saw it was four-twenty.

"Look what time it is, Ardella!" I exclaimed. "Daddy got off work at four o'clock."

"Quick, Katie Jane," she answered. "Yo' daddy comes right by Dr. Green's office on de way home. Let's get out on de side of de road and sees if we can catch him!"

"I'll go with you," said Mrs. Green, grabbing Beth by the hand. "Mr. Taylor will be more likely to notice all four of us."

We rushed out the back door and around to the front of the house. Lining up on the sidewalk along U.S. Route 41, all of us craned our necks to watch for Daddy's car.

As the minutes passed, I wondered if we had missed him. Surely not, I reasoned. Daddy had told me many times it took him about forty minutes to get home. But what if he got off early today? No, he never got off early.

It was stiflingly hot as we stood in the sun along the side of the road. Soon, perspiration plastered my dress against my body. I looked over at Ardella, Mrs. Green, and Beth as they stood beside me. They, too, had perspiration running down their faces, but no one made the suggestion to go back to the shade of the porch.

I thought I heard Daddy's car, but perhaps my brain was just playing tricks on me. No, I was right. The car that came around the bend was, in fact, our Plymouth. The four of us saw it about the same time as we all started jumping up and down together, waving and screaming to get Daddy's attention.

He saw us and pulled off the road in front of us. I ran ahead and jumped on the running board.

"Jimminey-Christmas!" Daddy declared. "What are you and Ardella doing on the side of the road in this heat?"

"Daddy, something's bad wrong with Josh," I blurted. "Dr. Green and Mama and Mr. Elliott have taken him to Grady Hospital. We tried to call you at work, but nobody answered."

A Different Kind of Trouble

"Oh God, not my boy," Daddy responded in disbelief. He looked past me at the doctor's wife, who had by now reached the car. "Mrs. Green, do you know what's wrong with Josh?"

"No, Mr. Taylor," she answered. "I only know what Katie Jane just told you. You better hurry to Grady's emergency room."

"Jump in the car, you two," Daddy instructed Ardella and me. "Let's turn this car around and head for the hospital."

Daddy looked at the doctor's wife again. "Mrs. Green, thank you for your help. If your husband should call, please tell him we're on our way."

"I will, and I'll be praying for little Josh."

On the way to Atlanta, I sat in the front between Daddy and Ardella, talking constantly, relaying all the events of the day to Daddy. I quickly realized I was the only one talking, so I, too, fell silent, matching their moods.

The hum of the Plymouth's engine, the whoosh of the wind blowing through the open windows, the rumbles of passing cars, and the occasional toot of a car horn barely got our attention. Our customary laughter and talking was silenced by our worry about Josh.

I looked over at Daddy. His face was drawn with anxiety. Then I looked at Ardella. Her face, too, was lined with worry. The thirty-mile drive to Atlanta seemed the longest ride of my life.

As we rode along, I remembered how excited Josh and I usually got when we came to this big city. Before today, a trip to Atlanta with Daddy meant a trip to Sears and Roebuck on Ponce de León Avenue. A trip in August was usually for new school shoes, a pair of overalls for Josh, and some blue jeans for me. A trip at Christmas was a time to see Santa, and a trip at Easter was for new Sunday clothing. Daddy sometimes surprised us with unplanned trips to Sears when he needed something for the house or farm, things he couldn't find at Smith's Hardware. I remembered back to the time Daddy bought the long galvanized tub from Sears, the tub Mama used twice a day to soak her legs.

Suddenly, in the distance, I saw the large red-lettered sign of Grady Memorial Hospital. I had seen this sign many times on our trips to Atlanta, but I never thought I'd be going there.

We pulled into the hospital's parking lot and drove to the emergency room entrance. I noticed Dr. Green's car under the big awning in front of the door.

Separate Fountains

As Daddy parked the car, Ardella broke the silence.

"I think I better sit in de car, Mistuh Taylor," she said. "You got enough troubles on yo' shoulders without havin' somebody my color following you in dem hospital doors."

"All right, Ardella," Daddy replied, " but I'm taking Katie Jane with me. Maybe if Josh sees her he'll feel better."

"Yessuh," she agreed. "And I's be right here, a-waitin' and a-prayin'."

As we walked across the parking lot toward the emergency room doors, Daddy held my hand. Pushing against the doors, he led me through the entrance into a huge room filled with people. I felt as though they were all looking at us. I saw Mr. Elliott sitting alone in a corner thumbing through a magazine. Daddy rushed over to him.

"Clark, where's Josh?" Daddy asked. "Is he all right?"

"I don't really know, B. J., Dr. Green took Josh and Katherine behind those doors as soon as we got here." He pointed to two doors that read "Staff Only."

As if on cue, Dr. Green came through the doors and walked straight toward us.

"B. J., I'm so glad you're here with Katie Jane," Dr. Green said. "Josh has been calling for her. I've arranged with the nursing staff to let Katie Jane go in and see him."

"What about Ardella, too?" I quickly asked. "She's in the car. I'll run out and get her."

"I'm sorry, Katie Jane," Dr. Green answered. "But Ardella's color is not allowed in the white patients' wing of the hospital."

"Dr. Green," Daddy interrupted, "What's wrong with my son?"

The doctor stared down the hall, avoiding Daddy's eyes.

"I'll discuss that with you in a little bit, B. J., but right now, let's get Katie Jane in to see if she can calm Josh down. He keeps crying for her. Please follow me."

I grabbed my father's hand and tugged him along, trying to rush him as we followed Dr. Green through the swinging doors. As we followed, the cleanliness of the hospital and the smell of disinfectants and medicines were quiet noticeable.

We passed nurses pushing patients on rolling beds. Other nurses pushed patients in wheelchairs or helped them walk in the corridors.

A Different Kind of Trouble

We passed doctors dressed in white, some with caps on their heads and some with nose and mouth masks hanging around their necks.

Still following Dr. Green, we turned into another corridor. A sign with an arrow pointed to the left, Wing B—Children's Ward.

Dr. Green kept a fast pace, staying several feet ahead of us. I sensed he was rushing away from us, not to be rude, but because he wanted to avoid a discussion of what was wrong with Josh. I felt uneasy.

We stopped in front of another set of double swinging doors. On one of the doors, in capital black letters, was the word "Children's." On the other door, in the same lettering, was the word "Ward." Behind the doors, I heard an eerie, muffled sound—whuuuf, whoooo, whuuuf, whoooo. Over and over the noise repeated, like the wind rushing in through a hundred car windows and then strangely pushing back out. Over and over—whuuuf, whoooo, whuuuf, whoooo. I didn't think the sound had anything to do with Josh.

Dr. Green stood in front of the doors, looking first at Daddy and then at me.

"When I open these doors," he said, "you'll be able to go in and see Josh for about fifteen minutes. Katie Jane, it is extremely important you stay calm and reassure your brother he's going to be all right."

"Dr. Green, I'm not going to take another step until you tell me what's wrong with my son!" Daddy demanded in a harsh, strained voice that startled me.

"This is hard for me to tell you, B. J.," Dr. Green said sympathetically. "You know how I feel about Josh and your whole family."

"For God's sake, Dr. Green," Daddy interrupted with panic in his voice. "What's wrong!"

Dr. Green's voice trembled, "Josh has polio."

Not waiting for us to answer, Dr. Green turned and pushed open the doors. He stood aside for us to enter.

I gasped in disbelief. The sound of a giant's breathing filled the room. At the far end of the ward I saw Josh on a table, encased in a big steel cylinder—an iron lung—with only his head sticking out. An iron lung is a large, metal tank with an attached pump used to help a person breathe in spite of paralyzed chest muscles. Elsewhere in the room were other children in identical chambers.

I saw Mama sitting in a brown, metal folding chair beside Josh. Her back was toward us. Daddy and I walked slowly toward them, in shock at the scene before us. Overwhelmed by the powerful noise of

Separate Fountains

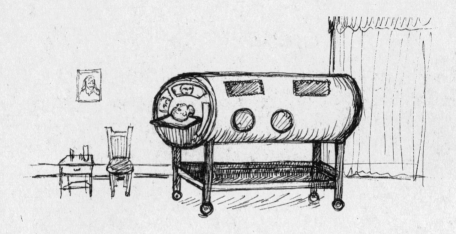

the machine, I soon realized it was breathing for Josh. All of a sudden, I was painfully conscious of my own breathing.

As I got closer, I could clearly see Josh's face in the mirrors attached to the sides of his iron lung. The mirrors allowed him to see anything going on in the room as he lay confined, completely dependent on the device to force air in and out of his lungs. The frightening rhythm of Josh's artificial lung seemed to pull me into the vortex of the sound.

I suddenly remembered that I had heard these sounds before, when Aunt Ruth was in the hospital dying of pneumonia. To me, the use of a breathing machine signaled impending death. Whuuuf, inhale, whoooo, exhale.

Seeing us walking toward them in one of Josh's mirrors, Mama turned around, looked up at us, and smiled slightly. Deep lines etched across her brow and there were black circles under her eyes. Her face looked like she had aged a hundred years since I had seen her earlier that afternoon. Her fragile body appeared drained of all energy.

In the overhead mirror, I saw Josh cut his eyes toward us. He strained to look up, but he did not attempt to speak.

As I watched, I understood the true benefit of the mirrors surrounding his head. The mirrors were a constant reminder to him that he was still alive. The mirrors connected Josh to his family and his environment by the use of the only physical movement he had— the movement of his eyes.

Daddy bent over and kissed Josh on the forehead.

"I love you, my son," he said softly.

A Different Kind of Trouble

Josh acknowledged with a slight smile.

"Remember, you're my sugar lump, and you'll be going home with us soon—to our blue heaven," Daddy said, trying to make the smile stay on Josh's face.

Josh tried to nod, but he could hardly move his head. Terror shone in his eyes.

The realization struck me like lightning—my little brother was paralyzed. He could not turn his head; only his eyes moved as he struggled to look at us. I wondered if he could speak.

I, too, leaned over and kissed his head.

"Josh, you've got to get well so we can ride the Greyhound bus," I teased, knowing he would smile at our private joke. He did smile, and it seemed so natural that for a second I forgot he couldn't move.

Dr. Green, standing behind me, spoke to Josh. "Son, you're a mighty brave boy. You'll soon be out of this iron lung. It's to help you breathe, just for right now."

Josh tried to nod again, but his head hardly moved.

Daddy walked over to Mama. Kneeling down beside her, he caressed one of her hands. Using his other hand, he gently ran his fingertips down the side of her face, as though trying to brush away her worries.

"I'm going to stay at the hospital all night and be right here with you, Josh," Dr. Green said.

Josh again acknowledged with a smile.

"I'm going to insist your Daddy take your Mama home, Josh," Dr. Green continued. "She can come back to see you in the morning."

Josh's eyes widened with fright, tears started to roll down his flushed cheeks.

"Oh no, Dr. Green," Mama interrupted in a strong, demanding voice. "I'm staying right here with Josh."

"But Katherine, you're not physically able to do that," Dr. Green scolded. "You can't possibly keep up with the routine I've prescribed for you if you stay here."

"I'm not leaving my baby alone in this hospital," Mama insisted. "B. J., you and Katie Jane go on home and have Ardella send fresh clothing for me when you come back tomorrow."

"But Katherine, you're not in good health," Daddy protested. "Dr. Green will be right here with Josh. Why not come home tonight?"

"I'm not leaving my baby, B. J. Taylor!" Mama cried out.

Separate Fountains

"If that's what you want to do," Daddy said, knowing he couldn't change Mama's mind.

"Get some rest, my son," Daddy continued as he leaned over to kiss Josh on the forehead, "and will you do Daddy a favor? Watch after your Mama for me."

Josh nodded his head in agreement.

Frightening thoughts continued to race through my mind as I stood there. Can Josh talk? Can he move any part of his body other than his head? Will he ever be able to run and play again?

"Don't worry about Katherine, B. J.," I heard Dr. Green say. "I'll have one of the nurses put up a cot for her right here."

Josh's eyes lit up with approval.

Daddy stooped to Mama again. Putting his arms around her wilted body, he leaned over and kissed her on the cheek.

"Try to rest, Katherine. I'll be back early in the morning."

Daddy stood up and looked at the doctor.

"May I speak to you in the hallway for a moment, Dr. Green?"

"Yes, of course. I'll walk with you and Katie Jane out to the emergency room where Mr. Elliott is waiting."

As Dr. Green and Daddy moved toward the door, I walked back over to Josh and kissed him good-bye.

"Josh," I said, "tomorrow I'm gonna bring you a surprise."

All of a sudden, a smile spread across Josh's face, and I saw something in his eyes that gave me hope. His eyes danced with mischief. I knew then my brother was still alive on the inside.

I walked over to Mama and threw my arms around her. I wanted to cry, but I knew I had to be brave for Josh's sake. "Mama, I'll help Ardella pick out fresh clothes for you tomorrow," I said. "I promise we won't forget."

Mama hugged me tightly, holding on as though she would never let go. I felt her tears on the side of my face, and as I pulled back, I brushed her cheeks dry with my fingers. I stood between her and Josh's mirrors so he could not see her crying. "Don't forget to tell Ardella to send me some clean gauze to wrap my legs in," Mama whispered.

Stepping back from Mama's side, I waved good-bye toward Josh and walked quickly toward the exit door.

I was deep in thought as I walked.

Once Mama and I had run and played, but now she could barely walk. And now, my brother, my constant companion for six years,

A Different Kind of Trouble

was paralyzed. My world was crumbling, and I was tired of being strong. Emotions welled up inside me, and I struggled to contain them. I wanted to cry. I had to get outside before my feelings exploded within me.

My body was trembling with silent sobs as I pushed open the doors. Before they swished shut behind me, my tears flowed uncontrollably. With teary eyes, I saw a blurred outline of two men standing in the wide hallway. I stopped for an instant to wipe away my tears on the sleeve of my dress as I walked toward Daddy and Dr. Green.

"You don't understand, B. J.," Dr. Green said. "The medical profession knows very little about polio. It'll take some time to diagnose the extent of Josh's paralysis."

"What will the treatment be?" Daddy asked.

"There are no medicines to cure polio. All we know to do is try to keep the fever down and apply physical therapy in warm water baths. And prayer, B.J. That's all we can do."

Daddy hung his head as though the weight of the world was upon him. He covered his face with his hands and sobbed. Pain twisted inside me as I saw his whole body shaking. I saw something I'd never seen before—my daddy crying. I, too, began to sob. What would happen to us now?

Grady Hospital faded away. Only my daddy and I existed in that moment. I threw my arms around his waist. "Don't cry, Daddy," I pleaded. "Josh is gonna be all right."

"Be assured, B. J., I'll do everything I can do for Josh," Dr. Green consoled. "Why don't you take Katie Jane home and get some rest. You've both had a long day."

Daddy wiped his tears with his hankerchief and blew his nose.

"Thanks for all you've done for us today, Dr. Green. I'll never forget your devotion to us."

"I just wish I could have done more," Dr. Green replied.

The doctor stooped down beside me and put his hands on my shoulders, "You've got to help Josh pull through this, Katie Jane," he said, as he looked me straight in the eyes.

"I know," I said.

"There is one special request I have Dr. Green," Daddy said as we started to walk down the hall. "We both know Katherine's not well and shouldn't be at the hospital twenty-four hours a day. Can you make some special arrangement for Ardella to sit with Josh for a few hours tomorrow while I take Katherine home to rest?"

Separate Fountains

"I'm sorry, B. J.," Dr. Green said, "but like I told you earlier, Grady Hospital will not allow a colored person to visit this floor designated for white patients, and that includes the polio ward."

"But, Ardella is like a mother to Josh," Daddy pleaded.

"I know, B. J., and if I had my way, she would be up there right now. But, as you and I both know, colored people have no rights at this hospital. They are allowed only in the basement rooms marked "Colored.""

Anger flashed across Daddy's face.

"When is our society going to stop being so ignorant!" Daddy yelled out, again shocking me. "Skin color has nothing to do with what's inside a person's heart. Are the bigots ever gonna learn that?"

"I don't know the answer, B. J.," Dr. Green answered solemnly, putting his hand on Daddy's shoulder to calm him.

Daddy turned, bashing the swinging doors to the waiting room with his fists as he pushed through them. I followed closely and quietly behind him, not sure how to react to my father's sudden violent anger toward society. As I walked through the doors behind Daddy, Mr. Elliott stood up and came to meet us.

"How is Josh?" he asked.

"The diagnosis is infantile paralysis—polio," Daddy answered.

"Oh no!" Mr. Elliott responded.

The three of us stood in silence, looking at each other in disbelief.

"Thank you again, Clark," Daddy finally said. "I don't know what would have happened to Josh if you hadn't helped Katherine get him to the doctor."

"I was glad to help," Mr. Elliott replied.

"Let's go home," Daddy said, turning toward the exit door. "There's nothing else we can do here tonight."

As we walked to the parking lot, Mr. Elliott continued to make conversation. "B. J., you should be proud of the way Katie Jane helped out today. And, I know Josh, he's a strong little fella; he'll be well in no time."

"I pray you're right, Clark."

"I'm gonna bring Josh a surprise tomorrow," I spoke up.

"That's the ticket!" Mr. Elliott said. "Keep Josh looking forward to the next day."

When we reached the car, we saw Ardella still in the backseat. Mr. Elliott went around to get into the front passenger seat. I climbed in the back, next to Ardella.

A Different Kind of Trouble

"What's wrong wif our baby?" Ardella asked anxiously.

"He's got polio," Daddy answered quietly without looking at her.

"Lawds-a-mercy, no. Not our baby," she exclaimed, shaking her head. "Not our baby."

She began a sing-song moan, repeating over and over, "Poor lil Josh, poor lil baby. Oh, Lawds-a-mercy, wat we gonna do?"

As we headed south on Route 41, no one said a word. Exhausted, I lay my head against Ardella's arm. I watched Daddy in the glow of the dashboard lights. He was a changed man, no longer the laughing, carefree Daddy to whom I was accustomed.

His physical appearance had become like Mama's, drained and tired. In one afternoon, Daddy had changed into one of the old men who sat on the bench every day in front of Thornton's grocery store.

Ardella was the first to speak.

"Poor Miz Taylor. How she gonna git her hot baths? Who gonna wrap her legs in gauze? I know she be stayin' by Josh and you cain't drag her away. I wish things wuz dif'nt so I could hep her watch over our baby."

"So do I, Ardella," Daddy said. "I asked Dr. Green to let you stay tonight."

"Then why ain't I a-stayin'?" she asked indignantly. "We both knows Miz Taylor need to be home in de bed."

"Dr. Green said the hospital rules won't allow you to stay in the white children's ward."

"Dat's wat I be 'fraid of, Mistuh Taylor."

Ardella paused, then continued, "Some people shore has a funny way of lookin' at things, judgin' people by the color of de skin God give dem."

Silence settled over the car again, with only the rumble of the engine and the rush of the wind through the car windows to fill our ears. It reminded me of the sound of the iron lungs in the children's ward.

Ardella spoke again. "Mistuh Taylor, where you gonna git de money to pays all Josh's hospital bills?"

Separate Fountains

"I don't know. I'm so worried about Josh right now I hadn't even thought about the bills. I'd give everything I have just to see him well again."

"Yessuh."

We rode a little further, and Ardella spoke up again. "Mistuh Taylor, I's work for you fer free til you gits Josh's bills paid."

"How sweet of you to offer to help us like that, Ardella," Daddy said, "but I'll make out somehow. Anyway, you need your wages for your children."

"Yessuh."

"Just keep Josh in your prayers."

"Yessuh, dat's where he be. Dat's where he be."

Chapter Fourteen

New Routines

"Wake up, Katie Jane," Daddy said. "It's time to get up!"
"What time is it?" I asked sleepily.
"It's 5:30. We have to pick up Ardella earlier than usual today. She has to get Mama's clothes ready."
I sat up quickly, rubbing my eyes with my fists. Yesterday's events came rushing back to me, dampening the day before it even started.
As soon as we got back to the house, Ardella bustled around getting Mama's clothes ready. She got underwear from the bureau and a blouse and skirt from the closet. She folded everything carefully and placed them in a brown paper sack. Then, she tore off a piece of waxed paper to place over the clothing, to separate them from the toiletries she placed on top. She folded the top of the sack over and over, deliberately creasing the fold so it made a sturdy handle.
"Dere!" she said as she placed the package on the table. "Dat be what Miz Taylor needs."
She walked away muttering, a habit she had when life was frustrating for her. She thought no one was listening but I caught her words.
"Dat what Miz Taylor needs since she gotta stay dere de whole time in dat Grady Hospital. Dat what she needs since dey got dem stupid rules for coloreds. Won't lets me stay wif our baby—dat baby I takes care of since the day he was born."
Suddenly, I remembered my promise to Josh. I needed to take him a surprise. I didn't have to think but a minute about what it would be. I ran to the bookcase and picked up *Mike Mulligan and His Steam*

Separate Fountains

Shovel. I knew Miss Ada Belle wouldn't mind my taking the book to the hospital for a few hours.

I held up the surprise for Daddy's and Ardella's approval.

"I's git you a carry bag fer dat," Ardella said as she rummaged around in one of Mama's dresser drawers. She pulled out a fluorescent chartreuse and orange bag with long straps and shook it hardily.

"That's the gypsy bag I tease your Mama about, Katie Jane." Daddy said. "Don't you remember she purchased it at Mr. Solomon's sale?"

I loved the bright-colored bag, but Daddy always teased Mama by calling it her gypsy bag. Because of his teasing, she carried it only on family outings, never to town or church.

"This will be Josh's surprise bag," I announced as I put the book inside it. "Every day I'll take something different to him in this bag."

"Well, the whole hospital staff will notice you as soon as you walk in," Daddy laughed.

As Ardella helped me put the bag's straps over my head and across my chest, the telephone rang.

I listened closely to the conversation.

"Yes, Dr. Green, we're just leaving for the hospital now," Daddy said.

Whatever the doctor said next made Daddy smile. Josh must be better, I thought to myself.

Daddy listened some more, then put down the receiver softly, as though he feared he might break it. He looked up at me and let out a whoop!

"Whoopee, Josh's fever's gone!"

"Praise de Lawd!" Ardella shouted, looking up to the ceiling.

"Dr. Green said Josh's temperature's back to normal, and he's beginning to turn his head more from side to side."

"De Lawd hast shorely blessed us," Ardella said. "Thank you, Jesus!"

"You're right, Ardella," Daddy agreed. "We have been blessed."

Turning to me, Daddy continued, "Come on, Katie Jane, let's get outta here and go to Atlanta to see Josh and your Mama."

As Daddy and I rushed down the steps to the car, we heard Ardella calling. She ran out the door behind us carrying the sack of clothes Mama had requested.

"Mistuh Taylor! Mistuh Taylor!" Ardella yelled as she ran down the steps. "You done forgit Miz Taylor's clothes. All you men is alike. You would forgits yo' head if it wasn't stuck on."

Daddy and I laughed. It felt so good to laugh.

New Routines

"You're probably right, Ardella," Daddy jovially popped back. "I don't know what we'd do if we didn't have you to help us. As Milton Berle says, 'You're top banana in this bunch.'"

We all laughed again.

"Quit yo' joshin' Mistuh Taylor and git on up dat road to Atlanta."

On the ride to Atlanta, Daddy's happy demeanor quickly faded. I could tell he was deep in thought and distressed. I knew he was worried about Josh, and Mama, too. I also knew that when he didn't go to work, he didn't get paid. Knowing my father as I did, I knew he was thinking about something always on his mind—providing money for our family's existence.

Was he wondering about Josh's mounting hospital bills? Where was he going to get the money to pay them and Dr. Green? Would we have to move to the Poor Folks Farm?

I knew for sure that all of Mama's bills weren't paid. When Dr. Green came by the house to check on her only a few days ago, I overheard Daddy telling him he would pay some more on her bill at the end of the month.

"Daddy, are you all right?" I ventured into his silence.

"Why do you ask, sugar lump?"

"Your face just looks tired."

"Oh, it does, does it?" He looked at himself in the rearview mirror. "Well, Katie Jane, I am tired. I didn't get much sleep last night. I kept worrying about Josh."

"Ardella says life gets tiresome for everybody sometimes, no matter who you are, no matter how much money you have, no matter the color of your skin. She says when life's not going the way you want it, your body just gets to feeling worn out, or as Ardella puts it, 'you jes' git plain weary.'"

"Ardella's probably right, as always," he said with a smile.

"She says we just have to accept life gets tedious sometimes, but we must keep on going and trusting the good Lord will pull us through."

"Well, I'm trusting in the good Lord to help Josh get well, and I'm hoping and praying He'll help me find a way to pay the hospital bills."

"How's the good Lord gonna help you pay them, Daddy?"

"I don't know, sugar lump. I don't know. He'll have to figure that one out."

Separate Fountains

We rode for awhile in silence.

"Oh by the way, Katie Jane, when I talked to Dr. Green today, he said he wants to see you as soon as we get to the hospital."

"Why?" I asked, puzzled at why the doctor would want to see me.

"Since you were with Josh when he came down with polio, Dr. Green wants to give you a gamma globulin shot to boost your immune system."

A shot! The word filled me with dread.

"But Daddy, I don't want a shot," I whined. "The penicillin shot Dr. Green gave me when I had the flu made my hip hurt so bad I could hardly sit down."

"You'll have to follow Dr. Green's orders, Katie Jane. It's for your own good."

"Yes, sir."

Until that moment, the trip to Atlanta had seemed to take forever. Now it flew by. In fact, it was the shortest ride to Atlanta I'd ever had.

After parking the car, Daddy enthusiastically jumped out. He was excited about seeing Josh and Mama. I wanted to see them, too, but my enthusiasm had been dampened by the impending shot.

Before entering the hospital's doors, Daddy stopped short and turned to me.

"We forgot something," he said with a grin on his face.

"The clothes!" we said in unison.

I skipped to keep up with Daddy's long strides back to the car. We laughed as we pulled the sack out of the backseat.

With smiles on our faces, Daddy and I passed through the entrance of Grady Hospital. We tried to hold onto them as we walked toward the children's ward. As we passed through the double swinging doors, I willed myself not to be intimidated by the loud, mechanical breathing that filled the room crowded with iron lungs.

We walked to Josh's iron lung. Mama was seated at his side.

I saw my brother's face was no longer flushed, and Mama looked amazingly rested.

"Look, Daddy," Josh exclaimed. He moved his head from side to side as soon as he saw us in the mirrors.

"That's great, son," Daddy answered as he leaned over and kissed Josh on the cheek.

New Routines

Turning to kiss Mama, Daddy placed the sack on her lap.

"See? I didn't forget." Daddy glanced over at me with a smile and winked.

Mama placed the sack under her chair.

"Aren't you gonna look inside, Mama?" Josh questioned.

"If Ardella packed it, I know it's got everything I need," she answered.

I started to giggle, knowing why Josh wanted Mama to look in the sack.

"Your surprise isn't in there, Josh," I declared. I patted the orange and chartreuse bag under my arm. "It's in here. This is gonna be your surprise bag. I'll bring you something every day."

Josh smiled.

"What did you bring me today?" he asked.

As Josh spoke, I noticed his eyes were bright and clear. My spirits soared. I knew my brother's alertness was a sign his fever had disappeared.

A moment later, Dr. Green walked through the doors. My exuberance was quickly squelched, for I knew what was in store for me.

"Good morning," Dr. Green said cheerfully. He smiled at all of us, ruffling Josh's hair. "I have good news for you, Josh. I've consulted with the other doctors on the hospital staff, and they agree with me that you should be out of this iron lung soon."

"All right," Josh responded. "When will I get to go home, Dr. Green?"

"Not for awhile," Dr. Green replied. "When you are taken out of the iron lung, you'll be moved to another ward, a special room here for polio patients, both children and adults."

"How long will I have to stay there?" Josh sounded apprehensive.

"I'm not sure, Josh. It depends on how well your body responds to treatment. Several people will be working with you. They're called physical therapists."

"What are physical therapists?" Josh asked.

"They are special hospital staff who work as a team with polio patients," he explained. "They will massage and exercise your legs and arms—and whole body—trying to restore your strength."

"Will they hurt me?"

"No, Josh," Dr. Green reassured him. "The therapists will be gentle with you as they flex your muscles. They'll work with you in a heated pool, helping you participate in water exercises. And guess what?"

Separate Fountains

"What, Dr. Green?"

"You'll even get to swim and play in the pool."

As I listened to Dr. Green talk, I reflected back to what I knew about President Franklin Delano Roosevelt's polio. At school, I'd seen a movie about him that showed scenes of him swimming in heated pools at Warm Springs, Georgia. In the clip, a therapist helped him move his paralyzed legs in the warm water, which bubbled naturally out of a mountainside. I thought, too, about the picture of President Roosevelt in his wheelchair that hung in the barbershop in Jonesboro.

The chain of logic, from warm-water therapy to President Roosevelt to a wheelchair, brought a frightening thought. Josh might be confined to a wheelchair for the rest of his life.

Still lost in my own thoughts, Dr. Green quickly brought me back to reality by calling my name. "Katie Jane," he said, "I want you to walk down the hall with me. You must have a gamma globulin shot to lessen your chances of getting polio."

"I've never heard of that kind of shot," I said.

"It's something new," he explained. "It's made up of antibodies that boost your immune system, and helps your body fight off any disease to which you've been exposed."

"Do I hafta have a shot?" I whined, hoping to play on his sympathy for a reprieve.

"Yes, Katie Jane," Dr. Green said. "We have to protect you."

"I'll go with you to get your shot, Katie Jane," Daddy said reassuringly.

I looked at Josh, determined to hide my fear.

"Josh, you've been in this hospital for two days," I said teasingly, "and you haven't had a shot yet. I've only been here for two minutes and Dr. Green's ready to shoot me in the behind."

Josh smiled.

"But don't worry, Josh," I continued. "I'll be brave like you. If you can stand that old iron lung, I can surely stand a little shot."

Josh nodded.

"I'll be back in a few minutes with a sore behind," I joked, "and then I'll give you your surprise from the surprise bag."

"Okay," Josh answered.

New Routines

I followed Dr. Green and Daddy down the hall to the nurses' station. As the two of them watched, a nurse weighed me to determine the dosage of the drug.

"What if I was fat?" I asked the nurse.

"You'd need a bigger dose of gamma globulin," she answered, "and it would take several of these syringes to give it to you."

I'm sure glad I'm not fat, I thought.

"You weigh seventy-eight pounds, Katie Jane," the nurse announced as she read the scales. "Since you weigh under a hundred pounds, you'll need only one shot."

Following her instructions, I bent over the examining table and pulled my dress up over my right hip. With one hand, she slid down the top part of my cotton panties. With the other, she shoved the needle into my hip.

I felt an instant, burning pain. I could feel the liquid spreading througout my hip. The pain seemed to slide into every part of my body. I whimpered. I wanted to cry out loud. Tears streamed down my face as I bit my lip.

When the nurse removed the needle, I gasped and began to heave. Daddy came running to me and put his arms around me.

"Just stay calm, Katie Jane," he consoled. "You're gonna be all right. Let's see if the nurse can get you a Coca-Cola to drink. Then you'll feel better."

Dr. Green hurried to the refrigerator in the back of the room and came back with a Coca-Cola. At the bottle opener nailed to the side of the door frame, he popped the cap off of the green glass bottle.

"Drink some of this, Katie Jane," he instructed. "You'll feel better."

I took several long swallows, and the magic formula seemed to calm my nausea.

"I want to go back and see about Josh," I said.

Daddy held my hand, still comforting me as we walked down the hall.

"I'm sorry the shot hurt you, Katie Jane," Daddy said. He put his arm around my shoulders and gave me a hug as we walked.

"I'm all right now, Daddy, don't worry about me," I said, trying to sound braver than I really felt. I still wanted to cry, but how could I when Josh was so sick?

When we got back to Josh, I pulled *Mike Mulligan and His Steam Shovel* out of the surprise bag. Josh's eyes danced.

"Please read it to me, Katie Jane," he said quietly.

Separate Fountains

Mama got up and gave me her folding chair so I could sit next to Josh. She and Daddy walked out into the hall.

I immediately noticed Mama was walking without Daddy's help. Did the scare of Josh's polio suddenly empower Mama with inner strength and willpower? Or, was she making herself walk for Josh's sake?

As I started to read to Josh, the words were so familiar I could almost recite them from memory. The last time I had read to him was at home just three days ago. That happy moment seemed so far away now.

When Daddy and I got home later that day from the hospital, Mr. Thornton's grocery truck was parked in front of our house. Mr. Thornton was seated in one of the rocking chairs on the porch, and in the other rocker sat Ardella.

As Daddy and I started up the porch steps, Ardella got up and ran over to open the screen door.

"Yawl come in here quick, Mistuh Taylor," she directed excitedly. "Come in dis kitch'n and see wat Mistuh Thornton brung."

"What's going on, Ted?" Daddy asked. "Why are you here?"

"Just follow Ardella into the house," Mr. Thornton answered with a big smile.

Exchanging puzzled looks, Daddy and I followed Ardella into the kitchen with Mr. Thornton close behind. On the kitchen counter were three large sacks of groceries.

"I didn't order any groceries, Ted," Daddy said, turning back toward Mr. Thornton with a puzzled look. "Why did you bring these to us?"

The grocer had a sheepish grin on his face.

"Calm down, B. J.," he said soothingly. "Someone in Jonesboro, who wants to remain anonymous, came to the store this morning. He said to deliver to your house all the groceries your family needs while Josh is sick. I told him I would only charge him wholesale prices, and I'd throw in a few groceries myself."

"Oh, thank you. But . . . I can't believe this. Who would do such a thing?" Daddy asked meekly as he touched the top edge of one of the sacks as though to make sure it was real. He had tears in his eyes.

"Oh, please tell that person thanks for me, Ted," Daddy said, standing there in disbelief. "We appreciate the help so much."

New Routines

"Well, getting food on your table is not going to be one of your problems right now, B. J.," Mr. Thornton replied. "Just come by the store every few days and get the things you need, or call me and I'll deliver them to you. You have your hands full trying to juggle work and running back and forth to the hospital."

"Thank you, Ted, thank you," Daddy replied, as he reached out to shake Mr. Thornton's hand.

Two weeks passed. Josh was finally liberated from the iron lung and moved to Grady's rehabilitation ward. The left side of his body was slightly paralyzed, but the right side appeared normal. When I saw all the other patients in the ward, I realized just how lucky Josh was. Most of the people I saw there wore metal leg braces and walked with crutches. Others, in wheelchairs, had no use of their crooked, shriveled-up legs. Some patients had lost so much weight you could, literally, see their bones under their thin skin.

Once again, our family changed its routine. Mama came home every night but stayed at the hospital most of the day. She depended on others to drive her to the hospital in the mornings because Daddy needed the car for work. Neighbors and friends took turns driving her to Atlanta. Daddy went to the hospital at night and brought her home with him.

On days when no one was available to drive Mama, Daddy got off work early and the three of us would go and visit Josh together. Most days, though, were long and full of worry as I waited anxiously for Daddy's work day to end so I could go with him to see my brother.

Ardella always had our supper ready when Daddy walked in the door. We gobbled down our meal while ignoring her warnings about the consequences of eating too fast. We would drop Ardella off at her house on our way to the hospital.

Josh's days were full of activity. He liked the reassurance of having Mama close by, and he had the full attention of a staff of doctors, nurses,

Separate Fountains

and physical therapists. They kept Josh on the move constantly, from the pool to the exercise machines to the massage tables.

The therapist moved and stretched and moved and twisted and moved and massaged the left side of his body—shoulder, arm, torso, hip, and leg—then the right side, all the same moves.

Because of Josh's confinement in the iron lung for over two weeks, he had to learn to walk again. With his left leg now partially paralyzed, his stride was like that of a small child—little steps, one at a time. Twice a day for thirty minutes, he had to practice walking in a maze with handrails on each side.

When Josh wasn't exercising, the staff was feeding him nutritious foods, trying to rebuild his health. He fell, exhausted, into bed every night.

For the next six weeks, Josh worked at getting well. His goal was to start first grade after Labor Day. His good attitude brightened the day for everyone around him, from doctors and nurses and therapists to other patients and their families.

"I'll get to go home tomorrow, Katie Jane," Josh announced one day. "Just in time for school."

"Yippee!" I yelled with excitement. "Josh's coming home!"

"And just in time for first grade," Josh said.

As I handed Josh his surprise for the day, a Blue Horse tablet that had been assigned as "My Portrait Book" when I was in fifth grade, I saw Mama reach over and take Daddy's hand. She led him to a nearby window. Their words floated back to me as I stood between them and Josh.

"Dr. Green came by today with some of the staff doctors," Mama said. "Although they're dismissing Josh tomorrow, we'll have to take him to Emory University Hospital two days a week to continue the warm-water massage and physical therapy."

As I listened, I turned the pages of the tablet for my brother, letting him guess the subject of each drawing. But my ears were tuned in to our parents' conversation.

"Emory University Hospital?" Daddy questioned. "Why, that's way over on the north side of Atlanta. Why there?"

"Dr. Green explained to me Emory's Medical School is doing a lot of research on polio, and their hospital has an outpatient program that's coordinated with Grady's polio patients."

New Routines

"I know Josh is not well and still needs treatment," Daddy replied, "but I wasn't expecting anything like this. Emory University Hospital is more than sixty miles from Jonesboro! How in the world are we ever gonna get him there?"

"We'll think of something," Mama said, but there was little conviction in her tone.

"How would we manage?" I thought to myself. We had only one car, and Daddy needed it to go to work every day. He could not take off twice a week. He needed a full paycheck.

After eight weeks in the hospital, Josh was finally released. The ride home to Jonesboro was like old times, with the four of us singing, telling silly stories, and laughing. It was so good to hear Josh's laughter again.

When we got to our farm's gate, Sherlock ran up the driveway to meet us. Daddy opened the car door for him to get in the backseat with Josh and me. I don't know who was the most excited about seeing each other—Sherlock or Josh. As Josh hugged him, Sherlock licked Josh's face.

Ardella was waiting for us on the front porch. As soon as the car door opened, she started in with her Hallelujahs.

"Hallelujah! Hallelujah! My baby's home!" she exclaimed as she ran down the steps, opened the car door, and pulled Josh from the car.

"Oh, my chile," she said, as she smothered him with kisses. Because of the segregation rules at Grady Hospital, it had been two months since they had seen each other.

Josh returned her affection by putting his arms around her neck and hugging her.

"I missed you, Ardella," he said, with tears running down his cheeks.

"Jes' keep huggin' me," she said as she carried Josh up the porch steps. "I's got yo' suppa all ready, with yo' fav'rit dessert, peach pie. I's gonna cook anything you want, yes I is. I's gonna spoil my baby."

After supper, Ardella helped Daddy get Josh settled on his cot and Mama settled on her bed. Both fell asleep quickly, exhausted from the trip home.

Daddy and I tiptoed quietly out the door with Ardella to take her home for the night.

Separate Fountains

When we got in the car, Daddy sat still for a few minutes, as if in deep thought. Then he turned to Ardella, reached over, and patted her hand on her lap.

"Ardella, I want to thank you for all your help these last few months," he said. "I don't know how our family could have survived without you."

"You know you welcome," she answered. "And I know one thing fer shore, Mistuh Taylor."

"What's that, Ardella?"

"I's got two fam'lies. One at my house and one at yores."

The next morning, after delivering Ardella to our house, Daddy and I went to Thornton's grocery store. As we rounded an aisle, we came face to face with Cletus Jones.

"B. J.! Katie Jane!" he exclaimed loudly. "How's Josh? I've been so worried about him."

"We brought him home from the hospital yesterday, Cletus," Daddy replied.

"That's great. How is he?"

"Better. However, he still has a long way to go to regain his health. For the next few months, he'll have to go to Emory University Hospital twice a week for therapy."

Daddy paused, then continued. "And I only have the weekend to figure out how I'm gonna get him there and go to work at the same time."

"Maybe I can help you figure out something," Cletus said as he moved his tobacco around in his cheek. "In the meantime, why don't you drop by my drugstore when you're finished shopping. I'll whip up a banana split for Josh."

Before Daddy could answer, I quickly answered for him. "Oh Daddy, Josh does like Mr. Cletus's scrumptious banana splits. It's one of his favorite things, and he hasn't had one in months."

Daddy chuckled, knowing that I wanted one, too.

"We'll be there shortly, Cletus," Daddy said.

I breathed a sigh of relief.

As Cletus headed for the checkout counter, I pushed our cart on down the aisle. "Do you think Mr. Cletus will help us figure out a way to get Josh to the hospital?" I asked.

New Routines

"I don't know, sugar lump," he answered, "but I do know we need a miracle. We'll just hope and pray Cletus Jones can work miracles."

"I've seen him work miracles in his drugstore," I said with a grin.

"That reminds me," Daddy replied, looking me straight in the eyes. "I've been wanting to talk to you about that, Katie Jane."

"What do you mean?" I asked, feigning innocence.

"You've been such a brave girl these past weeks," he said, "that today, I proclaim Cletus Jones's drugstore is no longer off limits to you. You've proved you have a good head on your shoulders, and I know you won't be swayed by anything you might see or hear there."

"You mean today is the day for Josh's first legal banana split?" I teased.

"I guess so," Daddy laughed mischievously.

We ignored the flim-flammers at Thornton's Grocery Store that day. We knew we were headed to the drugstore for Cletus's famous banana split.

When Daddy and I arrived at the drugstore, I couldn't believe my eyes. I saw five banana splits lined up on the soda fountain counter! Cletus was just putting on the finishing touches, carefully placing cherries on top of each one.

"One for everybody in the family, including Ardella," Cletus beamed.

Separate Fountains

"Thank you, Mr. Cletus, thank you!" I squealed with excitement as Cletus put the filled dishes side by side in a shallow cardboard box.

"Katie Jane, tell Josh I expect him to bring these dishes back himself," Cletus exclaimed with a wink.

I stood there wondering if Cletus was aware his store had been off limits to me until today. I wondered if he would spill the beans by telling Daddy about how many days Josh and I had spent in our booth in the corner, waiting to see the Greyhound bus. I wondered if he was going to tell how many scrumptious banana splits Josh and I had shared. Or, was his wink a signal to me that our secret was safe.

With Daddy carefully balancing the box, we started toward the door.

"By the way, B. J.," Cletus called after him. "I'll let you know tomorrow about Josh's transportation to Emory Hospital."

"Thank you, Cletus," Daddy said, looking back over his shoulder, "for your concern, and for the banana splits."

I turned back to Cletus. "Thanks again for the banana splits!"

"Come back here a minute, Katie Jane," Cletus ordered. "I've just thought of something else I want you to take to Josh."

I ran back to the soda fountain. I watched as Cletus reached under the counter and pulled out his checkerboard and the sack of checkers.

"Take these to Josh," Cletus said, "and tell him to win some games for me."

"Oh, thank you, Mr. Cletus. Thank you for everything."

Chapter Fifteen

Helping Ardella

When I awoke, I looked across the room at Josh asleep on his bed. So sure was I that life was back to normal now, I couldn't understand why he hadn't already bounced out of bed to wake me up like he usually did on a Saturday morning.

He wasn't even awake yet although Daddy had already picked up Ardella and the two of them were stirring around in the kitchen making the family's favorite breakfast of pancakes, ham, and red-eyed gravy.

I jumped out of bed and bounded over to Josh's cot.

"Wake up, sleepyhead," I exclaimed, tugging on his covers.

His eyes opened, but his usual sparkle of mischief was not there.

"I don't feel good," Josh said, in a grumpy voice.

I squatted down in front of him, rocking back on my bare heels, looking him squarely in the face.

"You'll feel better after you eat pancakes," I said.

"I'm not hungry," Josh whined, frowning at me as he spoke. "Leave me alone!"

Daddy started walking toward Josh's cot, singing one of his silly songs:

Have you seen the ghost of Tom—
Long white bones with the skin all gone?
Wouldn't it be chilly with no skin on!

I laughed at Daddy's song. I moved out of his way and drifted back over to my cot to make up my bed.

Daddy sat down on the side of Josh's cot.

Separate Fountains

"Come on, my sugar lump," Daddy said. "Let me help you to the bathroom, then we'll eat breakfast."

Josh whimpered as Daddy picked him up. I noticed how lethargic Josh looked as Daddy carried him into the bathroom, then brought him back to the kitchen table where Mama, Ardella, and I joined them.

Josh slumped in his chair, still frowning with a sluggish look on his face.

Daddy, Mama, Ardella, and I chattered, pretending this was any normal Saturday morning. We delighted over breakfast, how light the pancakes were, how delicious the ham was, how tasty the red-eyed gravy, but Josh didn't say a word and could only be coaxed into trying a few morsels of food.

Josh didn't want to eat. He didn't want to get dressed. He didn't want to go outside to play. He whined and whined, saying he was tired and wanted to crawl into Mama and Daddy's bed, which he did.

Mama got Josh settled under her covers and went back to the kitchen to help Ardella. As she stood at the kitchen sink scraping food off the dishes, she looked out the window.

"Look, everybody, there's a black car at the gate."

Jumping up, I looked out the living room window.

"That looks like Cletus's new Cadillac," I said confidently.

"Maybe he has news about how he might help us," Daddy said, pushing back his chair from the kitchen table, and headed for the front door.

I followed Daddy and was so excited I ran right past him as he opened the screen door. I jumped off the porch.

"I'll go open the gate," I yelled back to Daddy, already starting to run up the driveway.

When I got to the top of the hill, Cletus was standing outside his car, waiting. He spit a line of tobacco juice toward the side of the road.

"Open this confounded gate, Katie Jane," Cletus said, all baffled. "I've got some good news to tell your daddy if I can ever get down to your house."

I laughed. I knew exactly how he felt about that confounded gate.

"Just a second, I'll have it open."

After I opened the gate, Cletus drove through, then stopped his car to wait for me as I relocked it.

"Hop in the backseat," he yelled out his rolled-down window.

Helping Ardella

I opened the door of the shiny, black car. My heart started pounding with excitement.

Oh, what a thrill for me! A chance to ride in Cletus Jones's new Cadillac! Yes, I knew all about his fancy car. It had been the talk of the town for weeks. People said he had paid cash for it from the money he made selling moonshine.

I didn't have much time to dwell on its plush interior or new car smell, though. My attention was immediately drawn to another person, dressed in a police uniform, sitting in the front. I recognized Mike Brewster, one of the town's policemen.

"Hello, Katie Jane," Mike said, as he turned back toward me. "How's Josh?"

"Not too good," I answered. "He's tired all the time."

As we drove toward the house, I instantaneously thought of Ardella. How would she react to Cletus Jones coming to visit us? She almost refused to eat the banana split Cletus had sent her yesterday. She felt like his drugstore was the place "de devil don picked to be his home in dis here town."

But then again, I thought, Ardella would be mighty grateful if Cletus Jones could help Josh get to Emory Hospital.

"Come on in, Cletus," Daddy shouted with enthusiasm from the front porch. "And Mike Brewster, what in the world are you doing here? Come on in both of you."

When we entered the room, I saw Mama was propped up against the headboard of her bed, lying beside Josh. Still exhausted from all the days spent at the hospital, she, too, needed rest. Stroking Josh's back as he rested, she watched us come in with Cletus and Mike.

"Is something wrong, B. J.?" Mama quickly asked, her voice reflecting alarm when she saw a policeman with Cletus.

"Nothing's wrong, Mrs. Taylor," Cletus bellowed with delight. "Mike and I have something special to tell you."

Glancing toward Josh, Cletus quickly slapped his hand over his mouth to quiet himself, realizing Josh was asleep.

"It's all right, Mr. Jones," Mama responded, "Josh's not asleep, he's just resting."

"Well, B. J.," Cletus said, "we've come up with a way to get Josh to Emory University Hospital. Sergeant Brewster's gonna tell you all about it himself."

Mike Brewster stepped forward.

Separate Fountains

"Mrs. Taylor," he said, looking toward Mama, "you probably don't know me, but I know your husband very well from his many visits to Jonesboro. All of us at the police station have been concerned about little Josh since the day he turned ill. We've been trying to come up with a way we could help your family out."

"Thank you for your concern, Sergeant Brewster," my mother said politely.

"After Cletus closed his store last night," Sergeant Brewster continued, "he walked down to the police station where I happened to be on duty for the night. He was upset over trying to figure out a way to help you get Josh back and forth to Emory University Hospital."

"And, the Jonesboro police force has come up with a solution," Cletus interrupted.

"Yes, we have," Sergeant Brewster said.

"So what's the solution?" Daddy asked.

"This is the plan," Mike continued, with a twinkle in his eyes. "The city of Jonesboro has three police cars, but we only seem to use the two newer ones. The old '47 stays parked at the station's garage all the time. I'm here to tell you the Jonesboro City Council has decided to let the police staff use the old car to transport Josh back and forth to the hospital."

Josh moved on the bed.

I could see his eyes were open now, but he showed no interest in what was going on.

"Hey, boy. You there on the bed," Cletus said, having noticed Josh's movement about the same time I did. "How would you like to ride to the hospital tomorrow in a police car?"

Josh suddenly jumped out of bed. He stood up straight, like a soldier at attention. As if by magic, a sparkle came to his eyes and a smile broke out on his face.

"Are you a-kiddin' me, Mr. Cletus?" Josh asked.

"No, I ain't a-kiddin'," Cletus laughed. "Sergeant Brewster has tomorrow off. He's gonna pick you and your Mama up in the morning in a real police car and take you to Emory University Hospital."

"Oh boy, I can hardly wait!" Josh yelled out. "Can Katie Jane go, too?"

"Of course," answered Sergeant Brewster.

Helping Ardella

Everyone laughed. This was the first time we had seen Josh happy about anything connected to a hospital.

"All the policemen have volunteered to carry Josh on their days off," Cletus continued. "Even the police chief has volunteered his time."

"You mean," Josh said excitedly, "that I'm gonna ride with Chief Bob."

"Yep, that's right, boy," Cletus said.

"Thank you, Mike," Daddy said, rushing over to shake the policeman's hand. "This news is almost too good to be true."

Mother, too, looked like she was overwhelmed by the surprise plan.

"I thank you, too, Sergent Brewster," she said. "It's so generous of the police force to donate their time to help Josh."

"We've even got our wives' approval," the policeman joked.

Daddy rushed to Mama's side.

"Oh Katherine, we are so lucky to have so many wonderful friends."

"And Cletus is my best friend," Josh piped up, now standing next to Cletus.

Cletus's famous toothless grin spread across his face.

"How can I ever thank you enough for coming up with a plan to help my boy?" Daddy said, as both men turned to exit through the front door.

"Don't worry about the thanks, B. J.," Captain Brewster said, as he shook Daddy's hand. "We just want to see Josh well again."

"I want to see that boy running into my drugstore and ordering a banana split!" Cletus yelled back toward Josh, again showing his famous toothless grin.

Now, rather than dreading his physical therapy, Josh looked forward to it. I, too, was excited about the trips in a police car. I knew that until school started I could ride along and be Mama's legs when she needed something at the hospital.

Jonesboro's six policemen took turns driving us to Emory University hospital. Wearing their starched blue uniforms, they were very professional in their attitude toward helping us. Josh always sat in the front seat, and Mama and I sat in the back.

Separate Fountains

Because Mama was shy and reserved, she had very little to say during the ride to Atlanta. However, Josh and I talked constantly to whoever was the driver for the day. Josh was fascinated—and pleased—that he could sit in the front seat with a "real" policeman. And boy, did he ask the questions! If Ardella had been with us, she would have said what she always said to us when we asked her questions: "You knows, curiousity killed a cat."

Josh wanted to know how the siren worked and how fast the car would go. He wanted to know if the policeman had ever been in a dangerous situation and had to use his gun. He wanted to know all about police training and police work. When Josh wasn't talking I usually talked of the latest town gossip or pointed out the sights we saw on the road between Jonesboro and Emory University Hospital.

As the days went by, Josh continued to improve. I could tell he was getting stronger because he didn't sleep as much, and he was putting on weight. His goal to be ready for school was foremost on his mind, but that ended one day when Dr. Green stopped by at home to check on him.

"I need to tell you something you are not going to like, Josh," Dr. Green said as he flexed Josh's leg muscles.

"What?" Josh asked, looking directly at the doctor.

"You're not going to be able to start school after Labor Day like we'd hoped," Dr. Green said.

"But," Josh whined, "the physical therapists say I'm better."

"You are better, but your body's still not strong enough for you to attend school every day," Dr. Green replied.

"Can I start after Christmas?" Josh asked.

"No, Josh," the doctor said sternly. "You're going to have to wait until next fall to start first grade."

"Noooo, Dr. Green! I want to go to school," Josh cried out pitifully. "Can't I just sit in the classroom and listen? I promise I won't go out to play."

"Listen to me, Josh," Dr. Green said kindly. "You're not physically able to sit in class all day. You need a lot of rest because your body is still tired from fighting the polio virus."

Josh looked to me for help.

"Katie Jane, you tell him," Josh pleaded. "You tell Dr. Green to let me go to school. Please Katie Jane, I want to go to school with you."

Seeing Josh so emotional upset me, but I knew Dr. Green needed some help.

Helping Ardella

"You have to do what the doctor says, Josh. You don't want to have to go back into that iron lung again, do you?"

Josh shook his head no.

"Will you keep helping me with my letters and numbers, Katie Jane?" he whined.

"Of course I will, and I'll give you my new Blue Horse tablet and Coca-Cola pencil, too."

"Will you really do that for me?"

"Just for you, Josh, I promise."

"I guess you'll have to teach me to read, too, Katie Jane. Just like you did Ardella."

"She be good at teachin' readin', chile," Ardella joined in. "I can tell you dat, for sure."

Josh laughed.

As if Josh's laughter was his signal to leave, Dr. Green packed up his medical bag. He waved good-bye to Mama as he walked out the front door.

After Dr. Green told Josh he couldn't start school, Josh seemed to lose his enthusiasm for recovery. He spent most of his time on his cot, where he slept most of the day. The only bright spots in his life were the two days each week a policeman drove him to the hospital for physical therapy. On these two days, Josh came close to being the happy, bright-eyed brother I had once known.

Josh was no longer my easy-going companion, talking and laughing and playing games with me. He was demanding, always wanting his way. He complained of headaches, and of feeling either too hot or too cold. And, he constantly ordered me to bring him a glass of water.

On some days, Josh refused to eat. Ardella tried to whet his appetite by cooking things he requested, from fried chicken to homemade vegetable soup to his favorite food, peach pie. Because his hand muscles were weak, Josh was embarrassed at the table when he dropped his fork. He couldn't hold his glass steady when he drank his milk. The only way Mama could get Josh to eat was to feed him like a baby.

Every day after school, I became Josh's teacher. Although I tried to make learning fun for him, his attention span was short, and he gave up easily on any assignment I gave him. He would become frustrated when he could not hold his pencil correctly to write his letters and would angrily throw it across the room. He didn't even want to hear *Mike Mulligan and His Steam Shovel*.

And, Josh missed his daddy's attention. Daddy, burdened down with the worry of paying Josh's hospital bills, continued working two jobs—his regular job at the Army base, and his night job at the peach packing plant. After the peach packing plant closed down for the season, Colonel Bartlett kept Daddy on the payroll to rebuild some of the older machines and bring them up to date with modern parts. Daddy worked on the machines every night until after midnight and was home just long enough to sleep a few hours before going back to work.

Mama's health didn't improve either. She continued to depend on Ardella to run the household and to help take care of Josh. After each meal, Ardella helped Mama to her bed, then carried Josh over to Mama, propping him up beside her. Mama read to Josh or colored with him in his coloring books. When he fell asleep, she stroked his back. Many times, when Mama thought I wasn't looking, I saw tears rolling down her cheeks as she sat there with her legs wrapped up in gauze, almost helpless.

I sensed Mama's hopeless feelings. She didn't know if her son would ever get well. She didn't know if she would ever walk normally again. She didn't know if she would ever be the strong companion she once had been to her husband.

Looking back now, I realize Mama's love of reading is probably what kept her sanity. She loved to read biographies of famous people, and she avidly devoured the biographies Miss Ada Belle sent her. Because of Daddy's busy schedule, he did not have much time for pleasure reading so Mama often shared her most recent book with him late at night, before they went to bed.

With my required bedtime of nine o'clock, I was always asleep when Daddy came home from the peach packing plant, but his

Helping Ardella

entrance to our house usually awakened me. While Mama and Daddy thought I was asleep, I would lie on my cot listening to their conversations at the kitchen table while Daddy had a snack.

"Miss Ada Belle chose a wonderful book for me this week, B. J.," my mother said one night. "It's about President Roosevelt and his struggle with polio."

"Oh, I bet that's inspiring," Daddy said, as I heard him stirring his spoon in his glass. I knew immediately Daddy was having his favorite nighttime snack, Ardella's leftover cornbread and buttermilk.

"Did you know President Roosevelt was thirty-six years old when he contracted polio?" Mama stated.

"Just think, he led our nation for almost twelve years from a wheelchair," Daddy said.

As I dozed back and forth from my sleeping and the reality of listening to Mama and Daddy's conversation, I thought of the time when my family saw the train carrying President Roosevelt's body back to Washington, D.C., after he died in Warm Springs. The president's flag-draped casket, along with uniformed soldiers standing at its side, was displayed in front of the train's windows as it passed slowly through Georgia. As it rolled through the small towns and big cities, citizens were given a chance to pay their last respects to the fallen leader. I remember hearing Daddy say people came from far and wide just to get a glimpse of the train that carried the president's body.

My Uncle Bud, from Marietta, Georgia, was a fireman for Southern Railroad at this time and had the honor of accompanying President Roosevelt's body on this solemn journey to Washington. Aunt Dorothy and her sons, Jimmy and Gene, came from Marietta to go with Mama, Daddy, and me to nearby Red Oak, Georgia, to see President Roosevelt's train go by and hopefully wave hello to Bud. Although I was only four years old, I faintly remember the train and the big crowd. One reason I remember was Uncle Bud stood on the side of the train's engine and handed three small American flags to Aunt Dorothy, requesting she give them to their sons and to me.

Separate Fountains

"I know you get discouraged, Katherine," I heard Daddy say, bringing me back to reality again in our one-room house.

"I worry about you, B. J., because you have so much to do. Things I should be helping you with."

"Don't worry about me," Daddy said. "The time you spend with the children is priceless . . . and the time you spend with me is precious."

I heard a staccato of kisses.

I knew Mama and Daddy loved each other.

I turned over, and fell asleep.

As I was walking home from school in the pouring rain, Mr. Elliott stopped his truck beside me. "Need a ride, Katie Jane?"

Grateful for his offer, I jumped in. He delivered me right to our gate.

"Thanks, Mr. Elliott," I said as I slid out of the truck.

Holding aloft the umbrella Ardella made me take that morning, I opened the gate and ran down the hill. After leaving the open umbrella on the porch to dry, I hurried into the house.

Ardella glanced up, but she said nothing since she was busy with Josh.

Mama looked over and winked at me, acknowledging she was glad to see me.

"Ardella baked some gingerbread cookies today," Mama said. "Get some for you and bring me one, too."

I got the cookies, and sat down on the end of Mama's bed. As she and I started to eat our cookies, we turned our attention to Josh and Ardella.

It was time for Josh's warm water massage, the second one for the day. I heard him whimper as Ardella helped him out of his favorite cotton pajamas—the ones with the red fire engines running along the sleeves and down the pant legs. Mindful of his need for privacy, Ardella covered him with a towel, then carried him to the tub of warm water.

Carefully placing Josh in the tub, she took a seat in one of our kitchen chairs she had placed beside the tub. Reaching over with a wash cloth and a bar of Ivory Soap, she washed his body gently.

Helping Ardella

After bathing Josh, Ardella began his massage routine. Having him turn to one side, she told Josh to hold onto the metal tub to balance his body while she massaged him. She rubbed him gently, trying to put strength back in his body.

"I'm tired of this," Josh whined.

"I knows you is, baby, but we's jes' 'bout through now," she said. "Let's turn you over to yo' other side. Dr. Green sez we has to do both sides."

Josh turned over like a programmed robot as he followed her instructions. Ardella massaged him again, from head to toe. When she finished the massage, she lifted him out of the tub onto a big towel she had spread across her lap. She patted him dry and carried him back to his cot to help him put on clean pajamas.

"Do you want to take a nap, or do you want yo' Mama to read to you?" Ardella asked Josh.

"I want Mama, and I want my books," he said in a grumpy voice.

I jumped off the bed and got the books I had brought from Miss Ada Belle's library two days earlier.

"I want you, too, Katie Jane," he whined, like he was afraid I was going to leave him.

"O.K., Josh, I'm just getting our books."

Ardella carried Josh to Mama's bed, and I climbed up beside them. As we read, Ardella pulled the tub to the back door, then lifted and emptied the soapy water into the back yard.

As Ardella finished cooking our supper, Daddy came in from work and found me sitting in Mama's rocking chair reading one of my library books. Josh and Mama had fallen asleep on Mama's bed, so Daddy decided to leave the food on the stove, and we tiptoed out the door to take Ardella home.

As Daddy, Ardella, and I rode along, I noticed the rain had stopped. The water droplets on the autumn leaves shined like jewels. There was a nip in the air, creating a delicious anticipation of fall.

We dropped Ardella at the edge of Colored Town, since the red clay roads were impassable after such a drenching rain. As we turned, I watched her slosh along the edge of the road, still wearing the yellow rubber galoshes my father had bought her so many years ago.

Separate Fountains

"How are things in school," Daddy asked on the way home.

"Well, I've finally figured out how to get to all my classes," I said. "It sure is different to have to change rooms every hour."

"What about Pepe Rodriguez? Is he in any of your classes this year?"

"Yes, all the gypsy children are back. Our teachers are requiring some of them to take make-up courses because they missed so much of school last spring."

"I guess it's hard to be a gypsy child, traveling from town to town with no roots," Daddy said. "I sure hope nothing happens this year to cause Don to take Pepe out of school early."

"Me, too."

We rode on further down the road, my mind still on the mystery of the gypsies.

"Oh, Daddy, I forgot to tell you something. Today in school I told Pepe about Josh's polio. He asked if he could come out sometime to cheer up Josh with some of his magic tricks."

"That would be great."

"I'm running out of ideas, Daddy," I said with a sigh. "Josh just doesn't have as much curiosity as he used to have. He doesn't seem interested in anything any more."

"I know, sugar lump, I've about run out of ideas, too."

Several days later, Pepe and his father rode their horses out to our farm to see Josh. Mr. Rodriguez rode the black horse my father had given him a few months earlier for helping hide Sam from the Klan.

As Mr. Rodriguez and Pepe stepped through the front door, I noticed Mr. Rodriguez carried an odd-shaped package, wrapped in newspaper and tied with a string. I noticed it had a yellowed envelope attached to it, a get-well card I presupposed. Mr. Rodriquez placed the package on our kitchen table.

"Don't open it until we've gone," Mr. Rodriguez instructed. "It's a surprise gift for the whole family."

Josh immediately perked up. One thing Josh loved was having company, especially when they came bearing gifts.

Pepe came prepared to entertain Josh. Although Pepe was shy with adults outside the gypsy camp, he was comfortable with schoolmates.

"Josh, do you like magic tricks?" Pepe asked confidently, standing by Josh's cot.

Helping Ardella

"Sure," Josh answered enthusiastically, as he sat on the side of his cot.

"Well then, just watch the magic of my hands."

I was as enthralled as Josh was when Pepe made gold coins come out of Josh's ear.

"Do it again, Pepe! Do it again," Josh begged.

Josh and I both oohed and aahed when Pepe pulled a long line of red silk scarves from Josh's pajama pocket.

"How in the world did you do that, Pepe?" I asked.

"Next time, I'll promise to pull a bird from a hat," Pepe said, "That is if Josh promises to have on a hat."

"I promise," Josh answered with glee.

Daddy and Mr. Rodriguez laughed.

"Come, Pepe," his father said. "We must not tire Josh. We'll come back another day."

"I'll be back soon," Pepe said.

"Promise," Josh said.

"I promise."

"Thank you, Pepe and Mr. Rodriguez," Mama said. "Your visit has been a tonic for all of us."

The gypsy elder bowed toward Mama.

"Mrs. Taylor, it has been my pleasure," Mr. Rodriguez said. "Your husband has been a benefactor to me and to my troupe of comrades, and your daughter has been a true friend to my son. Please accept the small gift we leave on the table as a token of our appreciation."

Daddy and I stood on the front porch, watching as Mr. Rodriguez and Pepe mounted their horses and rode up the hill. Before they even got to the gate, I was pulling on Daddy's hand to get him back in the house.

"Hurry, let's open the package, Daddy. Let's see what Mr. Rodriguez brought."

Daddy and I walked to the kitchen table. He lifted the package and quickly dropped it back on the table with a bang.

"Jimminy Christmas! That's heavy as a rock," he said. "What in the world can it be?"

He tried to pick it up again and almost fell as he dropped it back on the table.

Separate Fountains

"I give up," Daddy said. "Whatever is in this package is a mystery to me."

"Bring it over here, Daddy," Josh said. "So I can see."

"It's too heavy, Josh. I'll come get you and bring you to the table."

Daddy pulled the yellowed envelope off of the package and handed it to me.

"Here, Katie Jane, take this envelope to your Mama," Daddy instructed. "We'll let her read it before we open the surprise."

After I gave Mama the used envelope, she opened it with her nails and pulled from it a yellowed, tattered sheet of paper.

She read these words out loud to us: "To the Taylor family, our friends, From Don, Carlita, Pepe, and Rosa Rodriguez."

"Ready to open the mystery package?" Daddy asked jokingly, still standing by the package.

Josh climbed off Mama's bed as fast as he could. In his usual slow, unsteady gait, he struggled across the floor to the table.

"Open the package, Daddy!" Josh shouted out.

As Daddy pulled the string off of the newspaper-wrapped package, gold coins began to fall out. They showered onto the kitchen's lineolum floor with radiant sparkles like nothing I'd ever seen before.

Josh and I started yelling with glee. "It's gold!"

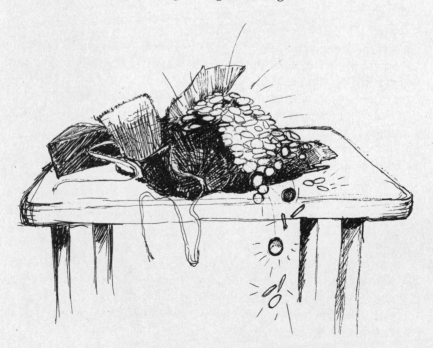

Helping Ardella

We fell to the floor and quickly picked up some of the coins in our hands. I studied each coin—inspecting them, smelling them, and pressing them hard between my fingers. Were they real?

"Is it real gold, Daddy?" I asked.

I saw that Daddy was also scrambling around on the floor examining each coin he picked up, studying the inscriptions closely.

"Yes, it's real!" he shouted. "It's real gold!"

Daddy scooped Josh up into his arms, then he reached down with his free hand and grabbed my hand. Holding Josh and pulling me, we circled the table in a jubilant dance.

"It's real gold. It's real gold," Daddy chanted as we skipped and danced around the room.

"Can you use gold to pay bills, Daddy?" I shouted above his chanting voice.

"Yes! Yes! Yes!" Daddy shouted, beside himself with excitement.

Daddy suddenly stopped dancing and let go of my hand. He put Josh down and rushed over to Mama. He swept her up from the bed and started dancing with her in his arms.

"Oh, Katherine," he exclaimed. "Our friends have helped us again!"

Several nights later, after we'd just gone to bed, I heard footsteps on our porch. Surprised and alarmed, Daddy ran to the screen door and flipped on the light. Through the screen, I could see three black men standing there, shading their eyes from the porch light.

"Sam! And Homer, and Mose!" Daddy exclaimed. "What are you doing here this time of night?"

"We wants to see you, Mistuh Taylor," Sam Gilbert said. "I's sorry we be here so late. We started out fer yo' place when we all gits home from work, and it took awhile to walk dis far."

"That's all right, Sam," Daddy reassured him.

"We climb over yo' gate and walks down de driveway, but we be quiet," Sam continued. "We's 'fraid de wrong peoples might hear us'sons."

As Daddy stepped outside, I bounded from my cot and ran to the screen door. I knew all of these black men. They were workers at the peach packing plant in the summertime.

"Aren't you fellows afraid to be out here this late at night?" Daddy questioned. "Are you in trouble? Is the Klan after you?"

Separate Fountains

"Naw suh," Mose answered. "We don't think so, but we has a heap of 'splainin' to do if we meets up wif dem dis late at night."

"You're right about that Mose. What can I help you with?"

"We don't needs yo' help, Mistuh Taylor," Homer said, "we come to do somethin' fer you."

"What do you mean?" Daddy asked, puzzled.

"Well," Homer started to explain. "All us colored folks dat work at de plant dis past summer has somethin' fer yo' family. Sam and Mose walks over here wif me to bring it."

I watched as Homer reached into his pocket and pulled out a crumpled brown sack. He handed it to Daddy.

"You be so good to us, Mistuh Taylor," Homer said, "and you hepped poor Sam here hide from de Klan. We all jes' decided we want to hep wif Josh's doctor bills. It ain't much, but all us pitched in some wages."

"Oh, thank you," Daddy said. "Thank you."

He hugged Sam, Homer, and Mose in turn, thanking them individually for their help.

"I can't believe you fellows walked all the way out here," Daddy said. "You really took a chance of running into the Klan."

"Yessuh, but we jes' decided on takin' de chance," Sam said. "You took a chance on heppin' me hide."

"And we had to git dis here money to you some how, Mistuh Taylor," Mose spoke up.

"What great friends you are," Daddy said, "And I tell you something right now—you're not walking back home. Get in the car, and I'll take you."

"Oh, naw suh, you cain't do dat. De Klan might sees you."

"I'm not afraid of the Klan," Daddy stated. "And, I'll never forget what you did for my family tonight. To deliver this gift, you took a chance that the Klan would see you walk to the home of a white man."

Daddy turned to me.

"Katie Jane, take care of your Mama and Josh until I get back."

"Yes, sir, Daddy."

I stood at the screen door and watched Homer and Mose get in the backseat. Sam got in the front with Daddy. As they drove away, I looked up at the sky.

"Dear God," I whispered, "wherever you are, please protect my Daddy and Sam and Homer and Mose from the Klan—tonight and every night."

Chapter Sixteen

A Miracle at the Gypsy Camp

In the spring, Josh suddenly began to get stronger. Although he still walked with difficulty, he began to follow me around the farm like he always had. Since his loss of mobility and our exposure to the polio patients in leg braces and wheelchairs, we had developed an awareness of how exciting life is when you can walk, run, and play.

Ardella continued to appease Josh with his favorite foods, and his appetite slowly improved. His energy level went up, and his frail body began to lose its gaunt look as he put on weight.

One day, Daddy came home from work with a wide grin on his face.

"Looks at Mistuh Taylor," Ardella said as she transferred pieces of fried chicken from the hot skillet to a flattened grocery sack to absorb the grease. "Dat mans got foolishness written all over his face."

Josh and I ran to him as he stood in the doorway.

"Guess who was in front of me on Route 41 this afternoon?" Daddy questioned.

"Who?" Josh and I squealed together.

"I'll give you a hint," Daddy teased. "I could smell soured milk."

"The Goat Man!" we chorused.

"Yup!" Daddy replied. "I was coming around the curve near Jester's Mill Pond, and I started smelling this gosh-awful smell. I thought it was a pole cat at first."

"But it was the goats!" Josh yelled out.

We doubled over with laughter.

Separate Fountains

Daddy was clearly delighted his story was having such a wonderful effect on his children.

"Goats, goats, and more goats!" Daddy said, throwing his hands high up in the air and waving his arms every time he said the word goat. "I hit the brakes so hard I almost lost control of the car."

Josh was laughing more than he had laughed in a long time. I looked over at Mama, who was watching Josh. I couldn't tell if the smile spread across her face was in response to Josh's delight of Daddy's story or to Daddy's story itself. I looked at Ardella, who was also smiling as she spread our dinner out on the table.

"I couldn't believe it," Daddy went on. "If I'd been driving faster around that curve, I'd had goats coming through my windshield and riding in the front seat with me."

Josh and I howled.

"How many goats were there?" Josh asked.

"Lord only knows," Daddy said, scratching his head like he was in deep thought. "I saw big goats and little goats, nanny goats and billy goats, baby goats and grandfather goats. Why, Josh, I saw more goats on Route 41 today than there is in the whole state of Georgia."

"Now, B. J. Taylor, don't stretch the truth too much," Mama teased, enjoying the occasion as much as the rest of us.

"Really, Daddy, how many goats did you see?" Josh asked.

"I'd guess about fifty," Daddy answered. "Every spring when the Goat Man comes through Jonesboro, he has a batch of new baby goats with him."

"I don't know how in the world the Goat Man can get by with going up and down the highway without someone hitting his wagon and the goats," Mama said. "You'd think the Georgia State Patrol would arrest him."

"But the Goat Man doesn't really bother anybody," Daddy said, trying to be serious although he still had mischief over his face. "He just comes to town for a few weeks, sells his goats' milk, and goes on to the next town. But, I must add, Katherine, it's a known fact that to get close to the goats, you almost have to hold your nose."

Once again, Josh and I crumbled with laughter.

"B. J.," Mama corrected him with a frown, "I'm afraid you're teaching the children disrespect."

"Oh, don't be so serious, Katherine Taylor," he replied. "The children know I'm teasing, but they also know I'm not teaching

A Miracle at the Gypsy Camp

them anything but the truth. Goats smell like goats!"

Josh and I guffawed.

"I don't mean to be disrespectful to the Goat Man and his goats," Daddy said, "but I do believe God likes us to laugh at some of His creations sometimes."

"I suppose you're right," Mama agreed reluctantly, not wanting to dampen the spirit of the moment. "It is a funny sight to see the Goat Man riding in his wagon pulled by goats."

"And followed by goats—and more goats," Josh said teasingly.

All of us laughed again.

"Daddy, will you please take me to pet the baby goats?" Josh pleaded.

"Me, too, Daddy," I joined in.

"Do you think the Goat Man has reached the gypsy camp by now?" Mama asked, knowing the Goat Man shared the old tourist court site with the gypsies when he was in town.

"I have an idea," Daddy said. "Let's all get in the car and go find out."

Stepping over to the kitchen area, Daddy began to pick up our supper from the table and put the bowls of food into the refrigerator.

"Wat you doin' Mistuh Taylor?" Ardella frowned, standing there in disbelief of his actions.

"We're all going to see the Goat Man," Daddy declared, "and then we'll take you home, Ardella."

"Yippee!" Josh shouted. "We're gonna see the Goat Man."

I put my arms around Josh and picked him up. Holding him, I started dancing around the room.

"We're gonna see the Goat Man! We're gonna see the Goat Man!" we chanted.

I quickly noticed Mama did not share our enthusiasm.

"B. J., we need to stay here," Mama said seriously. "Ardella hurried to have supper ready when you got home so we need to eat it now. Besides, Katie Jane needs to start on her homework."

"All that can wait," Daddy said. "I'll heat up the food when we get back, and I'll help Katie Jane with her homework. Besides, Katherine, you haven't been out of this house in ages."

"Ardella's fried chicken is just as good when it's cold," insisted Josh, trying to help convince Mama of the importance of our adventure.

"Get your pocketbook, Ardella," Daddy said. "We're going to see the Goat Man right now."

Separate Fountains

I was still holding Josh in my arms, and before Mama could say another word, I quickly carried him out the front door and down the porch steps to the car.

In a few minutes, Daddy, Mama, and Ardella were there, too.

"Lawds-a-mercy! Lets me squeeze in dat backseat wif yawl," Ardella said as she directed Josh and me to move over.

At the top of the drive, as I opened and refastened the gate for Daddy, the most wonderful feeling came over me. Suddenly, I felt a nearly forgotten surge of happiness. It was the same feeling I used to have with Josh when we were anticipating an adventure in town. As we rode away, I had a strange feeling something exciting was going to happen at the gypsy camp.

As we drove down the dusty road on our way to Route 41, I slid to the edge of my seat and leaned over toward my parents.

"Do you really think goat's milk helps people with stomach problems?" I asked, remembering our visits with Mama's brother, Howard, on his farm in south Georgia.

"Your Uncle Howard swears goat's milk got rid of his bleeding ulcers and saved his life," Mama said. "He has three goats on his farm now just so he can drink all the milk he wants."

"Aunt Ida Jane says the goats eat all her flowers and the clothes on her clothesline," Josh reminded us.

We all laughed.

"Dr. Green even prescribes goat's milk for people with stomach problems," Mama said.

"And dere's lots of colored folks who has a goat in dey yard jes' so dey can drink der milk," Ardella noted from the backseat.

"I wish we had some goats," Josh said. "They could pull me and Katie Jane in my red wagon."

When we arrived at the gypsy camp, many cars were already parked on the side of the road along Route 41. The goats smelled, but they were celebrities in this community. As we rode slowly looking for a place to park, we recognized many of our friends' cars, especially Cletus Jones's big black Cadillac.

A Miracle at the Gypsy Camp

"There's Cletus's Cadillac," Josh pointed out.

"Maybe he's gonna buy some goat's milk to make ice cream," I said.

"Daddy, can you make ice cream out of goat's milk?" Josh asked.

"I don't really know, my son," Daddy said. "You'll have to ask Cletus."

"Look" Ardella interrupted. "Dere's Jake's truck parked over yonder. Wat's he doin' out here?"

"It looks like Jake brought some of the workers from the peach packing plant with him," Daddy said. "I see Homer, Sam, and a few others."

"Does Jake have an ulcer, Ardella?" Josh asked innocently.

"No, I's don't think he duz," she said.

"It looks like everybody in town is here," Mama said. "There's Doctor Green and his family, and I even see Colonel and Mrs. Bartlett standing over by the Goat Man."

"Do you think Colonel Bartlett will change his peach farm into a goat farm?" Josh asked.

We all laughed again.

Daddy drove the car into the driveway of the tourist camp, in front of the gypsy wagons. He guided the car onto a grassy field near the crowd that had gathered around the Goat Man. Daddy parked the car, got out, and pulled the seat up to let Josh and me out.

"Come on, Katherine and Ardella," Daddy said, standing beside the car door. "You need to join the crowd."

"No, B. J.," Mama said. "You go on with the children. I can see from here."

"I's stay here wif Miz Taylor," Ardella joined in. "When you see Jake, Mistuh Taylor, tell him I's here and wants a ride home wif him."

Children and adults, whites and coloreds, were gathered around the Goat Man, his covered wagon, and his goats. I noticed Pepe and his father were there, having walked over from the gypsy campsite. I even saw Mr. Solomon and his wife. I wondered if Jewish people got ulcers, or if Mr. Solomon was making a deal with the Goat Man to sell his goats' milk.

Although I usually led Josh wherever we went, this time I followed him, walking slowly to match the speed of his halting gait. I

Separate Fountains

could sense his hesitancy, and I, myself, felt a little apprehensive about approaching the strange character we all called the Goat Man.

We stayed close to Daddy as we watched the Goat Man milk one of his nanny goats. He pulled and pumped the goat's teats, and we watched the milk spraying into a tin bucket. I smelled a stench like sour milk. The air around the Goat Man and his goats always had this smell.

The Goat Man's appearance was an attribute about him that one couldn't help but notice. His thick, wiry hair and beard left only his small mouth, nose, and eyes exposed. His clothing was unkempt, looking as though it needed ironing. He had no socks, and his bare toes stuck out the side of his shoes where the seams had broken.

The Goat Man's voice projected over the noise of the assembled group. Convincingly, he announced the health-giving properties of goat's milk. It was a real side show, with adults crowding around to hear his pitch. Fresh goat's milk in Jonesboro was as scarce as snowflakes, so people bought it when the Goat Man came to town.

I watched as the Goat Man sold some milk to Charlie Parsons. I wondered if Mr. Parson had stomach problems because of guilt from being in the Klan and stirring up all the trouble in the colored community. The Goat Man poured the milk from the tin bucket into Mr. Parsons's container, a clear glass bottle he had brought from home. Mr. Parson thanked the Goat Man and paid him.

Josh tugged on Daddy's arm.

"Will you give me a nickel so I can pet the goats?" Josh asked.

Daddy reached into his pocket and pulled out two nickels. He gave one to each of us.

"Thanks, Daddy!" we responded together.

This was one time I was not the brave one. As Josh hobbled toward the Goat Man, I followed like a shadow. He approached the bearded man and held out his money. The Goat Man responded with a noise that sounded like a grunt. I had noticed in the past that he was a man of few words when it came to talking to children. When we handed him our nickels, he motioned us toward the baby goats by the wagon.

Daddy walked along with us, and as Josh and I started petting the goats, he stood by us near the Goat Man's wagon. Joining the rest of the crowd, Daddy watched Josh, the other children, and me as we petted the goats.

I noticed the Goat Man looking over at Daddy, and then all of a sudden, he started walking in Daddy's direction. He walked through

A Miracle at the Gypsy Camp

the crowd of excited children and socializing parents and stood beside Daddy.

"Aren't you B. J. Taylor?" the Goat Man asked.

"Yes," Daddy responded, reaching out to shake the Goat Man's hand.

"When I was in Jonesboro today, I overheard some of the town folks talking about your son having polio."

"Yes," Daddy said. "We were lucky he had such a light case. He's walking better every day."

"I know all about the suffering polio can bring," the Goat Man said. "My cousin in Atlanta is so crippled she is confined to a wheelchair."

"I'm sorry," Daddy said.

"Isn't that your son petting the baby goat?" the Goat Man asked, pointing at Josh.

"Yes," Daddy said. "His name is Josh. When he heard you were in town today, he immediately wanted to come see you and the goats."

"Well, I have a get-well gift for Mr. Josh," the Goat Man said, "if you and Mrs. Taylor will let him accept it."

"What do you mean if we will let him accept it?" Daddy said, looking perplexed.

"I want to give Josh that newborn baby goat he is petting. His name is Buzz."

"Oh, gee," Daddy said in complete surprise, "that's nice of you, but you'd better talk to my wife Katherine about this. She's in the car."

Josh, along with me, was eavesdropping on the whole conversation. Suddenly, he began running toward the car to find Mama. Gone was his awkward walk. He was running—sprinting—to Mama.

"Mama!" Josh yelled at the top of his voice. "Mama! Mama!"

The entire crowd stopped their chatter and turned to look at Josh, wanting to know what had happened to him.

"Mama, please let me have a baby goat," Josh yelled. "His name is Buzz!"

"Run, Josh, run!" Cletus Jones shouted out from the crowd. "I knew you could do it!"

"Run, Josh!" others in the crowd begin to yell. "Run!"

People applauded and cheered his effort.

I watched Josh run across the open field toward our car.

Mama's door popped open, and she stepped out. At first she stood holding onto the door for support. She began to move, running her

Separate Fountains

hand along the top of the car to steady herself. Then, she let go and began to move forward, faster and faster. I saw my mother run for the first time in seven years.

"Of course you can have Buzz!" Mama shouted back to Josh.

When the two of them met, Mama fell to her knees, grabbed Josh, and held him close.

The crowd applauded and cheered again—only this time it was for Mama.

Daddy and I ran toward Mama and Josh.

Realizing that Ardella was still in the car, I ran past Daddy so I could get her. I yanked on her hand, pulling her through the door Mama had left hanging open. I continued to pull and tug on Ardella, making her run with me to our family.

The crowd applauded and cheered again, this time for Ardella!

I wasn't exactly sure what had happened, but I knew in my heart that it was supposed to be like this—all of our friends and neighbors there to witness this miracle of Josh and Mama running. To this day, I can still remember the silent hush that swept over the campsite. Everyone moved toward us, and there seemed to be an instant feeling of camaraderie that rippled through the crowd. For this particular moment in our lives, race and creed were irrelevant in the presence of the magical power of the human spirit.

We are sea and land.
It is not our purpose to become each other
—it is to recognize each other—
to learn to see the other and honor him for what he is—
each the other's opposite and complement.

Hermann Hesse (1877–1962)
German author

Epilogue

Charlayne Hunter and Hamilton Holmes, the two black students who integrated the University of Georgia on January 6, 1961, graduated from the university on June 1, 1963. Charlayne Hunter-Gault became a very successful television news journalist on *The NewsHour with Jim Lehrer* on PBS. In 1997 she moved to South Africa where she is presently covering the African continent for National Public Radio.

While at the University of Georgia, Hamilton Holmes was elected to the all-white national honor society Phi Beta Kappa, and during his senior year was accepted to the all-white Emory University School of Medicine. He became an orthopedic surgeon, hospital director, and an associate dean of Emory University School of Medicine. In 1995, at age fifty-four, he died in his sleep. Two weeks before his death, he had undergone quadruple bypass surgery.

I attended the University of Georgia on a four-year federal loan for prospective teachers, a loan whose repayment value was cut in half if one taught for five years. I married Harry Byars, also a University of Georgia graduate, and had two children. When I became a widow at age thirty-eight, Ardella showed her continued devotion to me by her loving emotional support of my children and me during our grief.

My brother's health improved, and he started first grade in 1954 when he turned seven. He was fortunate that his body was strong enough to win the battle against polio. Also in 1954 Jonas Salk developed the polio vaccine. My brother is a graduate of the University of Georgia and has a master's degree from the University of Florida. He is presently vice president of a bank.

Epilogue

Most of the characters represented in *Separate Fountains* are deceased.

Daddy and Mama are both deceased. The picture of them on the dedication page in the front of the book was taken on their wedding day, December 7, 1934.

Until the day Daddy died, he was full of fun and mischief—and always helping the less fortunate, no matter their race or creed. I always felt his love and devotion for Mama gave her the inner strength to carry on.

Mama's walking ability was poor for the rest of her life—but her persistence and determination to have a normal life was to be greatly admired. Looking back now, I realize she was a victim of the times she lived in. When she lost my baby sister at birth, the doctors ordered her to stay in bed for six weeks, and her lack of exercise brought about the development of phlebitis. There was no medical knowledge of phlebitis in 1946, and when the doctors insisted that Mama continue to stay in bed and keep her legs wrapped in gauze, her leg muscles and her health weakened over time.

Our family never did know who the benefactor was that paid for our groceries when my brother developed polio. That is one secret that has been kept in Jonesboro until this day. Daddy always thought it had to be the owner of the peach packing plant. Mama thought it had to be the owner of the building supply company and his wife. In later years, I surmised it was the owner of the grocery store. No one will ever really know!

The gypsies came through Jonesboro for a few more years, putting their children in our schools. Then one fall, they never showed up. We never saw their caravan of wagons on Route 41 again.

The Goat Man continued to come through Jonesboro until the traffic got so bad it was dangerous for him to travel on Route 41. While writing this book, I did some research on the Goat Man and discovered his name was Charles McCartney. Mr. McCartney, who never took a bath or washed his clothes, once boasted in a newspaper interview that nobody but his goats could stand the smell of him. He claimed to have visited every state except Hawaii. His goats couldn't swim that far, he explained, and if they could, they'd just end up eating the grass skirts off the hula dancers anyway. Charles McCartney is deceased. He was still known as the Goat Man when he died in 1998, at age ninety-seven, in a nursing home in Macon, Georgia.

After Daddy got all the medical bills paid, he and Jake built us a three-bedroom brick home. The Elliotts, our dear neighbors, were like

Separate Fountains

a second mother and father to my brother and me. Eunice Elliott, who died a few years after Clark, completely surprised us by leaving us her estate.

Jake wanted to buy a farm. Because he was black, had no property and no line of credit, the only way he could get a bank loan was for a white man to cosign with him. Daddy cosigned a loan with Jake, with Jake's signature being an X. Jake bought a small farm with a few acres. After he paid that loan off, Daddy cosigned with Jake to get another loan to buy additional land around his farm. He paid off the second loan, and got Daddy to cosign again on another loan to buy more land. Repeating the same pattern, Jake slowly acquired a farm with over two hundred acres of land—which he used to grow peaches and cotton. When an interstate highway was to be built through the Jonesboro area, some of Jake's farm land was in its planned path. The Georgia Department of Transportation paid Jake and Ardella a big sum of money for their property. Jake and Ardella are both deceased.

As the civil rights movement spread in the 1960s, integration of schools and public facilities became a fact—accepted by some Southerners and rejected by others. But, have the prejudices of the old South completely disappeared—or have they spread beyond southern borders to other regions of our country?

Daddy would have been heartbroken to see our nation still having so many racial problems. The laws have changed but prejudice remains very much a part of our society. People are still judged by their skin color—and not by their character and what they are really like on the inside.

Patti Wilson Byars
Author, May 1999
E-mail: Byarspatti@aol.com

---

*No talk of racial healing can succeed
until all players consider life in another's shoes—
or skin.*

James M. Abraham
Associate Editor
Tallahassee Democrat
June 27, 1998